Where No Gods Came

Where No

Gods Came

Sheila O'Connor

UNIVERSITY OF MICHIGAN PRESS

Ann Arbor

First paperback edition 2004
Copyright © by Sheila O'Connor 2003
All rights reserved
Published in the United States of America by
The University of Michigan Press
Manufactured in the United States of America
♾ Printed on acid-free paper

2007   2006   2005   2004   8   7   6

A CIP catalog record for this book is available from the British Library.

Library of Congress Cataloging-in-Publication Data

O'Connor, Sheila.
   Where no gods came / Sheila O'Connor.
      p.   cm. — (Michigan literary fiction awards)
   ISBN 0-472-11365-8 (cloth : alk. paper)
   I. Title. II. Series.
   PS3565.C645 W47 2003
   813'.54—dc21   2003008360

ISBN 0-472-03051-5

For Mikaela, Dylan, *and* Tim, *who dreamed the dream with me*

ACKNOWLEDGMENTS

Sherwood Anderson. "American Spring Song,"
Mid-American Chants. *New York: John Lane and Co., 1918*

Walt Whitman. "When Lilacs Last in the Dooryard Bloom'd,"
Leaves of Grass. *1881*

*Heartfelt thanks to the following: Wendy Weil and Emily Forland
for their labor and leap of faith; my readers: Reid Jensen, Callie
Cardamon, Anne Hickok, and Kim Palmer; Stuart "Morley" Shaver
for that invaluable Legion lunch; the Minnesota State Arts Board and
the Bush Foundation for fellowships that made this book possible;
Charles Baxter and Nicholas Delbanco for choosing it; Chris Hebert
and the staff at the University of Michigan Press for delivering it into
the world; Mary Rockcastle for her infinite goodwill; Martin Case for
everything, always; and finally Dylan, Mikaela, and Tim, who believed
from the beginning and whose generous spirits sustain me. Without
you, nothing.*

"I had been long alone in a strange place where no gods came."

—"American Spring Song," Sherwood Anderson

Where No Gods Came

Faina McCoy   Where Is the World?

I go back to San Diego for my beginning, because I can't shake from my mind the old life: hot sand and salt water outside my window, my father's coffee left on the stove, the early morning silence of our house, my father always gone before I'm awake. And, in the last days, the stench of Wiley, fully clothed, asleep on our living room floor.

No, I won't go back to Wiley. Instead, I carry what I have to keep to tell my story: the clutter of my aqua bulletin board, the archery ribbon I won at the summer park program, my poster of Paul Newman as Butch Cassidy. A shoe box full of poems, words to songs I want to remember. Spiral notebooks I've been writing since fourth grade, full of margin doodles and daydreams I jotted down in class. A note with the initials of all the boys I liked in sixth grade, taped to the back of my underwear drawer. Next to my bed, my father's old black phonograph, my green case of 45s, my first and only album.

I go back to Mission Boulevard, the sidewalks sizzling and edgy, as though the whole city is close to exploding. Girls with tangled hair panhandle; their bare bellies flash over the tops of their filthy hip-hugger jeans. Navy men bristle and spit at the hippies who hand out flowers. Most of the shops along the boulevard have changed their names. The Place, Magic Carpet, Electric Avenue. They sell black lights, psychedelic posters, pipes for smoking grass. On the street corners, with their guitar cases propped open for donations, boys strum guitars and sing James Taylor, Cat Stevens or Crosby, Stills, Nash and Young. They sing off-key in high voices that sound nothing like the originals. What else have I saved? My daily visits to Keith's Coffee Shop where I've eaten breakfast since first grade. The powdered sugar doughnut and carton of chocolate milk quickly slipped my way, the cracked vinyl of my usual stool sometimes cutting into my leg. My schoolbooks spilled out over the counter so Keith can quiz me to see if I've learned anything. Keith, tugging at his red goatee, "Let's see what you know today, young lady." The folded dollar bill I pass him at the last second.

I go back there, am there, sitting next to my father at the horse track. School is just out for the summer; it is June 17, 1973. We've driven to Hollywood Park for my twelfth birthday. He hunches over the Form and says he needs to win big so we can buy groceries.

"What about your paycheck?" I ask.

"Spent."

I'm anxious to go prowling, to hang out at the windows and wait for the rush of bets. "Stay still for once," he tells me. In his mouth, the tip of his cigar is gnawed and wet. He shifts nervously in his chair, arches his back, stretches his arms behind his neck to crack his knuckles.

"Stop it," I say. "You know that bugs me."

Tense, his breath comes in shallow snorts. He falls into his old, distracted habit of tugging at the rim of his fishing cap. He's worn this cap since I can remember, because it hides his high, bald forehead and the smooth patch at the top of his head. His belly bulges against the pearl snaps of his cowboy shirt. "Goddamnit. Goddamnit," he says as his horse fades. "God damn it." His bets never win. "Son of a bitch." He slaps his palm against his forehead. "We gotta quit."

Out in the hot sun of the parking lot, he pauses with his hand on the car door. It's my birthday; he has something important to tell me. He hasn't had a handful of luck in six months. There are people breathing down his neck for bad debts. He flops his heavy arm over my shoulder. "My back's against the wall. You have no way of knowing."

This has happened before, and we got past it. "You've still got your job at the marina. You can pay it off bit by bit."

"It's not that easy."

"We can rent a cheaper place. You're always complaining about the rent anyway."

"This is different. It's the real thing."

Now he clears his throat, leans against the car, stares into the sun, tugs at his cap. He stuffs his hands in his pockets, won't look at me. "Faina," he says, "I got to get back this money. Swear to god, baby. Wiley's got a gig lined up, some oil rig deal; it's incredible money. The thing is, it's pretty far."

I listen to the wheeze of his chest. "How far?"

"Somewhere off the coast of Australia."

"Where?"

"How the hell should I know? They fly you there; I don't need a map."

"You. But what about me?"

"I'll send checks every month. That's the glory of it. This deal is one stop short of hell; there's not a damn place for me to spend the money. No gambling. I'll just be floating on the ocean saving up money, sending some home for you to get by on. I'll work off my debts. Come back for you as soon as I can. Maybe a year."

"A year? Back where? Where will *I* be?"

"Well, that's the good news," he says, shuffling his feet. "You'll be in Minnesota with your mother and Cammy."

"Minnesota!" I scream.

I know Minnesota—farms, fields, people in black rubber boots milking cows—we studied it in geography. I don't know my mother, don't want to. I climb into the car, slam the door, refuse to speak. He touches my elbow, whispers, "Listen to me."

I turn my back to him, stare out at the stretch of empty cars. My fisted hands tremble. Wiley. This is all Wiley.

"Faina, you're acting ridiculous. It's not forever. Besides, your mother isn't feeling well; she needs to spend time with you, face it. And you could get to know Cammy, too. She's your sister. Like it or not, these people are your family."

The inside of my nose burns. My face is numb. "Forget it."

"Fine," he says. "You can live on the street."

"Fine," I say. "Great birthday."

At home Wiley, lounging on our lawn chair, burps between swigs of beer. "Happy birthday, young lady."

I flip him the finger, slam the screen door in his face. I despise Wiley for showing up in our lives and ruining everything. Before he came around, we were happy. It was just my dad and me. Sure my dad gambled some; he even had his nights when he stayed out drinking, but after Wiley, he was always at the track, coming home past midnight with different women. Wiley hooting and hollering until the morning. Wiley, with his long sideburns winding down his face, his brown teeth. Wiley telling my dad it was a waste of a life to work for a living.

I know my father will follow me with a string of apologies, so I stretch out on my bed and wait. I've lived in this house since I can remember and I love my room, my bookcase of wood and bricks he built me, my green flowered bedspread. Outside my window, the sound of the ocean, the bits of conversation from people passing on the beach, the words I turn into stories when I can't sleep. This is what belongs to me.

I don't know my mother; she gave me to my father when I was a baby. She didn't feel up to raising more than Cammy. When I was little, she sent me a few cards, presents, an occasional picture. I used to dream about her, about what it would be like to live with her. I imagined her brushing my hair before school, taking me shopping for shoes, tucking me in at night. I used to watch other mothers with their kids to find out what sort of things I was missing. But then, after awhile, when people asked, I just told them she'd died. It saved me a long story.

Out on the front lawn, my father and Wiley are arguing. I crouch under my bedroom window and wait for my father to refuse Wiley's oil rig scheme.

"It's your big break," Wiley says. "Think of the money. Besides, you can see for yourself she's getting beyond you. A girl her age needs a mother."

"You don't know her mother. I don't think Lenore would be much help to anybody."

"That's not your problem, Bobby. You've done your time. Let her old lady pick up some of the slack."

"She doesn't want to go."

"For Christ's sake, Faina's twelve. You don't ask a kid that age what they want to do."

"But Australia?"

"Why the cold feet now? We're all signed up. You can't stay here, not with the money you owe. You think she'd be safe?"

"Liar. You don't care what happens to me," I scream, then slam down the window so hard the glass rattles.

My father shakes his head at me, buries his face in his hands. Wiley heaves his body out of the lawn chair, pats my father on the back and leaves.

When the clatter of Wiley's car finally fades down the alley, my father comes inside, knocks twice on my bedroom door and walks over to me. "I'm looking for the birthday girl. I've got something for you, honey."

"I don't want it."

"Faina. Please."

He hands me a small package with ballerina wrapping and a white bow. It's a blank book with a cover marbled like Easter eggs.

"I thought you could use this for your stories. Maybe a kind of diary. Who knows. Something to put down your thoughts while you're away from me."

I fall into his chest and for the first time in a long time, I'm crying. "You're not really going? How could you decide something like this without asking me?"

"It's so beyond us, honey. It's so beyond us."

Over and over again, he kisses the top of my head. I don't feel his tears drip on my hair, but I feel his chest and I know he's crying.

By the end of the week, a moving-sale sign is taped to our front porch; our two bags are packed and hidden in the hall closet. The things we'll take. My father's suitcase is small. He's packed only the few clothes he'll need for work on the oil rig, the wooden box I carved and painted for him last Father's Day, his leather shaving kit, pictures of me in an old Christmas-card envelope. My duffel bag is stuffed full of my clothes, a new gray sweatshirt jacket for Minnesota weather, all new underwear including the bra he asked the saleslady to pick out for me, a new toothbrush, a hairbrush and, of course, the diary. The rest of my keepsakes are loaded into a big cardboard box marked FAINA MCCOY and stored away in a locker somewhere near Chula Vista.

Everything else we own is priced with ragged pieces of masking tape. People rummage through our house, carry out the toys and games I've outgrown: Chutes and Ladders, Candyland, my Etch-a-Sketch. All that goes for a quarter apiece. The customers will buy anything: hangers, my chipped ceramic poodle bank, ice-cube trays, bamboo shades. Some arrive in beat-up trucks to haul out my bed, our couch, my bookcase. I sit at a card table and collect the money. Perched on an empty beer case, I add up the items, count out the change. When they want to bargain, I point them toward my father, who always says, "Have at it." Although it seems he's letting go too easily, I can't blame him. It's hard to haggle over the price of a torn lampshade. When the house is nearly empty, I hand him the shoe box of money, our lives worth a grand total of $327. "Don't knock it," he says. "It's your plane ticket."

"I'm going to Keith's," I say, banging the screen door closed behind me. I don't want to join my dad and Wiley for their farewell celebration—cold beer and beef jerky on the front porch.

At this time of night, only a few customers straggle into Keith's place. "Isn't it a little late for breakfast?" Keith jokes. "I saved you your usual. Too busy with the sale to stop by?" He slides the powdered sugar doughnut over the counter toward me. "I hope you eat better than this in Minnesota."

"We sold most everything." The doughnut sticks in my throat like paste. "Today's my last day."

Keith wipes his damp rag over the clean counter. He unscrews the lids from the half-empty ketchup bottles and refills them. "It'll be good to see your mother and sister again. What's her name?"

"Cammy."

"Yeah, I knew it was something unusual. Your folks really had a thing for original names."

I shrug, keep chewing. As long as my mouth is full I can't answer. Keith leans on the counter in front of me, lifts his pouch of tobacco and rolling papers out of his apron pocket. He sprinkles a dash of tobacco along the crease. "Your sister will probably take you under her wing."

"Yeah." To me, Cammy has always been just a tiny square of school picture, a snapshot who always appeared older and prettier than me. "A regular blonde beauty," my father called her. This year she was nothing, not even a Christmas card, and I was secretly happy. I had been wanting to lose her for a long time, to get rid of the ghost who stole my father's loyalty. "Why should she care about us?" I told him. "We're hardly even her family."

Cammy and my mother. My father and me. "That's the court order," he always said. "That's the way it has to be." From what I knew of it, we left them in Minnesota when I was a baby, or rather, my mother left me. My father moved the two of us to California so he could have a chance at acting, but he ended up in San Diego repairing boat engines. This is the life I know, San Diego. Not my mother, not Cammy, just the waves crashing me to sleep, the narrow back streets, the stray cats slinking down the alley, Keith.

"I had a friend," Keith says, leaning on the counter, blowing smoke rings, "who made great money on an oil rig. There's no doubt about it, it's good work if you can get it. Your dad is doing the right thing. In the old days, parents left home all the time to make money for their family. This is nothing new. You'll come back in a year, all grown-up and talking with one of those midwestern accents; we'll just be sitting here, drinking the same cup of coffee, and you'll wonder why you were ever sad to leave." Keith brushes the hair away from my eyes. "Write to me."

He prints his address on a paper napkin. I pass him the folded dollar bill like I've done every day since first grade. "Not today. This one's on me."

For the last time, I close the door to Keith's and listen to the bell ring.

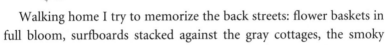

Walking home I try to memorize the back streets: flower baskets in full bloom, surfboards stacked against the gray cottages, the smoky smell of charcoal and burgers grilling, the sand scraping under my sandals. I welcome the lull of evening, the sun almost swallowed by water. This is where I belong, I repeat to myself. I live here. I can't imagine a life far away, I can't imagine a life without my father.

Back at our house, I curl into a ball on my bedroom floor, bunch my father's jacket into a pillow for my head. The walls are bare except for the gray stains where the pictures used to hang. I try to float away on the waves, let them rock me into dreams, but I can't sleep. I know my father is sitting on the front steps smoking; through the open window, I can hear him sigh. He's waiting to talk to me, to settle this uneasy silence we've lived in since my birthday.

"Come on out," he says, when he discovers me standing at the screen door. "You're getting too old to sleep in a T-shirt. Get a nightgown in Minneapolis with some of the money."

"Where's your good friend Wiley?"

"Oh, he's out enjoying civilization for the last time. This isn't his fault, Faina. If you're looking to blame someone, blame me."

"I do."

"What about a truce for our last night? This isn't the way you want to leave."

"Yes, it is."

"God, you're a stubborn kid." He yanks me down onto his lap, like he used to do when I was little, wraps me up in the warm circle of his arms. I give in, settle against his body, my back resting on his fat stomach.

"Don't forget about that book I gave you. I was hoping you'd write down your days for me."

I touch my chest. The key to the diary is hidden there, close to my heart, hanging from a purple ribbon under my shirt. "Maybe. Would you do the same for me?"

"Me?" he laughs. "Jesus, Faina, I can hardly sign a check. You're the one with all the brains."

"I don't want to go," I remind him, though I know nothing I say now will change his mind.

Ahead of us there is only the endless flat land of ocean and dark sky leading to nothing. After San Diego, where is the world?

"Is Minneapolis near the ocean?" I ask.

He laughs again. "That goes to show you don't know everything."

"You'll be on the ocean, won't you?"

"Constantly."

When I see him in my mind, I will picture him straight ahead of me, out our old front door, another mysterious ship in the distance.

"It'll go fast. You'll see." He presses his cheek against my head; I lean my weight into the nest of his body. Away from him, from here, will I disappear? After San Diego, where is the world?

Lenore A Smart Girl

The night Bobby sent Faina back to me, I stood at the window, watching her little cricket body climb out of the yellow cab, wondering how I'd let him talk me into this reunion. Cash, company, light housekeeping. Temporary. Until he was back on his feet.

When I heard the thump-thump up the stairway I steadied myself with one last swallow. My heart pulsed in my throat, my hands shook. I strangled my ratty bathrobe close around my neck, shivered while sweat rivered down between my breasts. We should have done this earlier, when I was still ravishing. The beautiful mother. The mother she never knew.

Through the peephole I scrutinized her, a scrawny stray no taller than my chest. A runt, the waste of a litter. And the indisputable truth: She was without question Bobby's daughter. It had given me such a great laugh through the years to wonder. But there was Bobby, in those dark eyes wild with challenge, the same half-smile sneer, stringy black hair. Clothes he must have bought her. A potato-sack dress, old canvas tennis shoes, drab from washing.

When I opened the door to peek past the chain, the driver held out his hand for the twenty. "Sorry I can't stay." Then he snatched the money, left with my change.

"How was your trip?" I asked, sliding off the chain for her arrival.

"All right," she said flatly, but I could see the storm in her black eyes.

"You can keep your things in Cammy's room," I told her. "It's this way." I teetered down the hallway, my heart twisted into a tight knot. Behind me, I could hear the constant swish of her duffel bag being lugged along the carpet. "If you're starving, nose around the kitchen. There's not much in the way of food but you're welcome to it. This is it." I opened the door to Cammy's room. "You can settle in in the morning."

"But where's Cammy? Will she be home soon?" Her voice broke like a snapped twig.

"Cammy? That's another story."

Out of the corner of my eye, I spied the slight quiver of her chin. She clutched the cloth handle of that enormous bag as if she planned to escape on a moment's notice. Like Cammy.

"I don't know what you expected," I said. "But this is it."

"I didn't expect anything," she said, staring down at her shoes.

"Well," I laughed. "It's a smart girl who learns that lesson early."

Faina Minneapolis

During the first few days, I pass the hours sitting on the floor, my back against the apartment door, my closed eyes pressed into my knees. This isn't my mother, I tell myself. I'm not really here. I just want to be ready, my suitcase next to me, so I can walk out the door when my dad comes to take me back home.

"Don't open that door," she warns me. "This is the city. We need to stay inside."

I write in my diary, everything I've seen so far. The outside of this battered brick building, Lenore's apartment over a bakery and a plumbing store, the filthy marble staircase, halls with peeling sea-green paint, black iron bars over the windows. A woman in a nightgown who won't get out of bed.

When the delivery boys come from Dakota Liquors or Kenny's Grocery, I'm ordered to keep the chain on the door, slip the check through the crack. "Don't talk to anybody."

While she sleeps, I snoop through Cammy's things. I'm living in her room, in the middle of her mysterious life. Worn moccasins. Velvet paisley fringe pillows tossed on her bed. A brass incense holder full of half-burnt matches and ash. Her macrame purse littered with lipstick, a lighter, loose tobacco, scraps of paper. In the afternoons, I close Cammy's door, turn on her fold-down stereo, and listen to her collection of record albums. Abbey Road. Carly Simon. Woodstock. I lie on her twin bed and page through her Jefferson yearbook. No signatures. But she's there, in the ninth-grade class, smiling in the same square photograph my dad kept in his sock drawer. Cammy. Wavy blonde hair, big round eyes, perfect teeth. Not my father. Not Lenore. Not me.

"I think you'll find I like my privacy," Lenore says when I ask about Cammy.

I work on the mystery my own way, piece together the clues Cammy left behind. I study the scribbles in her civics book, *The Needle and the Damage Done,* song lyrics copied in smudged pencil. I read through a box of old cards and letters. Love notes from boys with different names. Mark. Spider. Flash. Shane. In the back of her closet, I hunt through cardboard boxes of clothes, scuffed shoes, hot rollers, a plastic bag of make-up. I want to know my sister.

"WHERE IS SHE?" I write to my dad, on blue tissue stationery marked *airmail.* "I can't believe you did this to ME!" I lick the seal, slip it between Cammy's mattress and box spring. As soon as he sends his address, I'll mail them all. The whole horrible story.

The night we break our days of silence, my name comes to me in a dream. "Faina," a low moan. "Faina, help me."

My first thought is: It's Cammy. She's alive. She's finally home. But then I open my eyes to the shadowy world of Cammy's bedroom, and see Lenore, framed by the yellow square of street light, doubled over in the doorway.

"I'm sick," she whispers. "Help me."

I sit up in bed, pull the sheet close to my chin. The air is heavy with this clinging Minnesota heat, sticky, not a hint of breeze through the open window. "Do you want me to call an ambulance?"

"No, no. I don't have that kind of money."

I close my eyes tight and will her to disappear. When I open them again, I will be in my own bed in San Diego.

"I need something. Quick." She collapses to her knees, covers her mouth with both hands.

I grab the wastebasket and shove it in her direction, careful not to touch her. Curling into the corner of Cammy's bed, I press my palms against my ears to keep from hearing her cough and gag.

"I'm dying," she says, slumping face down onto the carpet. Blue legs, her nightgown twisted around her hips, the ragged edges of old underwear.

"Lenore, I've got to call somebody." I press a wadded ball of sheet over my nose to block the stench of vomit. "Please, tell me."

"It's okay," she mumbles into the carpet. "Don't call anybody. Promise me. It's just the flu."

Then she is completely still, except for short quick gasps, almost like hiccups. For a long time, I sit with the sheet over my nose, chewing on the damp edge, listening to the car doors slam outside my window and the last-call customers laugh outside Rusty's Tavern. If she dies, what happens to me? Where will I go? Who will take care of me?

Finally I swallow hard, pinch my nose, walk over and nudge her shoulder. She is lying in a pool of foamy vomit. I roll her body away from the slime that clings to her cheek. I lift her moist wrist to check for a pulse, the way we did in gym class after jumping jacks, but it's hidden somewhere under her sharp bones and besides I don't know what the count should be.

"Lenore." When I jerk her, her arm wiggles like Jell-O. I don't want to be alone with a dead body. "Lenore," I shout into her ear, "can you hear me?"

"Go away," she moans, rolling back toward the vomit.

"You can't stay here. Let me help you back to bed."

"I can't," she sobs. Her body shudders under my hands.

"I'll help you." I don't know how I'll do it, but I can't leave her here, asleep in her own sickness. "Come on." I wrap my arms around her waist and tug hard. Through the flimsy nightgown, I can feel the rattle of her frightening rib cage. "Lenore, please." She hunches up on her hands and knees; her weak arms wobble under the weight. "You can do it," I say.

The two of us begin to inch our way down the hall, Lenore crawling, me budging her forward with my hands on her hips. "We're almost there. You'll feel better in your own bed." When we get to her room, my stomach swirls from the smell of vomit and stale smoke. Snapping on her light, I discover another puddle next to her bed.

"Be careful," I whisper, sidestepping her past the mess.

Once I've settled her in bed, I turn the fan so the air blows directly over her clammy body. "Do you want anything?" I ask.

She shakes her head. "The light. It's killing my eyes."

In the kitchen, I dump a bottle of Pine-Sol into a plastic bowl. I have to get rid of the smell or I'll never be able to sleep. I tie a dishrag around my nose. When I bend down to scrub the carpet, I hold my breath. The Pine-Sol fumes burn my eyes, but I don't cry. I don't cry because, like my dad always said, I'm a tough kid who can survive anything.

"Maybe you should see a doctor," I tell her the next morning, as I change the sheets on her bed.

"I've been down that road already, and look where it got me. No, it was just a little bug. But I'm still going to go easy on the vodka."

After that we never return to that night. Instead we start on simple conversations: TV shows, my grades at school, books I like to read. To pass the slow days, I make myself useful. Dust the claw feet of the sofa, her vanity table, polish the mirrored tray that displays her bottles of perfume. I vacuum the lavender carpet in the living room, run a dry cheesecloth over the crystal prism lamps on each side of her bed.

I do my work between visits to her room, where we practice being friendly. Mornings, I bring her coffee and dry toast, sit on the edge of her bed and compete against game-show contestants on television. "Good girl," she says, slapping my knee and smiling when I answer a question correctly. "I'll tell you what, little lady; you get your brains from me. When I was your age I spent the summer trying to read the whole set of Encyclopedia Britannicas. Papa Roy bought them for me for my twelfth birthday. I had this dream to do research in my spare time. Crazy. But when I went back to school in September, the teacher was tired of me raising my hand. One day after school, my mother called me into the dining room, where she was polishing the silver tea set Papa Roy had given her. I remember she kept working the rag in these angry circles. 'Lenore,' she said. 'It isn't attractive to flaunt your gifts. Mrs. Pierre sent a note that says you're monopolizing the class-room. Let someone else have a chance. You're not as bright as you think.' Not as bright as I think. Can you believe that's what she said to me? But I showed them all. Class valedictorian of West High School at sixteen."

I try to listen past her, to hear the contestants make their best guess. Often, she begins a long sentence which seems to wander away from both of us, and her words are filled with a rage I have never known.

For lunch we share a plate of saltines, sometimes splitting a can of chicken-noodle soup. She sips the broth out of the bowl, while I scoop away at the big mound of noodles. I arrange the crackers on a china platter trimmed with pink and gold roses; hers are spread with butter and raspberry jam. "Sometimes I just need the extra sugar," she says, nibbling the corners daintily.

Afterward, I help her with her daily "hygiene." I backcomb her hair, ratting it close to her scalp the way she taught me. I try to keep my eyes off her dark roots, the white flecks of skin flaking off the ashen scalp. But at night, when I close my eyes, that image always comes back to me. "A beautician you'll never be," she says daily, studying her reflection in the magnified mirror. "One thing that's hard to lose is true beauty." She runs a cotton ball coated with Pond's cold cream over her eyes, wipes away old mascara in a glob of white grease. Then she begins again, with a heavy coat of fleshy powder caking her nose, a dash of lipstick over each cheek. Still, her yellowed skin shows through—the color of her nicotine-stained teeth. "You're not too young to put a little something on that face of yours. Your skin is so dark, you could use a good base."

When she's finished rubbing Cammy's CoverGirl into my skin, I stare into the mirror, my pores magnified into deep pits, the stubbly hair of my eyebrows dense and thick like whiskers. I return to the milky white spot of my right eye, the secret blindness I believe is coming. I trace my tongue along my jagged front teeth.

"You'll be pretty someday," she says to me. "But I'd try to stay out of the sun."

Minneapolis. Now I'm allowed out of the apartment on short errands. I pick up groceries, buy marmalade twists at the bakery downstairs. "Don't talk to anybody," she warns me, each time before I leave. "Don't answer questions. And don't tell the other tenants you live here."

Outside, on the sidewalk, I let the summer sun bake into my skin. If the bench at the bus stop is empty, I sit for a few minutes and soak in this strange city. The steady storm of traffic. The smell of stale beer from Rusty's Tavern mixed with hot blacktop. Delivery trucks pulling up in the alley. The Paradise Club, the neon palm tree dull in the daylight. Bread trucks unloading at Kenny's. The gutter a collection of candy wrappers and cigarette butts. At the end of the block, a grim black hearse in front of Mead's Mortuary and the roar of engines from the Auto Trade lot.

Thursdays, the bookmobile arrives at Dakota Park. Inside the narrow trailer, it's sweltering and silent and dusty. I take my usual place in front of Mythology. Last year at Ocean View, I won a blue ribbon for my project on Icarus: I wish I could show Lenore the story I wrote, my drawings of his beautiful bird wings. The bookmobile's mythology section is small: religion, fairy tales and gods all mixed together. Today, I choose *Greek Goddesses* because I like the story of Persephone, the way her mother nearly died without her.

When I'm finished, I take out the list Lenore wrote for me this morning. "I used to love a good story," she told me, folding the paper and passing it to me. "Since you're going to the bookmobile, why not choose a book you can read to me on these long afternoons? Or at night, when there's nothing worth watching."

"I'm looking for *Little Women*," I tell the librarian.

"It should be right there in fiction under A. For Alcott. I'm sure we have a copy. It's not read much anymore."

The book is old, with gray pages and a drab brown cover. Four girls in full dresses pose around a piano. I can tell it's going to be boring.

"That's an excellent choice," the librarian says. "One of my favorites. And it's good to see a girl your age still interested in the classics."

"My mother and I are reading the classics this summer," I tell her.

"How wonderful. Your mother must be a remarkable woman."

"Yes," I say, setting my two books on the counter. "She is."

I've slipped it past her before, but today she studies Cammy's library card, her eyebrows pinched together suddenly, her mouth in a frown. "You're not Camille McCoy."

"No," I say.

"I can tell from the birth date. You couldn't be sixteen."

"It's my sister's. She said I could use it."

"Of course," she says, sliding it back toward me. "But our policy is that patrons check out books in their own name."

"I don't have a card."

"Well, let's fix that today."

She lifts a white form out of a metal file box. "It'll just take a minute. Name?"

"Faina McCoy."

I remember Lenore's warning not to talk to anybody. Not to answer anyone's questions. I know if she finds out about the card, she won't let me come back to the bookmobile.

"That's unusual. Is it F-A-I-N-A?"

"Yes," I say, amazed she can spell it.

"Date of birth?"

"Could I just use Cammy's card today? I'm in a hurry."

"It will just take a minute. Besides, I can't let you use your sister's card."

"June 17, 1961."

"Address?"

I have to think for a minute, to picture from memory the black numbers over the door. "2126 Dakota."

"Are you new here?"

"Not really."

"I thought I noticed a little accent."

I chew my lip. I've said too much already.

"Well, Faina, you can check out three books while your card is being processed. Do you want to look around for one more before we finish?"

"No." I only check out one a week, one I can finish quickly, so every Thursday, Lenore will let me come back.

"Sign here." She points to a narrow rectangle with a large black X. "Use your best penmanship. It's a permanent record."

Faina McCoy, I write. And for the first time, I realize I live here.

Evenings, I save the cherry cobbler from my TV dinner and pass her the cooled tray. A fresh glass of vodka sweats on the bedside table. "Move the fan closer to the bed," she says. When I read *Little Women* aloud my voice wobbles in the wind. "Try to read with expression," she tells me.

We keep a box of Kleenex propped between us. In her deepest sadness, she forgets to correct my pronunciation.

"Someday you'll know what it's like to lose somebody," she says, closing her eyes as if she can see that person's face on the dark screen of memory. "When Papa Roy died, I sat at his grave and bawled like a baby. I was nearly crazy with grief. He was the only one who had ever loved me. It's strange to be someone with just one person in the world. But that's how your heart is like mine, little Faina. Because I know you're your daddy's girl. Always will be."

I nod, swallow down the new lump in my throat. I know she is off on that peculiar road of recollection, and when she starts in on Papa Roy and how much she misses him, I always end up walking my own path.

She gulps down the last of her *last* nightcap. "I've got to have another to make it through this heat."

I lift the hair off the base of my neck, turn to let the breeze of the fan cool my spine. My shirt is a layer of wet skin. "Do you think I should finish reading first?"

"I've had enough tonight. Mix me a fresh one, and we'll come back to it tomorrow. I think I'm going to pass out from this humidity."

I try to make the next one weak, but she catches me, sends me back for another shot. "Grab me a book of matches while you're at it," she calls. Every night, as I pour the last glass of vodka, I think: What if I wake in the morning to her dead, face down in the hallway, a pool of vomit under her cheek?

After I've given her a fresh drink, I flap her bed sheets to let in a last breath of air, shut off her light. "Don't read ahead of me," she says, giving my hand a feeble squeeze.

"Be careful of the tenants in this building. They'll try to trick you with their questions." This is my drill every day, before I'm allowed to go outside. "I don't want them to know you're my daughter. You're just visiting. It's none of their damn business."

I understand why she doesn't want to explain me, the daughter from California, the daughter they've never seen. Mornings, when I go downstairs for Lenore's marmalade twists, the woman at the bakery asks all the questions. What did you say your name was again? Never heard of such a thing. Where are you from? How long are you staying? Why don't we ever see Lenore anymore? Or Cammy? "Can't be much fun up there for a girl your age," she says, slipping the twists into a white bag. "I'm sure you know what I mean." Every day she waits for me to reveal the truth, pausing too long before she passes over the bag.

"Good girl," Lenore says. "Let them guess. Families deserve their privacy. That Frances is an old bitch. She's been watching me for years. But the one to steer clear of is Hank of Hank's Plumbing. He's the caretaker of this building."

When I meet Hank in the alley, I know it's him because his name is stitched into the pocket of his blue uniform. Before I can get in the back door, his hairy hand is on my elbow. "You that little girl living up with

Lenore?" He clenches a toothpick between his teeth, narrows his eyes at me. "Come here, I got something to show you."

"I'm late," I say, trying to step past him. I don't like his gravelly voice, or the snake tattoo on his dirty arm.

"Won't take but a minute." He clutches my elbow, shoves me through the gray steel door that leads to the basement—a place Lenore has forbidden me to go. At the bottom of the dark stairwell, he jingles his ring of keys, struggles with the padlock, then flips back the latch. He kicks the door with the toe of his heavy black boot, then shoves me into the storage room: a row of tall wooden lockers, a laundry tub, an antique washing machine. It's musty and cold, concrete blocks covered with gauzy webs.

"There," he says, pointing to a broken window.

"I've got to go."

He tightens his grip on my arm. "What's your hurry?" Hank smells like the garage at my dad's marina, oil and metal. "You tell Lenore I'll add that window to her rent." He steps on the shards of glass, points to a patch-work quilt heaped in a corner. "Tell her that kid of hers has been here."

"Cammy?"

"She got any more?" He winks at me. "You tell her to put it in her August check. You've seen the evidence."

"Okay," I say, but he won't let go of my arm.

"One more thing, Fina McCoy," he says, pulling an envelope out of his back pocket and handing it to me. My card from the Minneapolis Public Library. "Any chance this belongs to you?"

When I tell Lenore about Hank and the basement, I leave out the part about my library card. I don't want to add it to the broken window, I don't want her to know I told the librarian the truth, and now Hank knows my name.

"Let that bastard charge me. Close my door now, Faina. I need some sleep."

Out in the kitchen, I sweep the floor, scrub the sink, polish the top of her turquoise stove. When she wakes up again, I want her to be happy. I don't ask questions, because I know if I do, she'll close the door on our conversation. But if I wait quietly, she might offer a story.

In the evening, I help her out to the sink for her hair washing. She drapes a towel around her shoulders, positions her head under the kitchen faucet. "Check the temperature," she tells me, as I get ready to spray her with the black rubber hose.

I work the Prell shampoo into a lathery wig, stare at Lenore's spine, a narrow path of stones poking through her nightgown. The sack of skin on her arms flutters like a flag. "I love having someone else wash my hair. It reminds me of the beauty parlor."

When I'm finished, she wrings out a thin trickle of water.

"I always feel better clean."

After the white towel is wrapped around her head like a turban, she sits at the kitchen table munching cashews. In the chair, she shrinks into a small child, her bare feet dangling above the floor, her lower lip puffed out in a pout. I stand behind her, carefully creeping the comb through her thin wet hair. "Ouch," she screams, when I tug or touch the teeth to her tender scalp. "Remember, I'm sensitive." She reaches up and rubs her wet head. I divide Lenore's hair into perfect rows, streak setting gel through each damp section before slowly rolling it onto the prickly black curler. She gives me directions, passes me back the pins. "Let's do the rest of this in bed," she says suddenly. "I'm wiped out already."

When I've settled her into her bed, finished pinning down the last black curler, she turns her attention to me. "We ought to do something with your hair," she says. "It's so thin and straight; you could at least tie it back in a braid."

She makes me turn my back to her, so she can begin to weave together three long strands. "I used to love to do this to Cammy, when she was young," Lenore says. "It's relaxing. Of course, she was better at taking care of herself. You're what we called a tomboy in my day. I'm sure it comes from living with Bobby. But you're getting to the age where you're going to want boys to sit up and take notice."

"I don't care about boys."

"Oh, that will change."

"Not for me," I insist.

"Plenty of girls are late bloomers. But you'll need a husband some-day. I can still remember my mother telling me that. All the sons of her bridge-club cronies she invited over to meet me. Lemonade and egg-salad finger sandwiches served in the gazebo. But I wanted to go to college."

"Is that how you met my dad?" I ask.

Lenore pauses, balances the three strands in her still hands. Her sigh is long and slow, nearly as heavy as the heat on this July night. I hold my breath, wait patiently. If I'm silent, there's a chance the truth might come.

"Well, what did Bobby tell you? About us, I mean."

"Nothing. He's never told me anything."

She's quiet again, considering whether or not to go on. "Well, I'm sure he has his own story."

"Is the braid done?" I ask, reaching my hand back to feel her progress. "You can skip it if you want."

"No, no. You've got to get it out of your eyes." She picks up the rhythm again, gently tugging and weaving. "This is girl talk, I guess. I met Bobby at the Bryant Garage; he was fixing the brakes on Papa Roy's Cadillac. 'Hey, good-looking,' he said, when I came to drive it home. He seemed so bold, reckless. Nothing like the Kenwood boys I'd known all my life. Then, too, he was dark like you, black-eyed like a deer, twenty-two and already out of the Navy. Some strange mix of Romanian and Irish. I was typical sixteen. I went out with him to punish my parents. Especially my mother. Papa Roy hated him, but then, he hated all my dates because I was his sweetheart, his daughter, and it made him jealous to see me go off with boys."

"How long did you date before you got married?"

"Who keeps track? A couple of months, I guess. Not long enough, but I was a girl who didn't know how to wait. Papa Roy hosted an extravagant wedding for me at Kenwood Methodist. Not long after that, I had Cammy. I've probably said too much already, but there was never real love between us. I was Papa Roy's girl; that wasn't easy for a man to get past. And your father was from a lower class. He was too proud to take Papa Roy's money; he preferred to live like common poor. Of course, my mother was gloriously happy. She had Papa to herself, and the chance to see me suffer. She was right; I never made it to college."

She loops the rubber band around the end of my hair. "All finished," she announces, patting my back.

"Then how long were you married before you had me?"

"How'd we get on this subject in the first place?" she asks, settling back on her pillow and passing me her empty glass. "Put in an extra cube this time, sweetie. Let's forget all this talk. It's ancient history."

Lenore Ancient History

I can set the record straight. Tell you my ancient history. But it's a truth I would never want Faina to know.

Cammy and I were happy during those first few years. Bobby was gone all the time down at the garage, weekends hunting or fishing with his buddies near Moose Lake, poker games. From the start, Cammy was good company. I told her the worst of it. The phone numbers I found scribbled on little slips of paper, the nights he never came home, the crimson chiffon scarf I found in his coat pocket. Even as a toddler, she understood. She was born old.

We played games. "Shh," I'd say when we heard the doorknob turn. "It's Bobby. Let's pretend we're invisible." It was great fun, the two of us hiding in the closet until we heard him give up and leave. Then we'd creep out giggling and clapping.

I don't know what happened then. Papa Roy dragged me to doctors, but as usual they couldn't diagnose it. My whole body started sparking with electrical shocks. At night, my fingers and feet would tingle until I numbed them under icy water. Out of heavy sleep, I woke shivering. In the day, my mouth was a cave of sponge, my tongue sluggish and sticky.

"Get out of the house," Papa Roy said to me. "You're twenty-one years old, and you live like you're forty. I'll teach you my business. Learn it now. It'll be yours when I die."

Papa Roy owned so many things; he gave me the cleaners on Nicollet. I thought we would run it together, but Papa Roy handed it over to me like car keys. I hardly saw him; Mother told me he had a mistress named Gloria, a girl not much older than me he'd met at the Palomino Club. So Gloria had Papa Roy, and I had his cleaners: the chemicals, the customers' orders, the little white buttons I sewed on the businessmen's shirts.

Jess ran the press. He showed me the ropes, mixed the solutions, sorted through the clothes. He was a good-looking guy with thick lips, freckles, a forest of red hair. But he had this limp from a bullet he caught in Korea. "Jess," I said one day while watching the sweat streak down his back. "I think you're crazy about me."

Jess dropped his head into his hands and started laughing. "Jess," I said. "Admit it." But he was a decent guy, he knew I was married.

I blame this all on Papa Roy and Bobby. The men who had forsaken me.

Finally one night, we closed the cleaners at six, drew the shades over the front windows, and made love in the back room. I touched his scar, kissed it with my lips. "Jess," I whispered at the end. "I want you to marry me." I saw the three of us—Jess, me, Cammy—living happily ever after in a white colonial overlooking Lake of the Isles. I knew Papa Roy would buy it for me.

That night, for punishment, I seduced Bobby. I'd slept in Cammy's room for years to keep him away from me. But I went into his bedroom, woke him from a drunken sleep. I hoped he could sense Jess inside me; I wanted to give him a hint how it hurt.

Not long afterward, Jess left for a job at his brother's restaurant in Lincoln. Nine months later, Bobby named her Faina, after his mother, who'd died sometime that year. A strange name. But what did it matter to me?

I couldn't love her. She cried all the time; even in the hospital, the nurses said she would be a handful, stubborn, wrenching her face away from the bottle. All day she screamed, while Cammy crouched on the floor coloring, her sweet pictures ruined by Faina's gut-splitting shrieks. There wasn't even time for Cammy to curl up in my lap. I walked Faina constantly, jiggled her until her head bobbed like a dashboard ornament. I wanted my old life back: the cleaners, lazy mornings with Cammy, making love with Jess in the back room.

Bobby? I forgot about Bobby. He slept late in the mornings; nights he tended bar at a strip place down on Washington Avenue—Zorba's. Papa Roy offered to have him killed; he knew some people then who could do that kind of thing. I was too indifferent to want him dead.

Occasionally, Mother stopped by to remind me of how I had ruined my life. She spoiled Cammy, bought her ice-cream cones, dolls, bags of candy corn. When I asked her to hold Faina, she swallowed Cammy in her arms. "Ah, ah. Be careful of sibling rivalry."

No one wanted Faina. Not Papa Roy. Not Bobby. Not Cammy. Not even me.

"Why don't we leave Faina to live with Bobby?" Cammy said one night while I was rubbing soap over her perfect back. She was nearly five, old enough to know what she'd said. The words dropped from her mouth like stones, slid through the bath water and thumped on the bottom of the tub.

"Are you sure?" I asked. "You're sure you want to leave Faina and Bobby?" I didn't want Cammy to look back, and hold the decision against me.

"Sure," she said.

I packed the little that belonged to us. I thought we'd catch a bus to Nebraska. People didn't just fly in those days. I didn't even tell Papa Roy good-bye. Why should I? He was too busy with Gloria to bother with me.

When Bobby came home, Faina was asleep in the other room, her troubled body in the bassinet next to his bed. I took Cammy's hand in mine and said, "We're leaving."

He didn't say "So long," he didn't ask where, he didn't even bend over to kiss Cammy. Maybe he thought it was temporary. He thought he was off the hook, dumping the three of us like rotten fruit. I didn't mention Faina was in the other room, and he didn't ask about her. I think he'd forgotten he had another daughter. That's how little he was in our lives.

For years, I relished the terror he must have felt when he heard her first scream and discovered he was stuck with her. Stuck. Like me.

Hi Honey,

I know it's later than I promised, but if you saw the scene here, you'd know there isn't much time to scratch off a letter. And I'm not exactly a writer. Don't pretend to be either.

Are things O.K. there with Lenore? Tell her the cash is coming, it'll take awhile for me to get it all worked out. God knows she doesn't need the money. Her old man was loaded. I'm sure he left her plenty. Jesus, look at the way we've scrambled through the years. Did you hit it off with Cammy? I always thought it'd do you good to get to know your sister, your mother, too, for that matter. Well, here's your chance. I'm sure Cammy will show you the ropes, teach you to work the system—Lenore, school, Minn. Not exactly San Diego, is it?

Well, it's hot as hell here in the Indian Ocean. I cut the sleeves off my shirts just to survive the sun. This rig's so far out in the middle of nowhere, they fly us in by helicopter. Just water. Not another goddamn thing. The work is hard labor, prison would have been a vacation. I'm roughnecking, that means I'm on the drill floor. Too much to explain. Twelve hours a day of torture. Takes a whole shift to change a worn-out bit. Wiley got the easy gig working on the generators. No wonder he conned me into coming. I wish to god he'd told me what I was in for.

There's not a whole lot to report here. Can't write on my shift, no time. We drop into bed dead tired. Eat. Sleep. Work. Can't even get a cold beer. Guess they're afraid we'll get tanked up and kill each other.

Here's a card with the address of the co. office in Perth. We can get our mail there on our big week of freedom. Two on, one off. (Helicopter to Barrow Island, prop plane to Onslow, fly to Perth. Get it now? Way the hell out.) We're splitting a house in Perth with some other guys, hotbunking. It's not a palace, but the price is right. Remember that I love you. Dad

25

Cammy Missing

That summer, Tony was driving it up from a farm in Wisconsin. We could make a hundred bucks easy, just selling it to punks on the street. We were living high. Happy. I didn't think of going back.

Tony gave me a home in his basement place off Park Avenue. It wasn't much, but it kept back the heat. Days we slept stoned for free. At night, we hung out on the streets.

"I'd have to be dead broke to sell my skin for cash," I told Tony when we walked past the hookers.

"Won't be long now," he laughed, pulling me close against his hard stomach. Sometimes we'd dream about what I'd bring in, how rich we could be, but it never came to that.

I could have had the customers. Cars slowed when they saw me, but I just swung my hips, kept moving. Cops crawled along Lake Street like ants in honey, taking it all in, but it was rare you'd see them bust somebody. They were friendly with the regular girls, drinking bad coffee at the Lake Street Lounge. I learned early that a loose smile could get them to look the other way.

I made up my mind I wasn't going back to my mother, wasn't working as her steady nurse, pouring her drinks and rubbing the chipped polish off her yellow nails. Wasn't going back to the same stories she'd fed me for supper. Wasn't trying to save her again, just to have the cops nipping at my ass. She could drink herself to death without me. I wasn't her little girl.

The street was my family. I breathed the exhaust fumes, sour piss in empty alleys, and felt my blood rush. Tony lit my cigarettes and tangled my hair between his fingers. People were afraid of him, his temper and his rep. They stayed away from me.

It was months before he slapped me, his hand burning a mark on my cheek. He'd been drinking heavy, dope never made him so crazy. He threw me against the wall of the Salvation Army; the jagged bricks scratched the skin off my back. Bums scattered, but no one stopped him. We all knew enough to mind our own business.

"Come on," I said, leading him into the Poodle Lounge. "Let's get you something to eat."

When he was up at the bar, I snuck out the back door. I ran between houses, dogs barking and people drinking on their front steps. For a few miles I was sure I heard him behind me, but I never slowed down until I got to her building. The downstairs door was locked. I guessed right away she did it against me. I threw a rock through the basement window, climbed through a tunnel of sharp glass to safety. Then I passed the night huddled up in the corner, hoping for some sleep. I couldn't decide if I was desperate enough to go back to her, how low I'd have to sink before I came home.

In the morning I ripped off a box of Ritz crackers and a Coke from Kenny's Grocery. It was a smooth routine I'd polished through the years. Then I sat on the bus bench, letting the salt and soda explode in my stomach. I was still deciding. Tony or home? I suppose I was half hoping my mother would look out and see me, rush down the stairs and beg me back in. But then I pictured her, passed out in bed, too hung over to lift her head off the pillow.

This is the truth: I hated that girl when I saw her. When she stepped out onto the sidewalk, dressed in my Led Zeppelin T-shirt and jeans, it took me a minute to believe it. Faina? The girl from the picture, the girl who had stolen my father. That stray dog, my mother's lost daughter, my missing sister. Faina. She had come to take my place.

Faina The New Girl

By August, we've settled into a sleepy routine. Mornings, Lenore wakes slowly, giving her eyes time to adjust to the light. In the freezer, I keep a dish of frozen washrags, and I carry one to her bed and smooth it out on her forehead. Then I deliver her a strong cup of coffee, bitter with a bite, the way she likes it, and a cold Bloody Mary with a crisp celery stalk. While she comes back to earth in peace, without my *childish chatter*, I run downstairs to the bakery for her marmalade twist.

"How's the new girl today?" Frances says to me. Frances always calls me "the new girl," her greeting half-scolding, half-friendly.

When business is slow, she visits with me. All of our conversations are quizzes, a series of questions too long and complicated for me to answer. It happens everywhere I go—the bookmobile, Border Drug, Kenny's Grocery—everyone wants to know something about who I am, why I'm here, where I've come from. "You're not from around here," they say. "It's as plain as day; I can hear it in your voice." I've already lost track of the stories I've told trying to dodge the truth. A niece, a friend of the family, just a girl visiting from California. All of this I hide from Lenore, so I'm allowed to go out, sometimes in the daylight, and see a small piece of this strange city.

"So," Frances says today, placing her hands on her hefty hips. "Now that September is right around the corner, I suppose you'll be going home to California."

"I suppose," I say. With Frances, I've found it works best to agree.

"She shouldn't keep you up there all day. It's not healthy. Do your people know where you are?" She pats her meaty hand along her crown

of white braid.

"Yes, they know," I say. "I'll take the usual. Two marmalade twists."
I fiddle with the dollar bill I've wound around my finger like a bandage.

"Marmalade twists. She used to eat them every day, when she had the
old man to fetch them for her. Or the girl. She's always got somebody
doing her bidding. But it's been years since she's been in here herself.
Why don't you buy a nice loaf of bread? What do you people live on?
Sweets?"

"I don't have the money today. Maybe tomorrow."

"I tell you it isn't healthy. September is coming. Some of us are smart
enough to know what's going on upstairs. You belong in school. So did
the other girl. It's the law. And they'll catch up to you sooner or later.
Ask her."

That afternoon, we watch Lenore's soap operas: *As the World Turns,
The Doctors, General Hospital.*

"These shows are more real than people think," she tells me. She's
drawn a diagram of the characters for me in an old spiral notebook of
Cammy's. Between the names she's drawn dozens of colored lines
marked *marriage, birth, divorce, affair.*

"Check your outline," she says, whenever I ask a question. "I'm
watching."

To stay busy, I paint her nails frosty pink, ruby, even a blue raspberry
I found in Cammy's room. I file the sides up to a sharp tip. She loves the
attention, her hand held in mine, the slippery finger massage I give her
when I've finished.

"I guess we hit it off after all," she says, giving me a weak smile. "Isn't
it sweet?"

All of our days are sluggish, spent stretched out in her bed surviving
the humidity. So when the phone suddenly rings, we startle like
spooked horses.

"Should I answer it?" I ask, my heart pounding.

"Hurry." A nervous fear washes over her face. "It's Cammy."

I race down the hallway, eager to answer before the caller gives up on
us. "Hello?" Nothing. I press the plastic receiver against my ear, sit
down on the tapestry phone bench.

"Hello?"

There's a rustle of breath on the other end, but not the heavy prank-phone-call pant of slumber parties. "Hello?" I say again.

"Faina, is it her?" Lenore shouts from the bedroom.

"Hello?" I repeat, but then the phone goes dead.

When I return to Lenore's room, she's sitting upright at the edge of her bed, her eyes open wide, her hands clutching her satin nightgown. "Was it Cammy?"

"I don't know. They didn't say anything."

"It was her. I should have answered. Your voice must have scared her."

"How do you know?"

"Mother's instinct, Faina. It's Cammy. She's coming home."

The rest of that day we pass in a hush, listening for the next ring or the click of a key turning in the lock.

"Time drags when you wait," Lenore complains. "Let's do something."

We return again to the old red scrapbook she keeps under her bed, the fat album of photographs she loves to explain. I hold it on my lap, the leather cover gummy against my bare thighs, and flip the pages carefully so the snapshots won't spill from their tidy triangular corners.

"Always be careful with memories," she warns me.

We study the black-and-white images of the life that came before me, the strangers who are my family. Papa Roy and my grandmother, Eileen, people I'll never meet.

When Lenore touches them with her fingertips, it's as if she steps into the scene. "There I am standing outside the playhouse Papa Roy had built for me in the back yard of our Kenwood house. It was a magical place, full of tiny handmade furniture. A refrigerator. A stove. All the neighbor kids envied me, begged to play in it, but I preferred to be alone. Like most only children I suppose. Selfish. You never really learn to share. But Papa Roy and I spent hours in there, playing house. You can't imagine how strange it seemed to see a giant man folded into that small of a space. He let me serve him tea, make-believe cookies on a little platter.

"Look at me. That blonde halo of curls." She runs her finger under the caption, *Papa Roy's Angel,* written in white ink. "I'm surprised

Mother even wrote that. She detested his pet name for me. Later, he called Cammy the same thing. Mother hated his fondness for beautiful girls."

"What about me? Was I ever Papa Roy's angel?"

"Oh, you couldn't be. You were never blonde. The angel name came from our soft white curls. You were a different look entirely. Born dark like a gypsy. Like Bobby. You look just like your dad."

"No. I mean, did Papa Roy like me?" I try to picture him holding me as a baby, bouncing me up and down on his strong knee.

"Sure, he was crazy about you. Who wouldn't be? He kept your picture in his wallet until the day he died." She claps the cover of the album closed, slips it back under her bed. "I'm beat."

"Then why didn't you ever visit me?"

"Visit you? What do you mean?" She tap-taps her fresh pack of Salem cigarettes against her palm, pulls the long red cellophane thread, crumples the wrapper in her hand, and passes it to me. "Throw that in the wastebasket, would you, sweetie? I'm going to have one quick cigarette before my nap."

"I mean, why didn't you visit me? You and Papa Roy and Cammy." When I close my fist around her garbage, the cellophane crinkles into the quiet.

"Well, naturally, we couldn't go that far. We always hoped Bobby would bring you back home. It was his responsibility. I wasn't well, Papa Roy either. He had high blood pressure, heart trouble. I was always frail. Good health doesn't run in my family.

"I don't know what possessed Bobby to take you to another state. So far away. I left you with him so briefly, while Cammy and I took a trip to Nebraska. But when I got back, poof! You were gone.

"Mother, too. I lost both of you in the same year. Papa Roy and I sold the Kenwood house, it was too much to keep up, too much memory. He owned this property then, so we moved in temporarily. It was close to downtown, Papa Roy's haunts. A few years later, he let it go, and we became renters. Papa, me, Cammy. We were so happy then, living here, it never dawned on Papa or I to move on. Rent was cheap. It had to be. We were living off of Papa Roy's assets. We played cards all afternoon, read poetry, drank Manhattans before dinner, watched TV. There had been so many years with Mother between us, it was a relief to finally be alone."

I'm tired of her story, her straggling sentences, tired of the life she lived without me. "You could have written to me," I say. Those words have kept me company for so many years, when I finally release them, my heart stalls as if I've lost something.

"Write? What would I write about? In my condition? You've seen for yourself; there's nothing much to say."

———

By night, we're still waiting for Cammy's call. "The calm before the storm," Lenore announces, staring out at the hazy white sky. "I smell a tornado coming. I'll never be able to sleep."

"Do you want me to read?" We're three chapters into *Jane Eyre,* one of Lenore's favorites.

"No. I can't concentrate on anything." She ticks her nails against the edge of her glass. "Why don't you set us up for cards? The diversion will do us some good."

———

In the kitchen, I gather the supplies we'll need: a fresh glass of vodka, ice cold to take the edge off the heat, with a dash of Fresca for flavor. The rest of the chilly bottle belongs to me. I've learned to like the sour taste, the cool lime surprise. I pop a small batch of popcorn, shake the pan carefully, four inches above the burner the way Lenore taught me, so the kernels won't burn. Then I drench it in butter, a quarter of a stick, until the popcorn is soggy.

Finally, I retrieve the tin cigar box of coins from Papa Roy's desk. My betting money, the coins which used to be his, my keepsake. "He'd want you to have it," Lenore said to me. "He'd be amazed at the way you took to the game." I love the smell of it, old tin mixed with sweet tobacco, the way I imagine Papa Roy must have smelled when he held me to his chest. Whenever I open it, I open a memory, and I'm a baby in Papa Roy's big hands, being lifted up to the sky.

———

"You lead," Lenore says, passing my cards to me.

Between hands, we stuff our mouths with popcorn, lick the grease off our fingers to keep the cards clean. I'm winning, as usual, which makes Lenore happy. "You're sharp as a tack," she says, patting my knee. But she's far away from the game, half listening for that phone to ring. "I wish Papa Roy could see you play. You don't know what it's like to lose somebody." She stretches her arms up over her head, leans back in bed, then struggles to light a Salem with a wavering match. "My hands are so bad. Faina, I'm sorry, I'm not with the game. My nerves are getting to me."

"I know what it's like to lose somebody," I say. "I miss my dad every day." I think of the letters I write him each night, the mail that never comes for me.

"Oh," she laughs. "Your dad. It isn't the same." She presses my head down onto her shoulder, strokes my flushed cheek. "You're happy here with me." I close my eyes and smell her Fresca breath, her summer sweat, her smoky skin. "And you always will be."

Then abruptly it arrives, exploding into our night, the ring, Cammy's precious call.

"Help me," Lenore says. "I want to answer this time."

I pull her liquid body up in bed. It's always harder to move her at night, her legs too rubbery to support her own weight. I loop my arm around her waist, stagger her quickly down the hallway. "Cammy?" she says frantically, picking up the phone.

I inch her into the nook of the bench seat, untangle her nightgown from around her blue legs. Then I kneel there, barely breathing, staring at her veiny feet, the curve of brown nails curling over her toes.

"Leave us be," she hisses. She slumps over, hands the phone to me. "Hang it up," she says, dropping her head into her hands and burrowing her fingers through the dark roots of her hair. "I was wrong. It wasn't Cammy."

"What did they say?" I ask. Outside, there's a crack of thunder, then the flash of lightning.

"Not now, Faina. I should have seen it coming."

That night, the storm Lenore predicted arrives, not a tornado but a torrent of rain and hail that batters our building like stones.

When I wake, there's no electricity, the refrigerator is dead. In the freezer, Lenore's washrags are lukewarm, the ice beginning to melt.

"Do you want me to run across the street to Kenny's for fresh ice?" I ask. I'm perched on the edge of her bed, snapping my flip-flops nervously against my feet.

"Stop, please," she snarls, pulling the limp washrag over her swollen eyes. "It's so muggy in here, I can't think."

"The electricity is down. I need to go out for food."

"No more going out. You've done enough damage already."

"What damage?"

"If you wanted to go to school, you should have told me."

"School?"

"How was I to know September was coming? In my condition, the days run together. Now you've dragged Frances into our business. Who knows where the trouble will end?"

"I didn't tell Frances anything."

"Of course you did. Why else would she threaten me? I can't send you to school. Schools are full of perverts and thieves. It was school that took away Cammy."

Perverts and thieves? Not at Ocean View Elementary with the waves outside our classroom windows, the garden courtyard where we gathered each day to eat lunch. Green picnic tables and cobblestone paths, the tetherball pole, the old teeter-totter even the big kids loved. Mrs. Orr, my sixth-grade teacher who hugged me good-bye on my last day. *You've got a good mind, Faina McCoy. Don't be afraid to use it.*

"Besides, I'm too sick to be here alone. I'll teach you at home. Aren't I teaching you already? I'm a valedictorian, for heaven's sake. I can tutor a twelve-year-old."

"But Frances said it was the law."

"What are you now, an attorney?" Lenore tosses her wet rag down on the carpet. "I'll hide you up here, like Anne Frank in that attic. I shouldn't have let you go outside in the first place. I knew they'd take you away."

After that phone call, I'm her prisoner again. The bookmobile is forbidden, all the errands are done by delivery, we learn to live without our morning treats from the bakery. We go back to the chain on the door, the check slipped through at the last minute, the package picked up only when we're certain the footsteps have faded.

"I don't want to be locked inside forever," I tell her. "I don't care about school, but I want to go out in the world. I never stayed indoors at home. I miss the beach. I miss swimming and seeing my friends at the sno-cone stand."

"Look at me," she says. "I live without that, and I'm happy."

"But Frances knows I'm up here. What if she calls the police?"

"Faina, please. I'm trapped in a black hole. My nerves are nearly shot."

I mope in my bedroom with the door closed, write in my diary, refuse her requests to look at the scrapbook or watch TV. I've returned to the stubborn girl who arrived here six weeks ago. "I want to go home," I write to my dad. "Please come for me."

"Okay, you win," she says, handing me her empty glass for a fresh drink. I can hardly believe my good luck. She surrendered so quickly, after just a few days of chilly silence.

"Really? I can go outside? To the bookmobile on Thursdays? The bakery? Border Drug?"

"No. Stay away from those spies. You're going to school. Like Frances says, it's the law. It starts in a week."

"With perverts and thieves?"

"I've signed you up at Cathedral. It isn't cheap, but it's private and it's just past the park down Dakota. I'll make your father cough up the money. I can't enroll you at Jefferson, where I sent Cammy. Too much water under the bridge."

"Cathedral? What kind of name is that for a school?"

"It's Catholic. And you're lucky they're low on enrollment. Just twenty-eight kids in the seventh grade. You'll be safe."

"But I'm not Catholic."

"They won't know the difference. You're from a Kenwood family, that's qualification enough. Besides, Mother was raised Methodist. Methodist. Catholic. It's all the same thing. She took me to church on holidays; I can teach you enough to squeak by."

Once the decision is made, I'm back in her bed. We abandon *Jane Eyre* for Lenore's mother's Bible, an elegant ivory book with delicate pages edged in gold. Some of the stories I know already, from the Free Church Bible Camp I went to every summer on the beach. Adam and

Eve. Noah's Ark. Moses and the Ten Commandments. The Christmas story. The Crucifixion. I like the drama of the Old Testament best; it reminds me of Greek mythology: floods, famines, battles.

"This you can keep," Lenore says, handing me her mother's bookmark, a silky red ribbon with the Shepherd Psalm embossed in italic gold letters. "It's practically brand-new. You can see how much time Mother put into religion."

"The Lord is my shepherd," I recite, baa-ing on all fours like a sheep. "I shall not want."

"Don't make a joke out of this," Lenore says. "Those Catholic sheep herders won't think you're funny."

"But I'm not a sheep."

"I've got news for you, kiddo, you will be."

In the back of the Bible, under the section marked Family Record, I discover the Dahl Family Tree. They're all there on blue branches, their names and birth dates calligraphied in gold ink. Eileen, Papa Roy, Lenore, Cammy. Everyone except my dad and me. When Lenore's asleep, I take out my Bic ballpoint and draw an awkward black branch for me and my dad. Then I add our names, but even in my best handwriting, it's obvious we don't belong.

The day before school starts, my uniform finally arrives by taxi. We've been envisioning this plaid jumper ever since the day Lenore placed the order by phone. "The saleslady said it was a lovely wool blend, gray and blue plaid, very classic. At least we won't have to buy you a closet full of clothes. It comes with two white blouses. Hang them up. Keep them clean."

But when I take it out of the box and hold it up to me, it's huge. "Try it on," Lenore says. "It might not be that bad."

I look like a dwarf in it; the top half, from my shoulders to my waist, droops like a deflated balloon. The thick pleated skirt reaches my calves. "I can't wear this."

"Let me see the tag. It's a size twelve all right. I just told them to send a jumper a small seventh-grader could wear. Maybe the Catholics run big." She tugs the top away from my chest. "I can't fix that!" she says, laughing. "But how hard can a hem be?" She balances her cigarette between her lips, folds the fabric up to my knees. "There now," she mumbles through clenched teeth. "That's better. Go get Mother's sewing basket from the front closet for me."

I stand on her bed and pass her down straight pins while she tacks up my hem with twitchy hands. "A good ten inches will do the trick." When she's finished, it's my job to thread the needle and sew. "Just go in and out in a straight line. My hands shake too much for needlework. You better hope you don't inherit my nerves."

After I've knotted off the last bit of thread, I slip the jumper over my head, stand on her bed and look into the mirror. A bulky band of hem circles the skirt. Every few inches, royal blue thread pokes through the plaid. "I'm not wearing this. I look ridiculous. People will laugh."

"Don't worry, little girl, " she says, tickling the back of my calf. "You'll fit right in."

Lenore Departure

It was Frances who started the school trouble; it was Frances who burned the black hole into my bed.

By August, Faina had grown on me. Days, she stayed next to me, content to linger in my bed and study old family photos, her apple breath brushing against my ear. Asleep or awake, I felt her near me, the warmth of her little body soothing my ragged nerves.

Still I sent her. To save her from the authorities, the same people who threatened to take away Cammy. To save her from what was ahead.

The morning Faina left, the clouds were solid and low. Nothing like other sunny Septembers, nothing like the string of Cammy's "first days." Her starched cotton dresses always laid out the night before, her lacy anklets tucked into gleaming black shoes. Always a fresh pack of crayons, new paper, a pink eraser and a pencil box. When she was little, I'd pack a special cookie in her lunch with a cut-out heart that read, "Mommy misses Cammy."

From the start, I was shrewd enough to know they brainwashed children in school, lured them away from their families. In that respect, we might as well be Russia; Americans are snowed by democracy.

"Want anything before I leave?" Faina asked, setting my hot cup of morning coffee on the TV tray next to my bed. "Let me help you to the bathroom."

"No," I said. "Go. I have to get used to being alone. Now is as good a time as any. You look nice," I lied. I abhorred the woolen uniform, the Peter Pan blouse. I wanted her dressed in Cammy's old T-shirts, the long frayed jeans that whooshed when she walked. The pantyhose I'd lent her sagged around her ankles, and that enormous jumper made her skinny legs look like bowed saplings. From somewhere, she had scavenged a pair of blue pumps Cammy bought on a whim her first year at Jefferson. "Those heels give you some height," I said. "They're a real improvement over your tennis shoes. Wouldn't your father die if he could see you today? You're not even the same little Faina who landed on my doorstep."

"I need to get going. I don't want to be late."

The rush to escape wasn't lost on me. By second grade, Cammy forbid me to walk her to the bus stop.

"Faina, let me put on your face," I begged. "Braid your hair, so you look decent today."

"Hurry." Reluctantly, she flopped down on the edge of my bed, dropped her chin into my hand. Even with the morning shakes, I managed to camouflage her dark gypsy skin. I painted lavender over her dusky lids. "This is the first I've seen you look like a real girl. You could be beautiful."

"I don't want to be beautiful," she said, straining away from me. "I've got to go; I don't want to be late." She tripped over the toes of Cammy's shoes.

"Those are too big for you," I called after her, but she was already gone.

When I heard the door slam, and the rattle of her shoes tripping down the back staircase, my breath left me. I sat up in bed. Ahead, I saw the end of our world. She was gone. Like Cammy. I struggled to cross the room to the window. Only two months past her arrival, and already she was running away, down Dakota Avenue, with Cammy's old denim book bag bouncing against her leg. How would I survive without her small shoulder to support me? What would I do without my little Faina McCoy?

Hi Baby,

Got your <u>letters.</u> You do much besides write me? They were giving me crap at the co. office. Don't know how you find so much to say. Should of read them in order, I had to go back and check the postmarks to follow the whole story. If I got it right, things have finally settled down with Lenore. She can be mad as a rabid dog. It was something I couldn't prepare you for. You'll get used to her. I lasted five, six years, and I'm still alive to tell the story. Too bad about Cammy. The two of them were probably at each other's throats. My guess is she'll show up eventually. Teenage stuff. They all go through it. You will too. Maybe it's just as well she's gone now, gives you and Lenore a chance to get to know each other alone.

However hard you think you got it, I'm telling you I'd trade places tomorrow. The work is hot and dirty, backbreaking, mud spraying in my face all day. We're 13,000 feet down and still nothing. Heard there was an explosion up at Darwin—another rig. Starting to dawn on me this isn't real safe. I've almost been done in twice. Nearly lost a leg breaking up some pipe. Long story. Now I'm just hoping to make it back alive. I'm an old man in this operation, this is work for someone young. Young and stupid. The stupid I've got covered. They wouldn't have taken me if it wasn't for Wiley having the connections. Don't feel much like thanking him.

Made it into Perth twice. Some races. Harness. Dog. But I'm watching myself. Wiley's losing plenty. I know I need to save enough to dig us out. I will.

Remember, I've been watching out for you for twelve years. You got the brains to fend for yourself. Be a big girl. I'm just doing the best I can. I guess what I'm trying to say is, have you started to forgive me? That's it. I think about you every minute. Stay out of trouble. I love you. Dad

Faina Sheep

At recess, the girls follow me to the small strip of blacktop along the backside of the school. All together, there are twelve girls in seventh grade, and they gather on the stone wall that separates Cathedral from the back alley to hear the next chapter of my story. I let them finger the silver bracelet given to me by my sailor, the boy who writes from Australia. I pass around pictures of Cammy, glossy close-ups of a blonde model cut from an old *Seventeen* magazine. I tell them about the Del Mar Track, my father's family business, the race horses we bred, the days I spent in the stable brushing their knotted manes. In the spring, my chestnut colt, Secretariat, will arrive from California, and I will begin jockey training at a stable outside Minneapolis.

At first, even the popular girls are fascinated by me. I cross my legs, dangle one pump loose from my toe. The nylons I wore the first day have been replaced by proper, white, regulation knit knee-highs. Sometimes Sister Cyril strolls over to our cluster to loiter at the edge and eavesdrop. Whenever I know she's listening, I raise the stakes. I describe the way my sailor kissed me when he left for sea, that last dark night we spent alone on the beach. Sister pulls a hanky from the hollow of her sleeve and pretends to blow her nose, but I know she's taking in every word.

Mornings, our whole class gathers in a circle for prayer. We hold each other's sweaty hands, join the voice on the loudspeaker reciting the Our Father and the Hail Mary, prayers I've memorized from the *Daily Mass Book* I stole from the church pew on my first day. After the loudspeaker beeps off, it's time for special intentions. I offer petitions for Cammy, my older sister, who's off on modeling assignments in foreign countries. Italy, France, Spain. I tell Sister Cyril we have a map at home, with colored tacks to help us keep track of Cammy's location.

Sister Cyril raises her eyebrows, hesitates. *Lord hear our prayer,* she says reluctantly. "Fauna, who supervises your sister when she's traveling?" she asks, when we've returned to our assigned seats.

"It's Faina. My father, usually."

"Oh, really?"

"Really."

Sister says *oh really* after every question I answer. I know she's trying to trap me in a lie, but I've developed my talent for telling stories.

After prayers, Sister walks down the rows of desks for inspection. She lifts the girls' faces toward the fluorescent light, examining us for mascara, lip gloss, any *artifice that would prove distracting*. While she checks the girls, the boys slouch in their desks confidently, their long legs stretched into the aisles, their dirty hands crossed behind their heads. When she comes to me, she yanks my chin upward, studies me with her bloodshot eyes. Then she leans closer, sniffs my skin for powder or perfume. "Our boys don't fall for cheap gimmicks," she says, while the familiar buzz of snickers hums through the room.

Each time she lifts my chin, my cheeks sting with the memory of my first day at Cathedral when she made me scrub off my *war paint* in front of the class. The damp brown paper towel she waved like a flag, the fleshy stain of make-up splotched across it. *Acclimate yourself, Miss McCoy, if you plan to stay.*

We spend all day in the same room, crammed into worn wooden desks. In silence, we copy Sister's paragraphs off the blackboard, fill in the blanks in our workbooks. The textbooks are old, with tattered pages taped at the edges, and the names of previous readers listed inside the front covers. Andy Carver, '65. Carry Martin, '66. My classmates' older brothers and sisters. "Whose do you have?" they ask each other, and I wish there was a book with Cammy's name.

Everywhere in this dusty, yellow-brick building, there is silence. The silence of the sun on the linoleum floors. The silence of the empty hallways. The silence of the statues, the silent eyes of the saints. Sister's silence that stretches over our long days. The silence of the library where we are only allowed to choose books from three shelves.

At recess, I tell the girls about Ocean View Elementary, where the roses bloomed in the courtyard and we walked outside between buildings to switch classes every hour. We had choices about what we studied, electives you could sign up for at the beginning of the year. Last year I chose Greek mythology and pottery. During free periods, we sprawled on the grass in our bathing suit tops, gossiping. We ate corn chips and passed around cold bottles of Mountain Dew. Every class was a fresh mix of faces; with seven hundred kids you couldn't know everybody.

"Seven hundred!" the girls gasp. "Weren't you scared there?"

"No," I say. "Everyone had their own gang."

"I couldn't stand that," Emmy Atwood says. She towers over me, the fierce, blonde-haired leader of the girls' group, the one who interrupts my stories, the girl who orders my audience away when she's tired of listening.

"Why not? Think of all the friends you meet."

"I'd rather be with people like me. At Cathedral we can be sure of the kind of kids we're getting."

"Yeah," Carolyn Pugh agrees. She is Emmy's pasty reflection, Emmy's homely parrot, the girl who copies Emmy's every move. "Emmy and I have lived next door to each other since we were babies. We wouldn't want to be friends with just anybody."

"That's true," Emmy says. "I mean, I've known every, well, almost every, kid in this school since first grade. When my mom and I go to church every morning, Monsignor always gives us a special smile. We're an old family. My parents went here. We never, well, almost never, have to worry about strangers."

"Strangers aren't always a bad thing."

"That depends," Emmy says. "On whether or not they know how to take communion. Or if they're just pretending to fit in."

"What's that supposed to mean?" I know she's talking about Mass on my first day of school. "What are they saying?" I asked her, when Monsignor set the host on my classmates' tongues. One question, and she'll never let me forget it.

"It means what it means," Emmy says. "Let's go watch the boys play football." The herd of girls follows her to the wire-mesh fence that separates the two playgrounds.

"Sheep," I say. "Baa." But no one hears me.

Once a week, we line up single file and walk downstairs to music class. Sister Linette hands out mimeographed sheets with the lyrics from *Jesus Christ Superstar* printed in watery purple letters. We are not expected to sing along; our true work is to recognize the genius of the lyricist. Through rock and roll, we are coming to understand the drama of Christ's suffering.

When we've finished listening to one side of the record, Sister Linette takes out her guitar and turns into Mary Magdalene, strumming "Everything's Alright." The girls chime in, but the boys let their lyric sheets drift to the floor.

After class, Sister Linette puts her hand on my shoulder, pulls me out of the column of seventh-graders heading back to Sister Cyril's room.

"Faina, you know all the words?" she says, smiling.

"I do." Cammy owns the album; I've memorized it at night as part of my training.

"What does this story mean to you?"

I'm not sure what she's asking. I look down at her thin sandaled feet, which embarrass me, because compared to Sister Cyril in her full black habit, Sister Linette looks naked in this modern outfit.

"Faina, I see it in your face. You understand Christ's anguish. How tempted He was to second-guess God."

"It's a sad story."

"But He didn't, did He? He followed Our Father's plan. It's amazing how the raw pain of it can still strike you as new."

Sister settles her dewy brown eyes on me, and for the first time since I've come to Cathedral, I think I'm looking into the face of a friend. She lays her hand on the top of my head. "You seem to be a bright girl. I can see it in your eyes. I'm looking for an assistant to straighten the music room after school while I give piano lessons. You can decorate the bulletin board, fold the chairs. How would that be?"

I want to accept, but I know Lenore will expect me at home.

"It'll keep you out of trouble," Sister says. "Do we have a deal?"

"Yes." I know we don't, but I can't bring myself to disappoint her. "If my mother will let me."

"I'll be happy to talk with her," she says. "Would a home visit help?"

"No," I say. "I'm sure she'll let me."

"Good. Faina, you know I was just fourteen when I made the decision to join the order. Sometimes in hardship, God shows us our destiny."

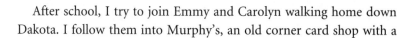

After school, I try to join Emmy and Carolyn walking home down Dakota. I follow them into Murphy's, an old corner card shop with a full rack of candy. We spend our quarters on red-hot jaw breakers with bubble-gum middles and long ropes of red licorice we wrap around our necks. The boys from our class are there, spending dollar bills they earned on their paper routes, and they shove past us to the counter where they unload handfuls of candy. Outside, they balance on their ten-speed bikes, their yellow paper sacks flung behind their backs, their pockets fat with treats.

They trail us on their bikes, back-pedal to keep pace with our slow strides. They spit sunflower seeds at my feet, their saliva speckling the sidewalk. Sometimes a gob of spit lands on my shoe or drips down my hair. "Get lost," I scream, flipping them the finger. "You're disgusting."

"Faina, it's your own fault," Emmy Atwood says. "You ask for trouble." She and Carolyn tilt their heads together, giggle, whisper about me, sneak the boys an occasional shy smile.

"Emmy, you coming to the game on Friday?" Tom Payne shouts. "We're going to kick Painter Park's ass."

Emmy shakes her hair so it cascades down her back like a sunny waterfall. "Maybe."

"Don't bring that little sailor slut. She'd be doing the whole team."

"Don't worry," Emmy laughs. She and Carolyn quicken their steps, hurry ahead of me. Then they take off running, their arms locked together at the elbow. I walk alone, wishing I could leave my body, fly free over the black lush canopy of elm trees.

"Sailor slut," they shout. "Put out. Put out."

"Go to hell," I shout back, but I can't stop them. They keep it up, a steady chant, until at last we're at Twenty-second Street and they pedal off toward football practice down at Dakota Park.

At home, Lenore sleeps. When I slip inside her dark bedroom, she opens her eyes, lazily, then returns to her dreams. "Wake me for supper," she murmurs. "I'm glad to see you're home." I empty her overflowing ashtray, crumple the empty packs of Salems, pick up her half-eaten serving of cottage cheese and canned peaches, dried into a heap on the china plate. Then I carry it all to the kitchen to wash up the few dishes left from the morning: my cereal bowl with the crust of milk, my crystal goblet of orange juice, Lenore's coffee cup. I wash them in scalding water, leave them to air dry in the wire rack.

In my bedroom, I step out of my uniform, hang up the jumper and blouse. I trade them in for Cammy's old jeans; they're huge on me, but I love the fringe hem and the Flower Power decal ironed onto the back pocket. I slip her Led Zeppelin T-shirt over my head, inhale the smoky smell of Cammy's clothes, Lenore's smell. For a minute, Cathedral disappears, and it's August again; I'm stretched out in Lenore's bed watching *General Hospital* or playing *Jeopardy.*

Then I remember my homework, and it's September, the trees changing to yellow, a thin layer of white frost splashed on the grass in the morning. I lie down on Cammy's bed, my chin propped on my palm, and puzzle over my religion workbook: *Values Clarification and Moral Development.* It's full of hypothetical situations we must resolve correctly. Tonight, I'm a parent whose child is dying of pneumonia. I'm too poor to afford the medicine. To save the child's life, I decide to rob the corner pharmacy. No one is killed. Did I act morally? Why or why not? If I argued my case in front of God, what would my justification be?

Every question paralyzes me. I am cursed with seeing every side, a trait Sister says proves my own moral ambiguity. She has instructed me to narrow it down to black and white. Is it right to rob a store? Is it right to let a child die?

I know the correct answer hides in the green *Teacher's Guide* on Sister Cyril's desk, and tomorrow she'll open it, read the response to the class to point out how far wrong I've gone. If I could steal the *Teacher's Guide* for one weekend, I could memorize the correct answers, and coast through the rest of the year. I'd get the straight A's I deserve, the straight A's I earned in San Diego. But instead, I'm stuck here, with the early darkness creeping over our apartment, wondering whether my child should live or die.

When Lenore finally wakes, I take my old place next to her in the bed. Although she's lost interest in our reading, she wants to sit, dozy eyes half-closed, and listen to me. "Tell me about your day at school," she says, closing my hand inside hers. "I'm so lonely here without you."

"It's sort of strange," I say. I don't tell her about Sister Linette and the rock opera, or the bulletin board she wants me to decorate after school. I don't tell her about the sunflower seeds or the stream of saliva stuck to my hair. I don't tell her about Emmy Atwood running away from me. Instead I say, "I don't think the kids like me."

"What do you mean?" she asks, her voice urgent and high. "Did you do something rude?"

"No, I didn't do anything."

"Then why wouldn't they like you? It's important you fit in."

"I fit in," I lie.

"Try," she pleads. "Don't let your coloring set you apart. It's important you do well there. I don't want anyone coming after me."

"No one's coming."

"You don't know, you don't know, you don't know," she repeats, her voice quivering. "We have enough trouble already."

"I won't. There's no trouble." Lately, Lenore tells me the same things over and over, as if she's forgotten she said them the moment before.

"Be a good girl, Faina. For me. I just want you to be safe and happy. I was never happy. Never happy."

"I'm happy, Lenore. Don't worry."

When I have calmed her with a cigarette and fresh drink, it's time for me to help her with her bath. In the summer, I used to wait outside the bathroom door while she took care of her privacy. Later, she would call for me, and I would help her stumble back into bed. But these days, she can't go far without me. The loneliness is too long for her. I fill the deep tub with hot water, sprinkle in Dreft, hang her silky robe on the brass hook. When she's ready, she lifts her brittle arms like a baby, and I raise her nightgown gently over her head. Together, we fold her naked body into the tub, the warm water splashing over the edge. I try not to look at her bare skeleton, the skin sucking in below her ribs, the sparse patches of strawberry hair. Before Minneapolis, I'd never been in the same room as a naked woman, and her body horrifies me.

I skim my shy hand quickly over the scabby sores, the scattering of raw wounds covering her back and butt. I try to keep my eyes on the pink and black hexagon tiles, the old grout brown and crumbling.

"I'm sorry," Lenore says. I know she detects my repulsion, my eyes that are always looking away. "I wouldn't ask you to help me if it wasn't necessary. I can't go without soaking these bedsores. I wish there was a way to get rid of them."

When she's finished, I loop my arms around her slippery waist to lift her from the tub. Then I set her down on the toilet seat, wrap the heavy terry towel around her shivering body. I will never have a baby, I promise myself. I'm filled with disgust for small and vulnerable things. My own tiny body. I hand her the robe, wait until she's closed it around her, and then I lead her back to bed.

In a few minutes, I will put her behind me, shut off her light and leave her to dream in the darkness. But still she follows me, the stench of her bedsores, the Dreft detergent, the smoke, the brittle bones.

Once she's asleep, I huddle inside Cammy's old peacoat, take my place outside on the fire escape. I like the darkness of the alley, the cool night air of autumn, the neon palm tree of the Paradise Club flashing, the smell of greasy burgers from Rusty's Tavern. Every night I come here, open my diary, write it all down.

But tonight, I have company—the dark-haired boy I've seen bagging groceries at Kenny's. He's down below, in the alley, hands hidden in the pockets of his loose leather jacket, staring straight up at me. "You got a smoke?"

"What?" I wrap my fingers around the cold metal rail, peer over the edge of the fire escape. "Are you talking to me?"

"Yeah. You got a smoke I can bum?"

"I got one inside. Hold on." I tiptoe back into Lenore's room, sneak out a Salem cigarette she'll never miss. Then I hurry back to the fire escape to get there before he disappears.

When I step outside, he's still there, grinning. "Any luck?" he asks. "I'm hard up."

I throw it down, and he catches it gracefully, one-handed in midair. "Menthols," he says, drawing in a deep drag. "It's like smoking a box of mints. But it's better than nothing. I think I've delivered groceries to your place. You live here?" He nods behind me toward the building.

I slip my diary into my jacket pocket. "Sort of. Temporarily. How about you? You live in the neighborhood?"

"I'm temporary, too. New Directions. Halfway house across the alley. That's why I've got to smoke before I get home. What's your name anyway?"

"Faina," I say.

"Strange," he laughs. "Strange name. Anyway, thanks for the cigarette. I guess we'll see you around."

Hi Baby,

So she put you with the Catholics. I had to laugh. I can still hear Lenore's old man calling me a fish eater. Not that I cared about the name, he called me plenty worse. But I wish he was alive today to see his golden girl, Lenore, kneeling next to you in the pew down at Cathedral. Dropping his cash into the basket. Amazing the way it all shakes out.

I did the God gig as a kid, guess that's why I never dragged you into it. Whatever you decide, I'm right there with you. There were things I took from it, all right. Some I find myself falling back on now that I've landed here in hell. Some you'll use. But let me set you straight. Whatever you missed along the way in terms of church was my mistake. Your soul, sweetheart, is A-O.K. You've been in someone else's hands since you sucked in your first breath. How else could we have made it this far down the road?

You're smart, you'll pick the program up. The whole nine yards. Kneeling. Letting the wafer melt to pieces on your tongue. Genuflecting. Don't forget to dip your fingers in the holy water dish. If I was home I could have run the routine past you. It's not something you forget. God knows Lenore's out of her league.

Just be happy you're not here. I'm still kicking myself for coming. Worst mistake I ever made. And I can't get off the rig. Not if I want a ticket home.

You're not missing anything. Some wallabies on Barrow Island. Sharks swimming around the rig. Perth's an O.K. break, but we're hanging in the slums. The ocean's ocean. I've had enough to last a lifetime. Don't even want to go back to the marina. Think we'll start over in Alaska. The cold looks good to me right now.

Now that school's on, you don't need to write so much. I don't want your fingers falling off. Besides, I can't keep up. There isn't time to write a word, let alone a letter. I've given it my best shot. This is more than I've 49 *written in a lifetime. I love you. Behave yourself. And while you're at it, light a candle and rattle off a Hail Mary for your old man. I could use the* 50 *help. Now and at the hour of my death. Amen. Dad*

Faina Ghost in the Graveyard

This Halloween, Emmy Atwood has decided the seventh-grade girls are too old to go trick-or-treating. Instead, she'll host a costume party with pizza, door prizes, and a seance to bring back John F. Kennedy.

"I invited all the girls," she told me. "Even you. It's a school rule. With so few of us, the mothers have agreed not to leave anyone out."

"Stay home," Lenore begs me. "This isn't a night to be out. I remember one year a black cat was stabbed on Halloween. On the news, they're warning parents to check the candy. Last year some lunatic tainted caramels with LSD."

I adjust Papa Roy's hunting cap on my head, button his orange vest. It isn't much of a costume, but it's the best I can do. I want to celebrate Halloween, see Emmy's house, call back John F. Kennedy with the rest of the kids. "It's a school rule," I lie. "Sister Cyril makes all the seventh-graders work the Halloween party for the younger kids. She's put me in charge of the costume parade. I'll be safe. Emmy Atwood's mom is picking me up at the bus stop out front. She'll drop me off by ten o'clock."

"I wish you had told me earlier. I would have given Sister Cyril a piece of my mind. A girl your age doesn't belong out at night. Just last year a runaway was murdered down at Minnehaha Creek."

"Lenore. I have to do it. I'm judging the costume parade. I don't want to start any trouble."

"I don't like it," she says, swallowing the last of her drink. "Be careful with Papa Roy's hunting cap. I have so little left of him. And pour me a fresh one, please. I'm going to need it to calm my nerves."

Outside, it's so cold I can see my breath. I love the woody smell of fall nights in Minneapolis, the musky leaves, the smoke rising from the chimneys. I pass New Directions, the halfway house where the delivery boy from Kenny's lives. I've been watching for him since the night we met in the alley.

Packs of trick-or-treaters run past me, their plastic orange pumpkins clattering with candy. I tell myself I'm safe out here, with parents everywhere pushing baby strollers or following their kids door to door. But then I remember the runaway murdered at Minnehaha Creek and I hurry toward Emmy Atwood's house. Maybe after the party her mom really will drive me home.

I think about Halloween in San Diego, my Batman costume I never outgrew, our neighbors sitting on their front steps passing out candy, offering my dad a shot of whiskey or a cold beer. "Now who might this masked man be?" they always asked, but they knew me. I think about the end of our night at Keith's Coffee Shop, the glass of milk he served me to wash down the chocolate, my candy spread out on the counter, my dad claiming the Almond Joys.

When I reach Alden Avenue, I leave behind the rush and hum of Dakota for Emmy's peaceful, dark side street, a part of the city I've never seen, the fancy world where Lenore must have lived with Papa Roy. All the huge houses are decorated for the holiday. Glowing pumpkins, scarecrows on hay bales, witches on brooms hanging from trees.

My feet ache from the cold soaking through my tennis shoes, and my hands are frozen into stiff fists. Shivering, I stop in front of Emmy's house. 2632 Alden. It looks just like I imagined it; a fairy-tale palace with pillars, balconies, a princess tower rising out from the roof. Bright jack-o'-lanterns line the winding brick walkway. I picture the circular staircase leading up to Emmy's room, and her canopy bed done in white lace. When I press the doorbell, chimes ring.

"Yes," Emmy's mother says, opening the door and smiling down at me. "Do you want to say trick-or-treat?" She hesitates before reaching into a bowl and handing me a giant Hershey bar. I can see Emmy in her: in the icy white hair wound into a hive on her head, the thin string of pearls on her pale neck, the sharp white teeth. "Trick or treat?" she reminds me.

"I'm here for the party," I croak out, before she closes the door.

"The party?"

"Is this Emmy Atwood's house?"

"Whom shall I say is calling?"

"Faina McCoy."

"Ah, yes. The new girl with the odd name. We haven't seen you at Sunday Mass."

Inside the entryway, I shudder from the sudden rush of warm air, the sweet smell of baked apples, Mrs. Atwood's heavy perfume.

"Is that a costume?" she asks me.

"Sort of. I came as a deer hunter. It's my grandfather's."

"How kind of him to lend it to you."

"He's dead."

"Is that right?" she smiles. "Well, I'm sorry."

"Is Emmy here?"

"Of course she is. It's her party. You're just a little late arriving. The girls are already feasting on pizza down in the rec room. Please leave your shoes on the mat, we don't want to scuff the floor."

The wooden floor mirrors the crystal chandelier, golden and glassy. I imagine Saturday evenings with Emmy playing piano, and Mr. and Mrs. Atwood waltzing over the polished sea.

"May I take your coat?" she asks, reaching out toward me.

"That's okay," I say. "I'm still pretty cold."

"I'm sure it's quite a change from. . . . Is it San Francisco?"

"San Diego."

"Yes, well, California."

I kneel down to untie my shoelaces, but my fingers are so cold they won't move.

"Your hands are blue. No mittens in this weather? Well, at least you had the good sense to wear *something* on your head."

At home, standing in front of the mirror, listening to Lenore praise Papa Roy's shooting skills, his cap had filled me with pride. But now I'm ashamed of it.

"I'm so glad you girls have decided to go out trick-or-treating. You should stay children as long as you can. Emmy's our baby, youngest of five, so of course we don't want to see her grow up."

I follow Mrs. Atwood through the shining rooms of the mansion, past the enormous leather furniture, the polished tables, the hand-painted china cabinet, the grandfather clock donging loudly in the long hallway where the wall is a gallery of Emmy's family.

"I suppose it shows—we can't get enough of our children," Mrs. Atwood laughs. "And Emmy's our delight. Our last little girl. Well, this is it," she says, opening a door to a paneled staircase.

In the rec room, a few girls from my class flock around silver platters of chips and dip, large glass bowls of candy corn and chocolate kisses. Along the bar, tiny orange pumpkin lights flicker on the half-eaten pizza slices abandoned on paper plates. The familiar burn of hunger returns to my stomach.

"What took you?" Emmy says. "We've been waiting." Tonight, with her lips painted blood red, and a black wig on her head, she's a witch in a long black satin dress. "Didn't you come in costume?"

"Not really." If I keep my coat on, she'll never see me in Papa Roy's orange hunting vest. "I didn't have time to put one together. We just got back from going out to dinner."

"Then what's that?" she asks, pointing at Papa Roy's cap.

"Oh, it's part of my grandfather's deer-hunting outfit. I brought it along for fun. It's not a costume really."

"I guess not. Deer hunting? Well, let's get going. We've been waiting long enough." Emmy swoops one arm over the girls and they rise together.

"Your mom said we were going trick-or-treating?"

"Don't believe everything you hear," Emmy says. "From my mom, especially."

I don't want to go back into the cold; my fingers and toes haven't thawed from my long walk. I want to stay with the greasy cardboard pizza boxes, the half-moons of crust, the cold cans of pop. Bring back John F. Kennedy. But instead, I scramble up the stairs behind the rest of Emmy's herd.

"Do you know where we're going?" I whisper to Carolyn.

"Shut up," she says, elbowing me in the rib. "You'll ruin it."

At the door, Mrs. Atwood gently glides the coats over the girls' shoulders. My classmates smile up at her, hoping to have their smiles returned. Sometimes she lays her elegant hand over a head, as a sort of blessing. "I'll see you precious goblins soon," she sings, passing us each a plastic trick-or-treat bag. "Save room for cider and my famous chocolate cake."

Then she lifts Emmy's hood over her head, tucking the black wig delicately behind her neck. "Be safe, Emmy," she says, kissing her quickly on the cheek.

"Mother," Emmy groans, rolling her eyes to the ceiling. "I'm almost thirteen."

"I know that, lovey. But when you grow up, you'll see the best mothers are the ones who protect their children."

Outside, under the glow of streetlights, we walk briskly behind Emmy, weaving in and out of trick-or-treaters. Most of the parents say hi to Emmy and Carolyn, while the little kids rush past us. "Have a good time," they say, waving us on. "Be safe."

When the wind steals Papa Roy's cap from my head, I chase after it, into the street, bending to catch it every few steps.

"Sad costume," Emmy says. "What a loser."

I return to the pack, the girls walking in rows, their arms hooked around each other's waists. "*Hey Jude, strip nude,*" they sing out, their voices broken in the rush of wind. They bump their hips against each other, shrieking. I try to latch on to the end of one group, but Carolyn twists away from me.

"Where are we going?" I ask, but they just keep shouting out the song. "Aren't we going trick-or-treating?"

"Grow up," Emmy says.

At the end of Alden, the big houses disappear. "Where are we going?" I ask again, terrified by the darkness.

"Lakeview Cemetery. Across the street," Carolyn says. "Now quit asking."

"Why are we going there? I don't like cemeteries." I've never been in one, but I know it's not a place I want to be on Halloween night. "They're creepy."

"You're creepy," Carolyn says to me. "It's a Cathedral tradition. We can't have girl-boy parties until the eighth grade, so the seventh-graders meet for Ghost in the Graveyard. It'll be great. Besides we think Dave Fadden is going to ask Emmy to go with him tonight." Carolyn loops her arm though Emmy's.

"Go where?"

"Go with him, stupid. Go steady."

I picture Dave Fadden sitting across from me in class, his desk stuffed with crumpled papers, the shreds of pink eraser littering the floor near his feet, the ink blotches on his fingertips, his spongy hand in mine during morning prayer circle.

"Dave Fadden? He's a worm."

"He's captain of his football team," Carolyn cries.

"I might not say yes," Emmy says. "I went with Jeff Feldman last year and it was so boring. All he did was hide sticks of gum in my desk. Dumb. I'd rather wait and see if an eighth-grader asks me."

"I wish someone would ask me," Carolyn sighs, her voice heavy with envy.

"Not me. Those boys in our class are jerks."

"They're only mean to you, Faina, because you bring it on yourself. You shouldn't brag about that sailor. It makes you seem fast. Everyone says so. Our boys don't like loose girls. They were fine until you came."

I shove my stiff hands deeper into the pockets of Cammy's peacoat, balling my fingers so they won't poke through the holes in the ripped lining. "I don't think I'll go," I say, stopping suddenly.

"What do you mean?" Emmy hisses, bumping into me.

"It's too cold. Besides, I thought I was invited to a party."

"Duh. This is the party. If you want to go back, go. But you'll go alone." I scan the circle of girls who have gathered around us; there has to be at least one who wants to turn back with me. "Don't show up at my house, you'll ruin everything."

"Faina," Carolyn says, pulling me by the elbow. "Don't be a baby."

I turn to look at the dark streets we've just crossed, the journey through Emmy's neighborhood I'll have to take alone. I remember Lenore's warning: *Girls are murdered in this city every day.*

"Okay, I'll come," I shrug. "But it's a stupid game."

"All right," Emmy says. "Let's get going."

When we reach the iron gate of the cemetery, we squeeze sideways though the narrow opening. On the other side of the wrought-iron fence, the hills of the cemetery dip into darkness. Everywhere there are headstones, and trees with branches that look like skeletons against the night sky.

"This is crazy," I whisper. "Let's go home."

"We must be early," Emmy says, searching the graveyard with her small flashlight. "I don't see the boys anywhere. Let's play while we wait. I'll go first. It's my party."

"What are we supposed to do?" I ask, shivering. My eyes tear from the bitter wind.

"I count," Emmy says. "And you run as far as you can. When I get to one hundred, I'll come looking. If you go over the second hill, you're out of bounds. Just freeze in one place until I find you with my flashlight. If you see me first, you run out and tag me and it'll be your turn. One, two, three," she says. "Get going."

Emmy turns her back to us, and we dash off in every direction. The only sounds are Emmy counting and the crackle of leaves crumbling under the stamp of feet.

"Don't follow me," Carolyn hisses, shoving me away. "Everyone finds their own hiding place."

I run straight ahead, trying to memorize the hiding places of my classmates. I want to stay close to the gate, close to the sound of Emmy counting. "Fifty-one, fifty-two, fifty-three." The cold air feels like fire inside my lungs, and a sharp ring of pain tightens around my chest. I drop down behind a marble tree stump, rest my back against a scroll engraved with the dead person's name and date. Between pants, I cough up a thick mucus that catches in my throat. Even in the cold, my skin is hot with a mixture of fever and fear.

When I can no longer hear the distant comfort of Emmy's counting, I press my knees into my chest and pull Cammy's coat down over my stiff legs. I listen for the sound of Emmy's footsteps and for the first time in my life, I pray for a miracle. I ask God to lift me out of this dark place, and deliver me home to Lenore. I want to be there next to her, tucked in safely, her familiar snore soothing me off to sleep.

"Please God," I plead. I'm down on my knees the way I've learned to do at weekday Mass. "Please save me."

But when I open my eyes again, I'm still here, surrounded by spirits and a dense forest of dangerous trees. *Yea, though I walk through the valley of the shadow of death, I will fear no evil.* I wish I had my shepherd bookmark with me, a lucky charm to keep me safe, the way I used to wear my dad's watch to the dentist.

"Emmy," I scream. "I'm leaving."

In the distance, the streetlights of Alden shine like moons. If I follow them, I'll find my way back to the gate, then I'll race down the street until I'm back among the lucky families, the happy trick-or-treaters, whose lives are nothing like my own.

"I'm leaving," I shout again, confused by the incredible stillness. Any minute someone should run up to me, or Emmy's voice should ring through the night: "All-y, All-y in free."

"Not so fast," a voice growls. I'm strangled backward by the collar of my coat. Rough wool gloves cover my eyes, and another hand whips Papa Roy's cap from my head. "Guess who?" he laughs.

"Careful, you'll get scabies," another voice says.

"Emmy," I cry out, but my voice is muffled under his hand. I kick back at his shins, thrash wildly against him. But he twists my arm, throws me face down to the ground, crouches on top of me. "Give up?" he says.

When he rolls me over I stare into Tom Payne's ghostly face, the raw red skin circling his mouth like lipstick.

"Get lost," I shout, rearing up my hips to throw him off, but he pushes the weight of his body into my stomach, presses his strong knees into my rib cage. He smothers my mouth with a scratchy wool glove that smells like wet dog and smoke.

"So she's a rag," Dave Fadden says. "Get off her." He stands over me, Papa Roy's cap perched on his head. "I'm a deer hunter," he says, his hand on his hip, his voice shrill like a silly girl's. "Aren't I just the sexiest thing?"

"She thinks she is," Tom Payne says. "But let's see."

His breath reeks of cigarettes and peppermint, some kind of sweet booze.

"Forget it," Dave Fadden says, nudging Tom Payne's back with the toe of his boot. "Let's go find the girls. I want to see Emmy."

"You go get Emmy," Tom Payne says. "Leave this one to me." He grinds a handful of leaves into my face; I blink back the dry specks of dirt crumbling into my eyes. "I just want to know if she's got anything."

"Who cares?" Dave Fadden spits. "She's a sleaze."

Tom Payne kneads his free hand into my chest, and the pain cuts through to my spine. *You bring it on yourself.* He presses one knee between my legs, tugs open the top of my coat until the button pops off.

"You're fucking crazy," Dave Fadden says. He nooses one arm around Tom Payne's neck and chokes him off of me.

I stand up to run, but Tom Payne trips me. The heel of his work boot slices into my ankle. Then he's over me again, his angry fist beating against my face. Warm liquid trickles down my lip. "Let her go," Dave Fadden yells, pulling him back again. "What the hell are you doing?"

"Deer hunting," Tom Payne laughs, and falls backward into the leaves.

I stumble up, take off running to save my life that seems somehow to be lost already. I choke on the blood and tears that stream down my tight throat.

"Faina," Emmy yells, her evil voice carried forward by the wind from her dark hiding place. "Faina, don't you dare tell anybody. It's only a game."

Lenore The Accident

As usual, I smelled the danger before her. And still, she insisted on that costume parade.

Weak as I was, I took care of her. I tucked her in next to me, dabbed her bloody lip with wet cotton balls, arranged my frozen washrags on her broken face. When I pressed my body next to hers to stop the shivering, her skin felt like a furnace.

She wouldn't go to school with bruises on her face. Why should she? She was ruined beyond recognition, her upper lip swollen, a deep gash dividing her eyebrow, her left eye the muddy blue of midnight, her cheek brown and round as a rotten peach. I told the principal she had bronchitis; the last thing we needed was that school snooping around.

"You'll go on," I whispered into her ear when she curled into a cold ball of sorrow. The truth was, I didn't know what would become of her face, how long the scars would last, if it would ever recover its original shape.

"Don't tell your father. He'll never forgive me for letting you go out at night."

"I'm sorry about Papa Roy's cap," she said to me. But that wasn't the only thing I'd lost.

I hungered for justice. If I had been another mother, I would have called the police, brought her into the emergency room, but it wasn't safe. Stronger, I would have searched those grim streets for the assailant myself, clawed out his eyes with my bare hands. I had dreams of slicing him open with a steak knife. Who was he? Some reckless man on a bike who drove his tire over my daughter's body, jabbed the pedal into her fragile ribs, smashed the handlebar into her sad face. Crushed her under his weight.

"It was an accident," she babbled over and over. An accident? Sure. Too fast around the corner, crashing into a little girl. But what kind of man would pick up his bike and disappear? What kind of monster would leave my daughter for dead?

Sweetheart,

What the hell kind of news is that? An accident? I couldn't make the pieces of the story fit together. Did they catch this guy on the bike? If I'd been there I would have tracked him down, beat the shit out of him. You know me. I'm starting to get worried. Is Lenore looking out for you? Sounds to me like it's the other way around.

Forget those kids at school. Forget them all. It's a short stint, remember that. You won't be there forever. Don't let them screw around with you. I think I'd feel better if Cammy was around, she should be looking out for you.

There was an accident here the other day. One of the roughnecks got hit on the head when some pipe fell from the derrick. Nice guy, Patterson, from Louisiana. Don't know whether or not he'll make it. This is young guys' work, most are in their 20's. I should've done it then, but I was swamped with you. Think raising you took most the fire out of me. Now I'm too damn old.

I'd come home tomorrow if I could. It's crossed my mind. Get on a plane in Perth. The only thing keeping me here's the money. How much I owe. How much I have to earn. Stay off those streets. Jesus, what kind of place is Minneapolis? I remember it as tame. I love you babe. Dad

Cammy First Snow

By late November, we were killing time waiting until the first snow fell. Life on the streets had gone to hell, it was so cold, even the dogs came in out of the alleys. Every few days a few flakes fell, but nothing steady. Still, we all knew how hard times would be ahead.

I took a job cutting keys and stocking hardware shelves at Sears. My boss, Clayton, was okay. Slow, but he had a thing for me. Bought me french fries every break at the food counter. I did a good job helping him with the inventory, ordering out-of-stock paints and sorting the tiny bins of nuts and bolts. If customers had big questions, I sent them over to Clayton. Nobody expected a girl like me to know the first thing about hardware.

It was decent money. Time-and-a-half on Sundays. When I got my check on Fridays, Tony cashed it for me at Chicago Lake Liquors, bought the two of us a bottle of Lambrusco to celebrate. We passed the icy nights with warm wine bubbling in our stomachs, splitting a frozen pizza, watching *Mannix* reruns on his black-and-white TV. Once or twice, I got the urge to call my mother, to let her know I was living a good life without her. To tell her I had a real home, I wasn't running. I wanted to know if she was still there, that skinny mutt, that girl whose name we'd almost forgotten.

When Tony would stop in on my shift, he'd case the place a bit. Get an idea of some things he'd like me to lift, check out the register, if I was ever left alone with the drawer.

"He can't come around," Clayton told me. "Mr. Durand says no."

Durand's rule was the start of the trouble. I was too many hours out of the house, too many hours leaving Tony to run loose and play his bad games.

The day the bleeding nearly killed me, Clayton found me doubled over in the stockroom. He brought me some wet paper towels to clean up the mess, soggy wads that shredded in my hands.

Weeks before, I'd gone down to the Sunshine Free Clinic; I wanted them to check out the boulder bulging in my abdomen. I filled out their two-page questionnaire, gave them my number of partners, sexual practices. I laid, legs spread open on their metal table, while they prodded my insides. The nurse ran tests for syphilis, gonorrhea, maybe a couple of other diseases, but came up empty. Instead of curing me, they put me in a dark room and ran a film strip through a projector. It was a stupid thing about teen pregnancy. How to prevent it.

"Go home, Cammy," Clayton said to me. He was a dumb guy, never married, and he was too skittish to see a female bleed. "I'll call Mr. Durand."

I could feel the blood seeping down the inside of my jeans. I kept my legs close together, leaned hard on Clayton's arm.

"Don't worry about the inventory," Clayton said. "I'll take you home." I knew he'd cover for me, tag and shelve the outlet covers before Durand had a chance to catch on.

Clayton's Mustang was souped up, roaring muffler and fuzzy dice dangling from the rearview mirror. It was clean as a plate inside, leather seats, the smell of cherry. The air from the heater blasted into my face.

"Turn it down," I snapped. "I can't breathe."

"Let me take you down to Abbott Hospital. It's a couple of blocks."

"No," I said. "I'll be okay." I was afraid of the law, the record checking. I didn't want to replay that day I'd taken my mother down to Abbott. The day that started it all. The day that sent me running. "Just take me to my place."

I didn't think ahead to Tony; the pain shooting through my brain made me stupid. But he should have heard us coming. When I flipped on the basement light switch, Tony was straddling her, his hairy chest greasy with sweat.

"Who the hell is that guy?" he shouted at me.

"I could ask you the same thing," I screamed.

"What are you doing sneaking home in the middle of the day? Hoping to catch me at something?"

"Cammy, let's go," Clayton said. His hand was on my shoulder.

I struggled free from Clayton and lunged toward the bed. The whore screamed, "Tony, Tony." But he couldn't save her, I beat her head into the mattress, her hair knotted in my solid fist.

"Jesus, Cammy," Tony shouted, over and over, dancing around me, naked. "Don't be crazy."

I forgot about the blood, the brick that throbbed inside of me. I had my old fight back. I scraped my fingernails over the whore's face, leaving her a deep scar for a memory.

"Give me back my money," I yelled at Tony. I knew there wasn't any left, but it was the principle of the thing. The months I'd been supporting his sorry ass while he screwed around on me. "Give it back to me."

"You're crazy," he said. He throttled my throat with his hands.

Maybe I was crazy. Clayton must have agreed, because he threw me over his shoulder, kicking and fighting, and carried me out into the cold. Who knows if Tony would have fought for me? But he was too smart to run stark naked into the street.

It wasn't until we were back in the car, engine revving, Clayton's arm pinning me into my seat, that I felt the wet clots oozing out of me.

"I'm taking you to my place," Clayton huffed. "My mother will understand." I didn't argue. I was too beaten to show up at Sears; I needed clothes, a place to sleep. I had no home. No mother to take care of me.

When we got inside his apartment, I hid in the bathroom, staring into the toilet while the slimy gray lumps slid out between my legs. Clayton opened the door, tossed in an old pair of work pants and a couple of dishtowels. I left them on the floor, wadded at my feet. My jeans were pulled down to my ankles, my legs covered in blood.

"Can you go to the store for me?" I asked.

"Sure, Cammy. Sure. For you I can do anything."

Outside the bathroom window, the first snow began to fall with a fury. Heavy white flakes piled on the trees. I remembered how, as a kid, I couldn't wait for the first snow. It felt like a promise. Like a new beginning. I tried to feel that again, but I was empty. I just felt cold and alone, crouched on the toilet, shivering, watching Tony's tiny baby slip clean of me.

Faina Jimmy Cordova

His name is Jimmy Cordova.

Winter nights when Lenore dreams beneath her down quilt, and the streets below our window are finally quiet, I take my diary outside to the fire escape, to write and wait for Jimmy.

Each time he crosses the alley, I pretend I'm there by chance.

"How was work?" I call down to him, my voice surprising in the still night.

"How could it be?" Then he climbs the fire escape, the metal stairs clanging under his leather work boots, to smoke one last cigarette with me before curfew at New Directions.

"How can you hang out here in the cold?" he asks, huddling down into his leather jacket, the fur collar pulled up to his chin.

I love the winter, the sparkle of snow in the streetlights, the hushed streets, the icy blue branches of the trees. I love the stillness, the muffled sound of footsteps.

"It doesn't bother me," I say, shrugging.

"Cigarette?" he asks, smacking a Camel from his pack and handing it to me. I stuff my mittens into my jacket pocket, press the fresh cigarette between my lips. When Jimmy's not here, I practice smoking, stealing a Salem while Lenore sleeps and sneaking outside for a quick cigarette. I've learned to love the hot smoke in my lungs, the cool mint on my tongue, the calm that crawls through my brain.

Jimmy leans toward me, offering a light off the flickering match he screens with his cupped hands. "Just one," he says. "Then I got to get trucking."

"How come I never see stars in this city?" Jimmy asks me. Tonight the sky glows the same pearly gray as the snow.

"It's the streetlights. They're shining so bright down here in the alley, it's hard to see the sky. When I lived in San Diego, the ocean was as dark as the sky, so that when you looked out into the distance, you couldn't tell the difference. It felt like the end of the world. Nothing."

"I'd like to see that someday," Jimmy says, flicking his ash over the edge. "Anywhere. I can't wait till I get out of this place."

"New Directions?"

"The whole scene. This goddamn city. I've done my time. Six months in Red Rock. Now this." He fiddles with the gold cross hanging from his left ear.

"What's Red Rock?"

"Ah," he says, spitting down into the snow. "A detention center mostly. Hell on earth. It's lockup. You know, electric fence, a watch tower. The whole works. I could tell you some stories, but I think they'd shock a little Catholic girl like you."

"Go ahead," I say. "Tell me."

"Not tonight," he reaches over and pinches my nose. "Maybe not ever."

I throw my cigarette down into the alley, pull my mittens out of my pocket. The hardest part of smoking outside in winter is how cold and stiff my fingers get. "I'm not that Catholic," I say, puffing warm air into my mittens.

"Cathedral? You got to be kidding. Besides, I know sheltered when I see it."

He unwraps a stick of Dentyne and sets it on my tongue. "Body of Christ," he says, laughing. "See I was Catholic once. Be smart. You don't want your old lady smelling it on your breath."

Winter in Minneapolis, the things I'll never forget. Cinnamon, snow, tobacco, Jimmy Cordova, his pink palms, his skin the color of caramel. "Our house is playing hockey at Dakota Park on Saturday. 1:30. Come on down if you want to see me skate. I used to be pretty good."

"I'll be there," I promise, although it will mean convincing Lenore.

"Good-bye, Faina McCoy," he says, standing. Before he leaves, he gives my stocking cap a little tug. "Go inside now, little one. It's freezing."

I creep into our quiet apartment, leave the lights off so I won't wake Lenore. Outside her bedroom door, I pause until I hear her snoring. By

9:30, she's disappeared into a sleep so deep, when I whisper, "Good night, Lenore," she doesn't even hear me.

Stretched out on my stomach in bed, I stare out across the deserted parking lot to the other side of the alley, where the warm lit windows of New Directions darken one by one. I know in one of those rooms, Jimmy sleeps, snuggled into a bunkbed probably, his shaggy hair fanned out on his pillow, his long eyelashes fluttering. I wish we could build an invention to connect us, a string with a pulley to send notes back and forth, or one of those homemade walkie-talkies with tin cans and wire. I try to send him a psychic message: *Jimmy, go to the window and look out at me. Jimmy, go to the window.* But he never does.

Finally, I give up, close my eyes and try to sleep. In just a few hours, Lenore will wake from a nightmare and scream my name until I appear at her bedside to calm her. "It's the nights that paralyze me," she'll say, clutching my hand. "If only I knew Cammy was safe."

On Saturday, I beg Lenore to let me go to Carolyn Pugh's house to finish our history project on Hiroshima.

"They expect too much of you at that school," she says. "Your face has hardly healed." She runs her hand along my cheek. "I hope you don't have permanent scars."

"It's daylight. Nothing will happen to me, I promise. Besides, I don't have a choice. It's assigned."

"I hate Saturday TV," she says, shaking her head. "Sports or old movies. I never should have sent you to school."

"I agree. But what can we do about it now?"

I stumble down the front stairs, clutching the wrought-iron handrail to keep from tripping in Cammy's high-heeled boots. Even with my jeans tucked into the white vinyl, the boots are so tall on me they jab into the back of my thigh. Outside, the glare of sun on snow is blinding. When I blink my eyes, white splotches glow inside my lids. I practice taking a few steps without wobbling. Through the frosty bakery window, Frances watches me, but when I give her a wave, she busies herself with her customers. Ever since the school threat, the bakery has been forbidden. I still crave the marmalade twists, but the trouble with Frances I can do without.

I teeter down to Dakota Park. I haven't been here since my bookmobile days last summer, and the old world of park benches and kiddie pool has been buried under a blanket of snow. I can't get over the strangeness of the seasons here, how the world looks brand-new with the weather. I trudge through the fields, sinking into snow like quicksand. Just a few months ago boys played baseball here, and I sat reading under the shady umbrella of elms. But everything's changed since then. Everything.

When Jimmy sees me leaning over the white boards, he skates close by and gives me a wink. He's so smooth on the ice, he's almost flying, his body gliding over the ground. Jimmy's speed makes it hard to keep up with the game, but when he scores a goal, he throws his hands over his head in a cheer of victory, and turns to make sure I'm watching. I don't know why, but I feel shy standing there, the only spectator, flinching each time the puck smacks against the boards.

Then suddenly, someone is slamming into Jimmy, pounding his body into the boards. My stomach sinks for Jimmy and for me, because I recognize that boy in the black stocking cap, the army jacket, that boy with the raw chapped circle of red on his face. Tom Payne.

I want to take off through these fields, run home and deadbolt my door. Instead, I pull my scarf up to my eyes, inch down my cap, hide inside my pea coat. If he sees me leave, he might tell Jimmy about Halloween, call me a slut, tell the sailor story. I don't want Jimmy to know the truth about Cathedral, the truth about me. When Jimmy skates by again, I see he's bleeding, a trail of blood trickling from his mouth. He wipes it away with the back of his leather work glove, winks again at me. "That's it," he says, skating off the ice. "Time for a break."

I follow Jimmy off the ice to a park bench frosted with snow. "Have a seat," he says, brushing a spot clean for me.

"That's it?" I ask. "So quick?"

"Nah, that was just a pickup game—you know, a little warm-up before the real thing." He runs his sleeve over his lip. "Shit, I'm still bleeding." Then he tucks his gloves between his knees. "Feel this," he says, pressing my face between his moist hands. "I'm burning." When he stares at me, his face flushed and wet, his black eyes glistening, I realize it's the first time I've seen Jimmy in the daylight, the first time I've really seen the cracked skin on his knuckles, the tiny emerald in the middle of his earring, his sharp side fangs. I lift my hand to my eye, hoping to cover the hint of scar that divides my eyebrow, the bluish bruise that's been with me since Halloween.

"I like your hair long," he says, lifting it up and letting it fall back to my shoulders. "Why do you always wear it in a braid?"

"My mom. She hates it in my face."

"Did you see I scored the winning goal? I'm hot today, even in borrowed skates. If I go back to Edison in the fall, I might go out for varsity."

"Yeah," I say, barely listening. "I can't stay. I need to get to the library to write a report."

"You're always writing," he says. "In that little diary. Ever write about me?"

"Why would I?" I burrow my hands down in my pockets, keep my eyes on Tom Payne. I want to get out of here before he sees me.

"Don't you think I'm interesting?"

"I got to go," I say, standing up. "I'll come and see another game."

"What's your hurry?" Jimmy says, pulling me back down on the bench next to him, so close our legs are touching. "Stay for a smoke at least."

"Here? We can't smoke here."

"Why not? The counselors don't care. We just can't smoke in the house." He pulls the Camels from his jacket, nudges one between my stubborn lips. "I got the Dentyne."

Maybe it's the blinding sun, or the sweat, or the rush of the game, but today Jimmy seems like a stranger. It was a mistake to meet him here, away from our secret world of the fire escape.

"Don't worry, little girl," he says, striking the match. "Just one smoke, then I'm going back for the real thing." He unzips his leather jacket, presses my hand against his drumming chest. "Feel that. My heart's pounding."

"Yeah," I say, pulling away. He rests his arm across the back of the park bench.

"Relax," he says, slumping closer to me. "You'll get to the library soon enough."

"Great boots, Fauna McCoy," Tom Payne shouts. "Really sexy." He's standing at the edge of the rink, hanging over the white board, eyeing me and Jimmy.

"That's the asshole who slammed me," Jimmy says, sitting up straight.

"You out sleazing?" Tom Payne yells.

"Get screwed," Jimmy shouts, flipping him the finger.

"Not by that rag. She's screwed everybody," Tom Payne screams. "Anyway, it looks like she's already busy with you boys from JD." Then he turns and skates back into the game.

"What the hell was that?" Jimmy asks. "He an old boyfriend or something?"

"No," I say, trying to hide inside my coat. "I don't even know his name."

"Well he knows yours," Jimmy says, lighting a second cigarette. "Sort of."

"He goes to my school."

"Well, he's got a thing for you." I let Jimmy believe what he wants to believe. I'll never tell anyone the truth about Halloween, or the trouble I brought on myself. "I'll kill that asshole," Jimmy mutters, huffing out a mouthful of smoke. "But he's right about one thing. Those boots make you look like a hooker."

"My mom's getting me a new pair for Christmas," I say, ashamed of Cammy's boots, the cracked white vinyl, the matted fur lining that doesn't even keep my feet warm. I wish I could tell Jimmy they're the only boots Cammy left me. "The snow soaks through my tennis shoes," I explain, but he isn't listening. He's staring off at the hockey rink, watching Tom Payne skate, and rubbing his fists down the front of his jeans.

"Next game, I'm going to beat the shit out of that punk," he says. "You wait and see."

"Leave him alone, Jimmy." I know if Jimmy goes after him, I won't be safe at school Monday.

"I don't walk away from a fight," Jimmy says, glaring at me. "You stay away from that kid: He's going to bring you trouble."

"What about Christmas?" I say, anxious to change the subject.

"Christmas? Who the hell brought that up?"

"You said you might get a pass. You know, to go home and see your family."

"Yeah, I did. Ten days."

"Ten days?"

He's still distracted, still hunting Tom Payne with his eyes. "Whatever that's worth. Holidays at my house are always a drag. My old lady cooks too much, my old man drinks too much. You know how it is with nine kids. The little ones get the best presents. Some crappy toy they've circled in the catalog. I end up with corduroy pants I wouldn't be buried in."

"You've got nine kids in your family?" This Christmas, Lenore and I will be alone, surrounded by decorations I've discovered in the hall closet: the Santa light with the burnt-out bulb, the miniature plastic tree I've set up in the living room, the porcelain manger set arranged at the side of Lenore's bed.

"The two oldest are off serving. And my sister Gwen's living with some loser who knocked her up, so my dad won't let her come home. My mom will spend the whole day lighting candles and crying for the ones who aren't there. It's always the ones who are missing that matter."

I think about Cammy's red stocking hung on Lenore's doorknob, her name printed with glue and gold glitter.

"Get some new boots," Jimmy says, standing suddenly. He zips his jacket, yanks his gloves back over his hands. "I got a game to play."

"You work tonight?" I ask, hoping we can go back to our fire-escape friendship, before I wore these ridiculous boots, before Tom Payne changed me in Jimmy's eyes.

"Nah, it's Saturday. I'll catch up with you some other time."

"*Angels we have heard on high.*" Sister Linette mouths the words to me, her hands clapping out the beat. We're practicing my solo for Friday's Christmas program. "Those who sing," she says to the class, "speak directly to God."

When we reach the chorus of Gloria, the whole class is supposed to chime in but, as usual, it's only the girls singing. And even then, they hardly raise their voices at all. Sister stops the song. "Cut," she shouts like a movie director. "I don't hear a single alto in the room." She tugs on her ear. "And the sopranos sound like a dentist drill. We'll sit here all day if we have to. In two days, your parents are coming to the Christmas program to see you perform, not to watch you take up space on the stage. Faina, you may rest while the rest of the class practices."

I take my place in the metal folding chair next to the piano and wait, wishing I didn't have to face my classmates while Sister Linette struggles to coax music out of the boys. They slouch down in their seats, their hands in their pants pockets, their eyes rolled toward the ceiling. The girls point at me, poke each other in the ribs and giggle. It's because of me they refuse to sing.

"Again," Sister Linette orders, throwing her arms out in front of her. "Or you can all come back at lunch and practice."

"Can I go to the bathroom?" I ask.

"You may go to the lavatory," she says. "Quickly."

When I return to the music room, the rest of my class has left. The brown folding chairs are scattered around the room, and the floor is littered with paper.

"Faina, I'd like to talk to you," Sister Linette says, ushering me toward her. "Come in and shut the door."

"I've got a math test."

"It can wait. I'll send Sister Cyril a note. Have a seat, please."

I smooth my uniform under my bare legs so my skin won't stick to the cold metal chair.

"I'm sorry your mother didn't give you permission to be my assistant," Sister Linette says, gently setting the cover down over the piano keys. "But I'd like you to sing your solo as part of the children's choir at Midnight Mass. You have a fine voice."

"Midnight Mass? What's that?" After Halloween, I'm afraid to walk by myself in the dark.

"Midnight Mass? It's on Christmas Eve, of course. Haven't you ever gone?"

"No, we go to bed early."

"Well, you're old enough now. It's quite awe-inspiring. I'd be happy to ask your mother when she comes to the program on Friday."

"No. I can't. Our house is always full of company on Christmas Eve."

"Even here?" Sister Linette asks. "I thought your family was new to the city?"

"We are, so it's possible we're going back to San Diego for the holidays."

"Faina, if transportation is a problem, I can make arrangements with another family. I'm sure your room mother, Mrs. Atwood, would be happy to give you a ride."

"No. Please." I blink to keep my eyes from filling with tears. I don't know why Sister Linette can't see it's my fault the kids won't sing.

Sister Linette sets her warm hand on my knee. "There are people here who are willing to help you. Are you having problems at home?"

"No," I insist, but the tears start falling. "I miss my sister, that's all. We don't know if she'll be home for Christmas."

"Where is she?" Sister Linette asks.

"In Spain modeling."

"Mmm-hmmm." Sister Linette says. "Spain?"

"Yes. At least that was the last we heard."

Sister runs her hand down my braid. "Faina, can we talk turkey?"

I nod my head yes, though I'm not sure what she means.

"There is some concern about you in the parish. Among your classmates' mothers especially. Something about a boyfriend who's in the Navy? Do you know what I'm saying?"

I nod again.

"You're too young to be with boys, Faina. To say nothing of a man who's old enough to serve in the Navy. Is it true he's written you letters? The girls say you've shown them the envelopes from Australia."

"Yes," I whisper, wiping my face with the back of my hand.

"You need to cut that off now," Sister Linette says sternly. "I want you to promise me."

"Okay," I say. That should be easy.

"And what about this other boy? Monsignor's had a call from a concerned parishioner."

"What other boy?" Another boy? I try to remember the other stories I've told. Maybe they've confused me with Cammy.

"Someone in a halfway house, apparently. You were seen smoking and kissing down at Dakota Park. Last Saturday?"

"That wasn't me."

"You're sure? Remember we agreed to talk turkey. It's time to be honest. We're both going to tell the truth."

"I am," I insist, my face tingling. "I've never kissed a boy."

"Is that the boy you snuck off with on Halloween?" Sister Linette keeps her eyes steady on mine to see if I'm lying.

"Halloween?"

"Halloween. When you were supposed to be at Emmy Atwood's party. The girls saw you sneak off with a boy. Mrs. Atwood said you didn't bother coming back to the house after trick-or-treating. Then you were absent for two weeks, and there was plenty of talk."

"I didn't sneak off with anybody. I was sick with bronchitis. I ran home."

"But you have marks on your face, Faina. Bruises and scrapes. We're all trying to make sense of it."

"I got hit by a bike that night. It wasn't anything big. The scars are fading."

"It isn't the physical scars that worry me. There is far more at stake than your face." Sister brushes the hair off my forehead with her fingertips. "Now, what about this one in the Navy?" Sister asks, lifting her eyebrows at me. "Didn't you tell the girls you used to French kiss? Minneapolis may seem like a big city, but our parish is a small town. Word gets around. There are very few secrets."

I squirm in my chair, pull my jumper down over my knees. "I'm sorry," I blurt out, burying my face in Sister Linette's shoulder. And I do feel sorry, very sorry. Sorry for my lies and the trouble I've brought on myself.

"Of course you are," Sister Linette says, rubbing my back. "Who wouldn't be? Your soul is all you have in the end. Come sing your solo at Midnight Mass, make an effort to turn things around."

At the school Christmas show on Friday, the gym is standing-room only. Parents and grandparents shout out names, wave from the crowd. The younger kids get the loudest applause. The audience laughs at their fleecy sheep suits, their tiny ears made of cotton. The third-graders put on the Christmas story with a Chatty Cathy doll wrapped up in a towel, while our class waits in the backstage darkness. We're angels in white bedsheets, with tinseled halos bobby-pinned to our hair.

"I got a boner," Tom Payne jokes, sticking his arm straight out of his gown while the boys fall against him choking back laughter. "For Mary." They pile on each other gasping for breath.

"Grow up," Emmy says, whipping her gown around like a cape.

"Oh baby, baby," Tom Payne says, rubbing against her with his tented sheet.

"Get away from me." Emmy barks. "You're disgusting."

"When the angels of the Lord fell upon them," the narrator reads loudly. On that cue we shuffle onto stage, my class taking their place on the back bleachers, me up front holding the narrator's microphone, waiting for the piano player to signal my solo.

"*Angels we have heard on high,*" I sing. Sister Linette is down on the ground, smiling up at me, her arms waving the way. "*Sweetly singing o'er the plain.*"

A high-pitched tone squeals from the microphone. The whole auditorium covers their ears.

Sister runs up and takes the microphone away from me. A new hush falls over the crowd. "You can do without it," she says. "Just lift your voice to the heavens."

I wait again for the pianist to plunk out the opening notes. Then I'm singing, the song squeaking out through the thin space left in my throat. Under my bedsheet my knees are shaking. But when I look at Sister, her eyes bright with pride, I keep going. I'm sure I'll bungle the next word, forget a verse, but somehow it comes out, word for word, the way I practiced it. The chorus is weak, a mumbling of low notes, even the girls are barely singing, but when my turn rolls around again, I sing to the heavens for Sister Linette.

Finally, there's the thunder of applause, and Sister Linette whispers "good job" as the curtain closes.

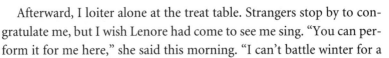

Afterward, I loiter alone at the treat table. Strangers stop by to congratulate me, but I wish Lenore had come to see me sing. "You can perform it for me here," she said this morning. "I can't battle winter for a song."

I choose another Christmas cookie, a buttery red bell from the platters of sweets the mothers have made.

"Did you see the mitten tree?" It's Mrs. Atwood standing beside me. I recognize her from the party, her high white hair, the pearls, the fur stole resting across her shoulders. She's talking about the huge ever-

green in the entry way of Cathedral. For Advent we've decorated it with donated mittens for poor children, and every day when we gather there for our Advent prayers, I think of all the lucky children who will have warm hands this winter because of us.

"Yes," I say.

"Well, I remember you weren't wearing any the night you came to Emmy's party. The donations are for poor children. Don't be ashamed to ask for a pair yourself."

On Christmas Eve, I count down the hours before I can go outside and say good-bye to Jimmy. Since that day at the skating rink, we've returned to our old ways. Dark nights. A last cigarette before bed check. But now we'll be apart for ten days, and I can't imagine how I'll survive Christmas vacation without him.

"Why don't you bring Cammy's record player in here?" Lenore says. "It isn't a holiday without listening to Perry Como's Christmas."

I set it up in the corner, light the holly and pine candles. "*Hark the Herald Angels Sing,*" Lenore sings along with the record. "Let me put your hair up," she says. "It wouldn't hurt you to look decent for once."

I sit on her bed and let her coil my hair up into a high bun. "This rhinestone clip belonged to my mother," she says, pinning it into my hair. "She wore it every Christmas." When she's finished with the bun, she rolls the loose hair along the side of my face into ringlets. "Isn't this fun?" she sighs. "It makes it feel more like a holiday."

"Hurry," I say, watching the clock. I'm meeting Jimmy out back at 1:30. "I want to get across the street before Border Drug closes."

"I hope you're not shopping for me. The one thing I really want, money can't buy," she says, her mood suddenly sullen. "You can't imagine Christmas without your child. If Papa Roy were here, he'd move heaven and earth to fix my broken heart."

"I wish I could find Cammy," I say, petting the top of her hand. "She'll come home soon. You'll see."

At 1:30, I'm out on the fire escape dressed in a velvet granny gown I found in Cammy's closet. I've come out without my pea coat so Jimmy can see me.

"What're you doing out here in that outfit?" Jimmy yells up to me. "It's freezing."

"Oh, I had to get ready for the company. We're having a big dinner party tonight. My mom made me wear something formal."

He runs up the steps two at a time to meet me. "Shh," I say, when he gets to the top. "I don't want my mom to hear us. She's awake."

"Right," he whispers.

Jimmy looks strange, too, dressed in tweed pants, his hair wet and combed in a wave away from his forehead.

"Self-respect. It's a New Directions regulation. What's with your hairdo?" He takes a step back to examine me. "Oooh, la-la." I fidget with the too-tight bun prickling my scalp.

"It's my mom's fault," I shrug.

"Well, one thing's for sure. It's not you. You look better with it loose. How come you're always trying to look older?"

I wish I could tell Jimmy the truth about my life, how I wear the things Cammy's left behind, how Lenore has dreams of making me beautiful. I wish he could see me in San Diego, in cutoffs and jeans running barefoot down the beach. "I'm not."

"Anyway, you're too young for me. Hey, remember that asshole at the hockey game? I slammed him up good, had a little help from my teammates. He was hurting bad by the time he left. I thought you'd be happy. Merry Christmas." Jimmy shakes his head and laughs. Then he reaches inside his jacket pocket and pulls out a small package wrapped in crinkled newspaper.

"What's that?"

"What's it look like? It's your Christmas present."

"But I didn't get you anything."

"Didn't have to," he says, dropping it into my hands. "It's nothing big, so don't let it blow your mind. It's a girl thing I made in O.T. And the way things are in my life right now, you're the only girl I ever see. So open it."

Inside the newspaper is a macrame choker made of thick purple twine with clear glass beads tied into it every few inches.

"Like it?" Jimmy smiles at me.

"A lot." I feel that familiar heat spread over my face again. "You made this?"

"Yeah, this weird artist lady shows up at the house once a week and teaches us all this crafty crap. I made a plant hanger for my parents." He takes the choker from my hands. "It's not too hard to do, you just got to get the hang of tying. The worst part is keeping the pattern straight. But I picked out these glass beads just for you. They're cool, you can look right through them." Jimmy lifts one to his right eye like a magnifying glass, squints as if he's inspecting me. "You should see what I see."

"What's that?"

"Nothing." Jimmy twists the choker around his hand. "So, you want to try it on?"

"Sure."

"Turn around. I'll tie it for you." I turn my back to Jimmy, hold the choker up against my neck while his frozen fingers fumble with the knot. "Merry Christmas," he says, stepping back from me. The twine scratches against my skin.

"I wish I had given you something."

"You could," Jimmy says. He stamps his boots against the fire escape. "How about a Christmas kiss?"

"Okay," I say, my heart leaping. I close my eyes and stand still as stone.

"It's been a long time," Jimmy says. He steps forward and takes my face in his hands like he did the day at the rink. "Here goes," he says, laughing. Then suddenly, his lips are moving over mine, his tongue slipping between my teeth. In a few seconds it's finished, but the taste of Jimmy's kiss stays with me. "Pretty good for a kid," he says, stepping back and staring at me.

"I'm not a kid."

"Maybe not," he laughs, again. "But I can't find out now. I got to go before the counselors catch me."

He flies down the steps the way he came, two at a time, and when he reaches the ice, he glides across the parking lot like a surfer, his hand slamming into the dumpster, his work boots leaving black streaks in the snow.

"Merry Christmas," I shout. I touch my fingertips to my lips. And I know as I live it, it's a memory I'll never forget.

Merry Christmas Sweetheart,

Don't know for sure when this will get there, after Christmas probably. I could of timed it better but there's no holidays in my world. Wasn't much here in the way of souvenirs, same stuff in every gift shop. The boomerang's an Australia thing, don't know if you've seen one, but thought you might have some fun with it. Show it to the kids at school. This one's handmade by the aboriginals, locals, the people who started it all. I liked the crocodile best, made me remember all those stuffed animals you used to sleep with, how I could hardly find you in your bed. Seemed you outgrew them overnight. Anyway, you're not too old for this croc. He needs some love. Like me. Treat him good. That's all for now. I want to get this in the mail so it makes it before next year. Drink some egg nog for me, honey. Merry Christmas. I love you, Dad

Lenore Winter Dream

It was Papa Roy who brought her home to me, it was Papa who heard my prayers. "Cammy's here," he whispered.

He was wearing his Christmas bowtie with the blinking lights. We were back at our old house on Lake of the Isles, a fire burning in the white stone fireplace, the colored light wheel splashing blue and green and pink over Mother's silver tinsel tree. Mother was playing the organ, "Oh, Holy Night," just as she did every Christmas Eve, while I sang along in French. "She's beautiful," I said to Papa. "Thank you for bringing her back to me."

"Is she who you asked for?" he said, stretching his legs out on the leather ottoman. "I didn't think you liked her. Come here to Papa."

I ran over and climbed into his lap, and Papa was big enough to hold me. He was alive, I could smell the cigars on his sweater. "I'm sorry I was asleep when you died," I said to him. Ever since the morning I'd found him, I'd been waiting to tell him I wish I'd been with him, holding his hand when his heart stopped.

"I'm alive now. Doesn't Papa Roy know what his little girl dreams?" He pointed toward the pile of presents he'd bought for me. Just like when I was his girl, there were packages nearly stacked to the ceiling, and all gift-wrapped by Daley's department store with the foil paper so popular in the fifties.

And then I saw her, yipping among the gifts, my little toy poodle, Yvette, with the red ribbons Papa had in her ears that Christmas morning. "Bring her over to Lenore," he said to Mother. "What are you waiting for?"

Yvette was so tiny, Mother carried her in a wicker basket. "I've knit her a little sweater to keep her warm in the winter," Mother said, holding the basket out to me. "You're a big girl now, Lenore. Remember to take care of her."

"I will, I will," I promised, snatching the basket. "Give her to me." I bent over to kiss her nose, the little black nose I'd loved for so many years. She was dressed in the coral sweater, the one with the zipper down the back, the one Mother knitted for Cammy. But when I picked her up to tuck her under my chin, she wasn't a dog, she was a baby no bigger than a doll. Only she was crying.

"This isn't what I asked for," I screamed at Mother. "Where's Yvette? I want the puppy Papa Roy promised me."

"She's here," Papa said, shutting off the lights of his Christmas bowtie. "Merry Christmas, angel."

When I opened my eyes, it was still night, and he was right. She was there at my side, shaking me awake. "Mom," she whispered. "Wake up. It's me, Cammy."

Faina Sisters

I have a sister. At night we sleep together in our narrow twin bed, Cammy's body clammy with sweat, her bare leg looped over my hip. "Don't go," she says, when I offer to sleep in the living room. "We're finally family." She nuzzles her nose into the back of my neck, closes her arm around my chest, and I lie there, falling asleep to the rhythm of her new warm breath.

"She's back," I write to my dad on Christmas night. "And you're right, she's beautiful."

"Let me see that," Cammy says, snatching it out of my hand. "Give me that pen. I want to add a word or two."

Hey what about you? Dropping my little sister off in another state? Nice going.

I want to know this girl, my sister with the black bikini underwear, the jeans so tight they stick to her skin. The thin slip of bare stomach at the bottom of every ribbed shirt, her ankle-high moccasins wet with snow, her suede fringed purse, the fake rabbit-fur jacket with the black vinyl collar and cuffs.

"What did I tell you?" Lenore says, lifting a handful of Cammy's blonde hair to her lips to kiss it. "My beautiful baby girl."

Now there are three of us lounging in Lenore's bed. Cammy's head resting in Lenore's lap. Lenore tickling her fingernails over Cammy's perfect white skin. "Do it again," Cammy yawns. "Draw something on my back."

Lenore never tires of Cammy's company, never closes the door on Cammy's conversation. "Give us some privacy," Lenore says to me. "Someday you'll understand."

When this happens, I wait in our bedroom, thinking of the questions I'll ask Cammy when it's our turn to be alone. I listen for the creak of the doorknob, the sound of Cammy's voice. "You get some sleep now," she orders, taking over my old job of pulling Lenore's covers up to her chin. Before she steps out, she snaps the shade closed, kisses Lenore on the lips. "You need your rest. Besides, I can't sit in here all day."

Then, I follow Cammy into the living room where we sit cross-legged on the stubbly lavender carpet, our backs against the ancient sofa. Surrounded by the scent of holly candles and the glow of blinking colored lights, we hardly notice the slow arrival of night.

"Smoke?" Cammy passes a Salem to me. "I thought she'd never go to sleep. You should tell her you smoke; she won't care. I've been smoking with her since sixth grade."

"I know. I'm going to tell her pretty soon."

I'm not ready to leave behind the girl I am in Lenore's eyes: a good girl, a smart girl, a girl with a bright future ahead of her.

"Papa Roy loved this room. He used to sit, late at night, smoking cigars in his leather recliner, his feet up, staring at nothing but the smoke floating out of his mouth. When I'd wake from a nightmare, I'd sneak around the corner to sleep in the little cave behind his chair. Later, he'd carry me to bed." When Cammy talks about Papa Roy she shares Lenore's sad voice. "He was the only one who could keep us happy. When he died, everything went down the drain."

Between cigarettes, we split a bowl of Ruffles potato chips, drink icy Pepsi, so cold it burns my throat. Sometimes, we sit like this for hours. "We're catching up," Cammy says. "It's been a long time living apart."

She wants to know everything about San Diego, her father, the man she barely remembers. I tell her about his job at the marina, our cottage on the beach, Wiley, Keith's Coffee Shop, the stores along Mission Boulevard, Electric Avenue with the black lights and posters, how warm the afternoon sun felt even in winter. I tell her how I got here, the gambling, the debts he couldn't pay.

"We'll go back there together," she says, stretching out on the carpet and resting her chin on her fist. "We'll wake up early and collect shells along the beach like they do in movies. Do you think my dad will like me?"

"Yes," I say. "He loves you already."

I tell her about her pictures and letters held together with a rubber band in his sock drawer. I invent stories of Cammy as a little girl, how sweet she was when she sat in his lap, the cute way she learned to say *cookie*.

"He remembers all that?" she asks, slowly running a strip of hair over her tongue. "My dad told you all those stories?"

"Sure. He talked about you constantly. He used to tell me stories about you every night before I went to sleep."

"Really? Every night?" Cammy says, opening her glassy blue eyes wide. She twists the wet strand around her finger. "Tell some to me."

"Well, he said you were Papa Roy's little angel. That Papa Roy loved you so much it made everyone jealous. Even me."

"That's true. I was Papa Roy's whole life. Next to Lenore. What else?"

"He said you liked to play pony on his back, and when he tucked you in at night, he sang you the same song he sang to me."

I'm running out of ideas for stories, mixing my memories with the details I've dreamed these last six months.

"What was that?" she asks. "I don't remember."

"'Anchors Aweigh.' From his days in the Navy."

"Oh, yes," she says, laughing. "I remember him singing that to me."

I wonder if my dad really did that with Cammy, or if she's fallen under the spell of my story. "Do you remember the way he'd rub his whiskers against your cheek after kissing you good-night? And how his fingers always smelled like engine grease?"

"Yes," she says, touching her hand to her face. "Faina, this is so weird. I mean, it's all coming back to me."

"What about me?" I ask, dipping my chip into the creamy pool of sour cream.

"What about you?"

"Did you guys ever talk about me?"

"I don't remember," Cammy says slowly, as if she's struggling to come up with the next sentence. "I thought about you, for sure. Who you were, what you were doing with my dad, that sort of thing. But while Papa Roy was alive, it was a dead subject. You know he hated my dad, and it upset my mom too much to mention your name."

My dad and my mom, Cammy insists, as if we're not really part of the same family. *My mom needs time alone with me, my mom feels better when I give her a bath, I'll pour my mom a drink.*

"Never? You never talked about me?"

"Not that I remember," Cammy says, lighting a fresh cigarette. "I want to live in San Diego so badly. I want my dad to know me."

"What about Lenore?" I ask. "Who would take care of her?"

"Who cares?" Cammy says. "I've done enough already."

Now that Cammy's home, we have food in the house. "I'm not living on TV dinners. I've had enough of that shit." She teaches me how to make Shake-and-Bake chicken, melt Velveeta cheese for vegetable sauce. "My mom liked to eat dinner when Papa Roy did the cooking." We make mashed potatoes from powder and milk, whipping the mix with the fork until it's thick. Some mornings, Cammy fries fluffy scrambled eggs with raw onions, serves them to Lenore in bed with a strong Bloody Mary. She scribbles the grocery list for me, her handwriting crooked and loopy. *Tomato juise, ry bread, baloney.* "Lenore wants me to stay out of Kenny's, in case the FBI is tracking me."

"Very funny," Lenore says, slapping playfully at Cammy's leg. "I just want to keep my family private. Is that so strange?"

"I don't mind going," I say, tucking the list into my pocket. In a few days Jimmy will be back, and I want it to be me, not Cammy, who stands at the cash register paying for groceries. Me, not Cammy, who watches Jimmy load the paper bag. I want to keep my family private, too. I want to keep Cammy from Jimmy.

All of our meals we eat in Lenore's bed, the sofa cushions propped behind our backs, our plates on our laps, our faces turned toward the TV. We sit like this for hours, through the *Sonny and Cher Show, All in the Family.*

"Honey, I'm just not hungry," Lenore says, when Cammy inspects her plate.

"Oh, for Christ's sake, Mother. Eat. Think about what happened last time."

Last time, Cammy says, and Lenore swallows another hill of cold potatoes.

"I'm taking Faina down to see Daley's eighth floor," Cammy announces. She's put on make-up: fleshy base, black raccoon eyeliner, a shiny coat of white lipstick. "It's New Year's Eve. The last day. I wouldn't want her to miss it."

"No," Lenore says. "You girls stay home here with me. It's ten below zero."

"What's Daley's eighth floor?"

"Oh, it's this cool display the department store creates every Christmas. You know, little mechanical dolls and elaborate decorations. Like window displays, only better. You walk through a dark room, and it tells a story. Every year it's a different thing. Rapunzel. Cinderella. All the kids go. Papa Roy always took me down to see it."

"Please," I say to Lenore, dropping to my knees and clasping my hands together. "Please let me go with Cammy."

"We'll only be gone a few hours," Cammy says. "Don't be a pain in the ass. You can't keep this kid locked in here like a prisoner."

"She isn't a prisoner," Lenore says, taking my hand. "We're happy. Please, Cammy. You've only been home a week. I'm not ready to let go of you."

"Mother, cut the dramatics. I'm taking her to see a Christmas display."

"Be careful," Lenore says, still holding on to me. "You girls are all that I've got."

"Go get your coat," Cammy says to me. "We're going to have a blast."

Outside we huddle together on the bus bench, and wait for the green 6B to screech to a halt in front of our building. "It's twenty cents," Cammy says, slipping two thin dimes into my mitten. "Just drop it into the slot."

On the bus, we zig-zag down the aisle to the farthest back seat, spotted with pink globs of gum and graffiti. "It's quiet today," Cammy says. "Holiday. But it'll start to fill up closer to downtown."

"I've always wanted to get on one of these buses. To go somewhere. But Lenore never let me."

"My mother's scared of her own shadow. I've walked the worst streets in this city, and look at me, I'm here."

We pass Loring Park, the Avalon Theater and Sex Shop, Raymond's

Shoe Store with metal grates across the windows. Off Dakota are old brick buildings, boarded windows, drunks passed out on icy front steps. Wet newspaper, beer bottles, and McDonald's wrappers litter the icy sidewalks and streets. "I used to live near here," Cammy says. "In a basement place off Portland. With my boyfriend, Tony. We'll go there someday. When the weather's better."

"Okay," I say, though I hope we never do. "Will we be home before dark?"

"Don't worry," Cammy says. "We're here to have a good time."

Inside Daley's, we ride the shiny escalator past the fancy jewelry department, fur coats, cosmetics and perfumes. I love the department store's waxy marble floors, the prism chandeliers, the bustle of customers. On the eighth floor, we step off the escalator and into a huge blue ice castle decorated with styrofoam candy canes and Christmas lights. "Isn't it cool?" Cammy says, taking my hand and leading me into a silvery room with snow sprinkled along the floor. "It's 'The Christmas Carol,'" Cammy whispers as if we're in church. "I love that story."

We linger in front of each display of mechanical figures—the women in long, elegant velvet dresses, the men in their formal wool coats, Christmas carolers in black top hats, the frightening ghost of Christmas past. Cammy rests her arm on my shoulder, pulls me close while she reads the story printed next to each scene. "That's just what Papa Roy used to do for me." When she stumbles on some of the words, I don't correct her; I let her keep reading though I'd rather read it myself.

"Don't you wish the world was really like this?" she whispers. We're standing in front of the Cratchit's dinner scene, the fat turkey and Tiny Tim's blessing. "God bless us, every one," she says. "Yeah, really. I used to dream of a Christmas like that when I was a kid."

At the other end of the display, there's a gingerbread house with a miniature door meant for small children. "Just duck," she warns, pushing me through the tiny opening. Inside, a stout woman dressed as Mrs. Claus polishes the glass counter.

"This is for children," she frowns at Cammy. "Besides, Santa's gone for the year."

"We just want a gingerbread cookie." Cammy jingles the coins in her jacket pocket.

"Ten and under," Mrs. Claus barks. "Read the sign outside." She studies Cammy, the black eyeliner, her tangled blonde hair.

"It's for my little sister," Cammy says. "Look at her, she's only nine years old."

"Nine?" Mrs. Claus says suspiciously. She hands each of us a soft brown boy with pastel icing. "It's the end of the season. They'll just wind up in the trash. But don't let me see you back here next year. This isn't set up for girls like you."

"Don't worry," Cammy says. She lifts a Santa coloring book from a wire rack. "These free?" She shoves me back out the wonderland door without waiting for an answer.

"For you," she says, handing the coloring book to me. "Merry Christmas. And hold off on that cookie, I still have another surprise."

Off the twelfth-floor elevator, Cammy grabs my sleeve, and pulls me after her. "Here," she says, stopping abruptly. "It's the Elm Tree Room. It's Papa Roy's tradition. I haven't come back since he died."

I glance into the elegant restaurant, the red luster of candlelight on the polished woodwork, the white tablecloths. "Here? What do you want to do here?"

"Eat. What do you think?"

It's late afternoon, but a few customers are still eating. Women in fancy dresses or matching polyester pantsuits, men in business suits and ties.

"We can't eat here. We don't have any money."

"So what?" Cammy says, pulling me inside with her. "Come on."

"Yes?" The hostess glares at Cammy's damp moccasins and faded tight jeans.

"We're here for lunch," Cammy says.

Pressing the menus to her chest, the hostess looks from Cammy to me, then back to Cammy. "You want to eat?"

"No," Cammy says. "We're here to take a bath." Cammy flashes two fingers in front of the hostess's blank face. "Table for two. Do you read me?"

The hostess shrinks under Cammy's fiery gaze.

"Come on, Cammy. Let's eat our gingerbread cookies on the bus ride home."

She snatches the menus out of the hostess's hand, storms into the restaurant, drops her purse on a vacant table. "Bring me an ashtray." I've never seen someone so solid, so dead set on getting their way.

"Cammy, we can't stay." I just want to get out of here, away from the staring eyes of the other customers.

"It's my tradition. Don't let them push you around."

The waitress slams our silverware down on the table. Cammy orders club sandwiches, a black coffee for her, a kiddie cocktail for me. "Club sandwiches. That's what Papa Roy and I ate every Christmas. Of course he had a Manhattan with his. Papa Roy loved his cocktails. Runs in the family. We'd come down to see the displays, Christmas shop, then stop here for a nice long lunch. Of course, Papa Roy got perfect service. He was so powerful, no one ever screwed with him."

"Where was Lenore?"

"Same place she's been as long as I can remember. At home in bed. Same place she is today."

"Was she always like this?"

"Not when I was little. But after a while she just crashed."

"How did she get so sick?"

"Sick? She's sick all right, but not like she wants you to think."

"What do you mean?"

"Stick around, you'll find out for yourself."

Cammy clinks her coffee cup against my kiddie cocktail. "Cheers," she says. The fruity ginger ale dribbles down my chin. She dunks her fingers into my drink and lifts out the soft red cherry. "I love these," she smiles, plopping it onto her tongue. She lifts the yellow umbrella out of my glass. "Look, it opens and closes," she says. "Another souvenir. You'll never forget this day."

"Cammy, how are we going to pay for this?" I ask softly so the other customers can't hear.

"Who cares?" she laughs. "We're here to have a good time."

"Come on, Cammy. Really."

"You worry too much. Ta da!" Like a magic trick, she pulls a fifty-dollar bill from her shirt sleeve and waves it in front of me. "You got to learn to trust Cammy. It's Cammy who knows the right tricks."

"Where'd you get that?" I don't want to eat a sandwich that was paid for with stolen money.

"That's my little secret."

"Cammy."

"You take all the fun out of things. This is our celebration lunch. My little sister is back; let me be happy."

I take another bite of my dry sandwich, the toast rough against the roof of my mouth, the bacon hard and brittle. When we're finished eating, we light our cigarettes from the candle wick, careful not to touch the hot wax.

"I've been living a hard life," Cammy says, licking the mayonnaise off her fingers. "But I was born for finer things."

"Cammy, where'd you get that money? Did you steal it from Lenore?"

"So what if I did?" she hisses. "She owes me a hell of a lot more than this."

We smoke through two more cups of coffee, Cammy wrapping her hands around the china cup and breathing in the steam. The restaurant is nearly empty except for the workers setting out fresh white tablecloths. "We're getting ready for dinner," our waitress says, handing our bill to Cammy. "Please pay."

"Bring me the change." Cammy gives her the fifty-dollar bill. "She can forget the tip."

"Let's go. Lenore's going to be worried."

"Lenore worries most about Lenore. Besides, I have one last surprise. I want to buy you a present."

"A present?"

"Yeah. That's the deal with the money. My mom gave it to me, so we could buy ourselves something for Christmas. She's given me money since I was about ten. Can't be bothered shopping. She said we should pick up something we need."

I think about the things I've needed so long: a new pair of jeans, a regulation navy-blue school sweater to keep me warm this winter, new boots.

"That money was for us? Why didn't you tell me?" My sandwich turns in my stomach. "We shouldn't have spent it on lunch."

"Why? It was my treat. Besides, we got some left over. And you don't always need money to get what you want."

"I do. I need boots."

"Boots," she says, wrapping her arm around me. "Come on, then. Let's get my little sister some boots."

In Daley's bargain basement, I find the ones I want; they're soft crinkled vinyl, rust colored with a fat layer of fleece. When I slide my feet into them, I'm warm for the first time this winter. "Cool. Do they fit?" Cammy asks, slipping on a pair of high red platforms. "Christmas clearance—it's the best time to buy."

I stand in front of the slanted floor mirror. The heels are thick wedge chunks, not high enough to make me wobble, and there's plenty of space around the calves to tuck in my jeans.

"Jesus, girl, you're so skinny," Cammy says.

The boots are two sizes too big for me, a woman's six, but I don't tell Cammy; I don't want to end up with a pair of red rubber pull-ons like the kindergartners wear. "I love them. Do we have the money?"

"Not if we're both buying. But that doesn't stop me." Cammy struts down the aisle, spins once, and comes back to me. "Too tight," she says, kicking them off.

"Does that mean I get mine?"

I can't wait until Jimmy comes back and sees me in my new boots. Two more days. When we meet on the fire escape, I'll look like a girl my age. I'll look like Emmy Atwood.

"Too bad we can't lift them," she whispers in my ear, her breath hot and airy. "The clerk's watching. Maybe if we come back next week."

"No," I plead. "I want to buy them now." I lift my foot like a horse so she can read the price sticker.

"Okay," she says, slapping my ankle. "They're yours. Just tell my mom they took the whole fifty." She stands behind me and kisses the top of my head. "Happy New Year, little sister. I told you it'd be a great day."

With Cammy, my secrets are safe. "You can tell me anything," she says, winding my new white cashmere scarf around my neck. It's a Christmas gift from Cammy, a surprise sister present. She sets the matching beret on my head, tilts it to one side until it touches my eyebrow. "There," she says. "That's what sisters are for."

We stand in front of the antique mirror, Cammy's chin resting on the top of my head, her golden hair framing my face. "You should try bleach. I bet Jimmy would like you blonde." Jimmy, my eighth-grader from Cathedral, Jimmy the boy who stops by on his way home from shoveling.

"I don't know. I think he likes me the way I am." I remember Christmas Eve, the hairdo Lenore made me wear. *Why do you always try to look older?*

"Don't be stupid," Cammy says, buttoning my coat.

Tonight Jimmy works his first shift back at Kenny's, and I'm impatient to see him, alone on the fire escape, away from Lenore and Cammy.

"When will you let me have a look at him, this Jimmy who's hustling my baby sister?"

"Pretty soon," I promise. "But wait until we're going together."

"Gotcha," she winks. "I've been there. But watch your step. Every guy's after one thing."

"Not Jimmy," I say.

"Every guy. But take your time, I'll cover for you. I'm a master at tricking my mother."

Outside on the back fire escape, the snow drifts down in fat flakes that stick to my eyelashes, melt on my tongue. The night is bright with streetlights and fresh snow. When Jimmy enters the alley, he strolls slowly through the falling snow, his leather jacket wide open, his cigarette cupped in his hand.

"So how's it going?" I call down. I'm trying to keep my voice calm and even, to hide the hammering in my chest.

"Faina," he says, looking up abruptly as if I've startled him out of some deep dream. "What's happening?"

"Nothing. How was your Christmas?"

"I survived. What about you?"

"Me, too." I hang over the metal railing so my new cashmere scarf can wave in the wind. I love the fuzzy yarn against my skin, how sharp the scarf looks with Cammy's pea coat. "You coming up for a smoke?"

"I guess," he shrugs. "Why not?"

As soon as Jimmy reaches the top, I can tell things are different between us. Instead of slouching in his usual spot against my building, he sits down on the staircase, stares out at the alley and the snowy rooftops peaking against the dark sky.

"So, I got new boots," I say, sitting down next to him.

He reaches over and squeezes my calf. "Pretty cool. They real leather?" He says this as if he's already forgotten the old boots, the day at Dakota Park, his fight with Tom Payne.

"I'm not sure. I got them at Daley's over vacation. I went downtown to see the Christmas display."

Jimmy nods his head. "Yeah. That. My old lady took me once when I was a kid. Aren't you past that yet?"

"My mom wanted me to see it."

"I think I went when I was nine or ten. All that Christmas crap is for little kids." He lets go of my boot, stuffs his hands into his pockets.

"I love the choker," I say quickly. I want us to go back to Christmas Eve, pick up where we left off. "I've worn it every day. Did your parents like the plant hanger you made?"

"As much as they like anything. It's hard to believe I'm going back there."

"Back where?"

"Back home. You know, I'm down to my last hundred. I kept thinking about that when I was there, what it'd be like living again in my old room, sharing a bed with my brother John. Listening to my old lady bitch constantly. But at least it ain't no halfway house."

"When do you go?"

"My free date's the end of April." He brushes the snow off his jeans, stamps his boots against the metal stairs. "If I can stay clean. I've tried to set my mind on turning my life around, but it's hard labor staying straight. I'm not sure it's for me."

"You can do it, Jimmy." I nudge my elbow against his. "You don't want to be locked up for the rest of your life. Remember you said you wanted to live in San Diego. You've got to be free to do that."

"Keep dreaming," Jimmy sighs. "I'll be living in this shit hole forever."

"You can save your money. You'll still have your job at Kenny's."

"Not a chance. We live over Northeast. I'll have to find work around my folks' house. Besides, New Directions will send Kenny another inmate to replace me."

"Then I'll never see you?" I'm staring at Jimmy's face, the faint mustache over his upper lip, his long bangs falling over his dark eyes. The face I'll never forget.

"You'll see me," he sniffs. He wipes his hand under his nose. I reach up and sweep off the snow that has settled on his hair like a veil.

"It'll be too strange without you."

"It's too strange with me," he laughs. "A girl your age shouldn't be hanging with a guy like me. Anyway, I'll stop by. But I'll tell you one thing, it won't be to sit outside and smoke in the middle of goddamn January. I got to go now, it's freezing."

"Wait," I say. "We haven't even had our cigarette."

"It's too late," he says, leaping down the stairs. "Besides, I've corrupted you enough."

Inside the apartment, I stick my head into Lenore's shadowy room. Cammy has forgotten to shut off the TV and an old *Bonanza* episode flickers on the gray screen. I can tell by the steady snoring Lenore's fallen asleep. If it were last summer, I'd crawl into bed with her, read her a chapter of *Little Women* to get my mind off Jimmy. Jimmy leaving. Jimmy not kissing me. Jimmy hardly noticing my new boots.

"Faina, is that you?" Cammy calls from the bathroom. "Come on in." Inside the bathroom, the air is thick with steam and the flowery perfume of Calgon crystals. Yellow light glows from the two votive candles Cammy has set at the edge of the tub. "How'd it go?" she asks, sinking down into the water. "Did he dig the boots?"

I'm embarrassed to look at her, the bubbles glistening on her shoulders, her hair in a rare ponytail, her cigarette smoldering in the ashtray. If I was Cammy, Jimmy would give me a second kiss. "Wash my back for me." She passes me the slippery bar of Yardley.

"Do you have a washcloth?"

"No," she says. "Use your hands." She turns and faces the wall, leaving me the pale curved surface of her wet back. "I want to hear about Jimmy. How far did he get?"

I slide the bar over her upper back, careful to stay away from her arms, her waist, the area hidden beneath the water. "How's that?"

"Use your hands," she orders. "I won't hurt you."

I push up the sleeves of my pea coat, tuck the scarf behind me. Kneeling on the pink fur bath mat, I circle my hands over her wing bones, her ribs, the small moles that freckle her spine.

"So? How far did he get?" she asks, lifting her arms to fasten a loose bobby pin.

"It isn't like that," I say.

"Then you play it too safe," she says, turning toward me suddenly.

When I jerk my hand back to avoid touching her breast, the Yardley slips down below the bubbles. "Help me find it," she says, fishing down into the hot water. "There's plenty of room for two. Strip down and climb in, little sister. I've taken baths with guys twice your size. Tell me what happened with Jimmy."

"Nothing happened. Nothing. I got to get ready for bed, I have school in the morning."

"School? You got to be kidding." She rises out of the suds, the water splashing over the sides of the tub, the bubbles gliding down her white skin. "I haven't gone to school for years. And look at me."

Cammy Family

Weekdays, my mother kept me in because of the cops. She was sure they were searching for me, sure Hank or Frances would blow the whistle. She had it in her head that the whole block knew our business. I humored her, because it was thirty below zero, so cold your spit froze in your mouth.

Faina was our break. At 3:30 my mother would sit up in bed, order me to wait by the window and watch. "The princess is coming," I'd call out, when I saw her little goblin body struggle down the alley. She was always hunched over against the cold, her eyes on the ground, her hands deep in her pockets. "I guess no one kidnapped her today. If you're so worried about her, why do you send her away?"

"It's the law," she said, her voice so dull she couldn't even convince herself.

On weekends we trained; I tried to teach Faina the things she might need. She was book smart in a worthless way, knew something about Greeks, but asked what I meant by *balling*. And I hated the way my mother encouraged her stupidity, urging her on like she was some kind of child prodigy put on the earth for better things.

"Faina's got my gift for language. She knows words you've never heard of. Tell some to Cammy."

Whenever she did that, Faina slumped into the chair embarrassed, let her hair fall in front of her face like a curtain. "I can't think of any."

"Well I can," I told my mother, laughing. "I know words that aren't even in the dictionary."

"Cammy, please. You inherited my looks, Faina my brains. You have no need for envy. An even split. Fifty-fifty. You're a beauty, but Faina will go to college."

My mother always talked about Faina like that, like she wasn't in the room.

"What brains?" I asked. I couldn't take my mother seriously. Couldn't look at her yellow face, the ratty orange hair, the stained teeth, and think brains or beauty. I couldn't imagine her as anything other than the drunk she'd been my whole life. "You live in a dream."

"Oh, Cammy! You know how good I used to be at crossword puzzles. And how quick I am at *Jeopardy*. I read voraciously as a child, before my eyes went bad. Voracious. Faina, tell her what that means. Papa Roy was so proud of me, he always said he never met a girl with a sharper mind. If it hadn't been for Bobby, and you girls slowing me down, I would probably be a doctor. Then, too, I lost so many years taking care of Papa Roy. But I had a gift for science. Chemistry, biology. Poetry too. I think I've told you how Papa Roy used to wake me in the night to recite poems to his company. *Remember me when I am gone away, Gone far away into the silent land; When you can no more hold me by the hand.* Christina Rosetti."

"I've heard it."

"Remember Papa Roy loved those sad poems so much? And I had the poem "Song" printed on his memorial card? *When I am dead, my dearest; Sing no sad songs for me.* I can never make it past the first two lines now. But I wish he was here to see Faina, to see how fast she learned to recite Wordsworth. Faina, go get Papa Roy's *Great Poems of the English Language*. The one we read last summer."

"Not now," Faina said, blushing. She sat there, in my mother's red velvet chair, her legs folded up to her chest, her face half hidden by her skinny knees.

"Mother," I said. "Give it up."

I had to defend Faina like that, to save her from the enemy, though she didn't have a clue who it was.

Faina was useful. I saw that immediately. She had an innocent look, from her age I guess, and that scrawny body. My favorite costume was her gray plaid jumper, the white knee-highs, the clean braid down the middle of her back.

I made her wear it on Saturdays when we did downtown: Daley's, Carlson's, Wentworth's—you name it. Never the same stores two weeks in a row. She worked the clerks, kept them busy with her school-girl manners and California accent while I lifted treasures. She didn't consider herself a thief. In the store, on the sidewalk outside, even in the crowded elevators, she refused to acknowledge me. We came and left through separate doors, breaking only for lunch at the LaSalle Deli. Salami sandwiches and hot bitter coffee. I taught her to like the taste.

Faina's job was begging. She was a master liar, a natural con. She could get us ten bucks by the end of the day. A dime for a phone call home, a quarter for the bus, a nickel for a newspaper. Old folks adored her, businessmen set down their briefcases and dug deep into their pockets. Some even passed her a buck. They loved to ruffle her hair, nip the tip of her nose, warn her to take care.

Back at home I surveyed my stash: silver rings, chokers, white eye shadow, the hottest 45s, even the little Virgin Mary night-light she'd admired in the Alleluia Shop. On good days I'd fill two shopping bags. Some of the items stayed with us, others I took back for cash. She never asked what I'd stolen. That's what I mean about her odd stupidity. She didn't like my games, but she played.

"We're going out rambling," I told her one night. I was dressing her in a new costume, one better suited for the role. A black ribbed turtleneck tight enough to show off her freshly stuffed chest. "You look great with tits," I said. "Too bad you're a late bloomer. If I were you, I'd stuff every day until I had my own. You can't get a guy without them." I pinched hoop earrings onto her lobes, painted her eyes with liner and shadow. I even ratted out her mouse hair to give it a lift. "Now that's better. You'll have to fight off the guys," I whispered into her ear.

"I don't want to," she said, suddenly crumbling. "I don't want to fight off anybody. I feel ridiculous dressed like this." She tried to flatten out the mounds of Kleenex, reached under her shirt to pull out my hard work.

"Don't," I said. "They look great. It's the best I've ever seen you. We're going to have a blast."

At Lord Leo's, a coat of ice draped the window. "Come on back," I said, leading her into the alley. We joined the huddle of regulars passing a quick joint between games. When they handed the roach to me, I pinched it carefully between my frozen fingers, sucked it into my lungs for a long drag. "Take a hit," I said, holding it to Faina's lips, but she shook her head no and looked away.

"What you got here?" one of the guys asked, nodding in her direction.

"My baby sister." I looped my arm around her proudly, pulling her shivering body in next to me.

"Adopted I guess," another guy laughed.

"It's a long story." I slipped my hand into her jacket pocket, wrapped it around her thick mittened fingers. In the back of my mind was an old secret, something my mother had said when I was young. *She isn't his. She isn't Bobby's.* I wondered if Faina knew the truth, or when a good time would come to tell her.

"Come on," she whined. "Let's go. I'm freezing."

"Wait," I said, tugging her in closer to me and wrapping my arms around her from behind. "I just want to stay for a good buzz."

"Well, look who's back," Leo said, when we walked into the pool hall. He slapped me hard on the ass. "Staying clean, babe?"

"Always," I winked. Leo and I went back a long way. I'd been hanging here since I was a kid, chalking sticks while I learned the game. I had dreams of making it big, but mostly I helped the regulars hustle. I played the distraction while they played the game, pretending to be their girl between shots, so it looked like they weren't concentrating. It was easy work, I earned a name and a small cut of the take. But that was before Tony.

"She's too young," he said, pressing his palm against Faina's chest. "They'll shut me down."

"She can pass for sixteen."

"In whose dream?"

I looked at her. The new breasts hidden by my huge peacoat, fresh mascara smeared under her eyes. Leo was right; she looked like she was ten.

"Let's go," she whined again.

"Leo, she's my baby sister. I'm showing her the ropes."

"She doesn't have your promise, Cammy," Leo said. He was sizing her up, from her new little boots to her cashmere beret.

"She's the one with the brains," I said, lifting my eyebrows at Leo so he'd give her a break. I could see the way she was shrinking down in her coat, burying her chin deeper into her scarf. "She can recite poetry."

"There was an old man named Drew . . ." Leo said. "Want me to continue?"

"Leo, give me a break." I wanted her to love it here, to love Lord Leo's the way I did, the cloudy haze of smoke, the jukebox, the smack of the ball as it spun into a pocket. "You let me in here when I was her age."

"You were never her age," Leo said. "You were twelve going on twenty."

"Come on, Leo, don't you owe me a little something?" I stood on my toes to tickle the tips of my fingers down the back of his neck. I knew what he liked.

"Take a back booth," he said, leaning over to lick my ear. "Near the fire exit. I'll be by for a visit."

"Send us over some Cokes and pretzels. I'll keep her away from the window." I pressed a ten-dollar bill into his palm, but he waved it away.

"A girl with your face doesn't pay. I thought you were showing her the ropes."

Inside the booth, I put her against the wall. "If you see a cop, drop under," I said, pointing to the floor. I was going down with her. I was sure they still had me in their files down at Hennepin County.

"Cammy, we shouldn't stay. Lenore will be waiting." Whenever she was nervous, she used my mother for an excuse. The two of them were always spooked. A match made in heaven.

"Faina, for Christ's sake, we just got here. Come on, have fun with me, please. I can't take you places if you always freak." I pulled her mittens off her hands, tugged her coat off her shoulders. "Live a little."

Leo served me my Coke just the way I liked it, with that secret splash of rum. He'd managed to serve booze for years under the counter; that's one of the reasons he kept his customers. "You remembered," I said, licking my lips.

"More than you know." He leaned over and kissed me on the nose. "Let me know what else you need."

Faina didn't mention anything about her drink tasting funny; Leo was the type to keep a kid's clean. I was tempted to switch, to loosen her up a little, but nobody needed a buzz more than me.

"You ever get high?" I asked.

"Not really."

"You should give it a try. Here, take a sip of my drink."

"No thanks," she said, shoving it away. "I've got one already."

"Mine's special," I whispered into her ear. "Come on. For me." She raised the glass to her mouth slowly, sipped a tiny bit, then wrinkled her nose up at me. "Yuck."

"Try again," I said. "You'll get used to it. I was drinking shots by the time I was your age." I lifted the glass to her lips. "Come on, take a big gulp this time." I tilted it, letting the first few drops dribble down her chin until she opened wide and swallowed for me.

"It's awful," she coughed. She wiped the Coke off her face.

"But you'll like what it does to your head," I said. "It makes you feel happy."

"I am happy." She smiled at me with that dark elf look, the stupid scarf still wrapped around her neck.

"Happier," I said. "It can make you really, really happy. You got to let it take over your heart, your mind, your body."

I tried to imagine her older, with breasts of her own, and a face that belonged to a teenager.

"Ever wonder why we don't look anything alike?" I asked her.

"I guess I look like my dad, and you look like Lenore," she said.

"Really? Do you really look like *our* dad?"

"That's what Lenore says. She says I'm from his dark side; she says that's where I get my gypsy look, like I'm from another country."

"Yeah," I said, taking another big guzzle. "Lenore's always one for a good story."

We split my next drink, and the next and the next. She took my advice and learned to like it. A few guys stopped by the table to flirt with me, dropping off bags of beer nuts and pretzels, but I made a point of letting them know I wasn't alone. Another night, maybe, but I wanted this to be for the two of us.

"Let's dance," I said, pulling her up out of the booth and into the back corner. Bob Dylan was singing "Lay Lady Lay," and his smokey voice reminded me of old nights with Tony. "I love this song."

"I don't dance, Cammy," she said, staggering a little. I wrapped her arms up around my neck, pulled her closer. "We'll slow dance. It's easy. Just let go, close your eyes, feel the music move through you."

I put my hands on her baby hips. She was so delicate in my arms, I felt like I was dancing with a chicken wing. "I'll take care of you," I said. "My baby sister." Her mounds of Kleenex rubbed against my stomach. When the song was over, I rested my head on her head, closed my eyes, and let her sway against me.

"You'll be beautiful someday," I said. It wasn't just the rum. I meant it. "Maybe not like me, but in a way that will be worth something."

Then I lifted her chin and studied her strange face, that crooked grin, those frightening black eyes, that odd pink gash across her eyebrow. I brushed my lips against her lips, so gentle and dry they startled me. "I can kiss you," I said, weaving her fingers through mine. "We're family."

Hi Honey,

So she's back. The missing Cammy. I had a feeling she'd show up before too long. It isn't easy making it away from home, I know that well enough. Left my folks' farm at 15, went hungry plenty. I'm glad you girls are hitting it off, no cat fights yet I hope. A house full of women. Glad I'm not there to see it.

Sounds like you were a hit there in the school show. Singing solo. Sure is strange the way things worked out. I never saw this ahead of us. Always thought the two of us would be together. At least until you left me for some guy. Not this Jimmy. It's good you got a friend, but be careful. I'm not too keen on you hanging with a teenage guy. Hand him over to Cammy. She's probably more his speed. I was 16 once. It occurs to me there's a lot we haven't covered, maybe Lenore and Cammy will fill in the blanks. We're in Perth for a week. Even when I close my eyes I can see the mud come flying at me. Can't shake the feeling I'm always on that rig. Work's so filthy I got to buy work clothes every time I get to town. Roughnecking. It's rough all right, but the tag can't do it justice. Wonder if it's worth it just to save my ass and skip a couple years of taxes. Wiley's conned me into the track, I got to have some fun. But guess what. I'm winning. Don't worry, I'll quit while I'm ahead. Say hi to Croc for me, the rest of the clan too. Lenore. Cammy. I love you, Dad

Faina Gifts

In April, when the archbishop comes to Cathedral to confirm Mrs. Lajoy's third-graders I will be with them, the only seventh-grader who hasn't made the sacrament yet. Sister Cyril sends me down to the primary wing for training. I sit in the back corner of Mrs. Lajoy's classroom, my knees banging against the top of the miniature desk.

We color in the pictures—amber and red flames burning over the apostles' heads, St. Catherine holding a torture wheel, St. Cecelia plucking her harp. I answer the worksheets, fill in the blanks. For fun, we play saint crossword puzzles and Name That Saint. I doodle Jimmy's initials in the margin of my workbook, J.C. J.C., and Mrs. Lajoy thinks she knows what it means, but she doesn't.

I'm happy to escape Values Clarification, the moral dilemmas I can never answer correctly. I prefer the Holy Spirit, the saints with their gruesome tales, the apostles speaking in tongues. Of all the gifts I've got coming, speaking in tongues is the one I'd like most of all.

"Does it happen right away?" I ask Mrs. Lajoy. "I mean as soon as the archbishop blesses us?"

"What? Does what?" She's staring out the window at the flurry of fresh snow.

"Our gifts from the Holy Spirit. Will they automatically appear?"

"You have to wait and see. I think."

"But can we expect to get them all? I mean this thing about tongues and prophesies. Is that for real?"

"I don't have the answers," Mrs. Lajoy says. "It's a mystery. Like faith."

Mrs. Lajoy assigns me to help with the children. I correct their answers, smooth bubbles out of their glued pictures, punch the holes for their construction-paper books. I like the work. The smell of kids just after recess, the way they cluster around my desk and hug me when I come into the room.

I imagine being Mrs. Lajoy someday, a gentle teacher in a long flowered skirt, a knit shawl wrapped around my shoulders, my hair bushing out in fuzzy brown curls, my voice always mild and kind. "You're good with children," she tells me, and I zip the next jacket with pride.

"Confirmation? What the hell is that?" Cammy asks. We're gathered together for our afternoon chat. When I come home from school now, they roll apart, make room for me in the middle of Lenore's warm bed, the quilt pulled up to my neck, the sheets still hot from their skin. "Cuddle up," Cammy says. Then she brings me a teacup of instant cocoa and a plate of oatmeal cookies.

"It's where you take a saint's name. Didn't you do anything like this, Lenore?"

"No," Lenore says. "I never got that far. Mother only took me to church on holidays. But I'm proud of you," she says, rubbing my arm absentmindedly. "You're such a good girl, Faina. Such a good girl."

"Sounds like crap to me," Cammy says. "Who's the archbishop, anyway?"

"Who knows?" I say. "But I'm going to need a sponsor." This is a subject I've been afraid to bring up to Lenore. Even though my confirmation is still months away, we already need the names of our sponsors.

"What's that?" Lenore asks, suddenly suspicious. She sits up in bed and pulls the pillow down her back. "I don't like the concept."

"I think it's just somebody who goes up with you when you make the sacrament. We need to draw pictures of them in our booklets. The trouble is, I don't really know anybody here."

"What about your teacher? Let her be your sponsor. Isn't that what those nuns are there for?" Lenore tugs at her hair nervously.

"What about me?" Cammy says. "I'll be your sponsor."

I look at Cammy hanging off the edge of Lenore's bed in her Grateful Dead T-shirt, red underwear, a ring of mascara under her eyes, her legs pale and whiskery.

"I don't think Monsignor will let you be my sponsor. I think it needs to be an adult." I blow on my cocoa to cool it.

"I can pass for eighteen."

"A Catholic adult. The sponsor has to be Catholic."

"Who would that be?" Lenore asks, lifting an oatmeal cookie off my plate. "We don't know any Catholics. And I don't like the idea of outsiders getting involved with our family."

"We know Faina," Cammy says. "She's Catholic."

"No, Faina's not Catholic," Lenore says. "She's pretending."

"You ever make your confirmation?" I ask Jimmy. We've fallen back into our old routine of meeting on the fire escape after Jimmy's shift ends at Kenny's. All the awkwardness of Christmas, that kiss, is behind us.

"Sure," he says. "In third grade. Like every Catholic kid. What about it?"

"I missed mine in San Diego. I guess the archbishop must have skipped my school. So I'm making it here at Cathedral. In April."

"Got a name?"

"Not yet. I'm still thinking. What's yours?"

Jimmy laughs. Shakes his head. "I'm not telling."

"Come on."

I give him a little shove, throw him off balance for a second, just enough so he has to reach out and grab the railing.

"Ama," he says, choking. He's laughing so hard he can hardly speak. "Amadeo."

"Oh, my god. That's awful. Amadeo. What's that mean?"

"What's awful is Faina; you got stuck with a name no one can even pronounce. Anyway, it's after my grandfather. It means something like the love of god."

"What's your middle name?"

"William, same as my father."

"James William Amadeo Cordova." It sounds ridiculous tripping off my tongue. It doesn't fit the boy standing in front of me smoking.

"Quit laughing," he says, yanking my beret off my head and tossing it down into the snow. "I told you I have secrets of my own."

"I remember." I run down to the parking lot to save my beret before the gritty snow bleeds through it. Now that it's January, the snow is always gray, and the cold is nothing like December. It's bitter, harsh, a wind that never lets up.

"I got a name for you." Jimmy's standing beside me in the parking lot, tucking my hair into the side of my hat. "Guinevere. It suits you."

"Guinevere?"

"It's the name of my favorite sister. Gwen. You remind me of her. And you know Guinevere was King Arthur's true love. I used to be all tied up in those round table stories."

"Okay." I hook my arm through Jimmy's arm. "Guinevere. I'll think about it."

"Guinevere?" Cammy says, shocked. "Like *Camelot*?" We're downtown, in an alley behind the Hollywood Theater, wedged between two dumpsters, hugging each other to try to stay warm. As soon as the early show streams out, she's sneaking me in to see Diana Ross in *Lady Sings the Blues.*

"I've never paid here," Cammy says. "I've been doing it since I was a kid. I've seen everything free, even *Last Tango in Paris.* That's why it reeks so bad in there now. The whole joint jacking off. You can still smell it on the seats."

"I never saw *Camelot.*" I try to steer Cammy away from this subject. Sex. The gory details she loves to describe.

"Well, she screwed Lancelot. I don't think that makes her a saint."

When the seven o'clock crowd pours out, Cammy grabs the back door, weaves in against the flood of customers. I follow, my usual few steps behind her, down the dark slanted corridor, past the heavy black curtain to the second row of seats. "Duck down," she orders. "Pull your hat down low on your head."

The theater stinks like disinfectant and old popcorn, stale smoke, mildew. The smell reminds me of Lenore's dark basement, the day Hank threw me in there. The walls are covered in scarlet flocked wallpaper, peeled away in scabby bare patches. I scrunch down into the bristly seat, my face buried in my coat, my boots making a sucking sound against the sticky floor.

"Keep your feet up, Guinevere," Cammy whispers. "They've had rats."

I curl my legs under me, wrap my scarf over my nose.

"Want any?" Cammy says, passing me the box of Milk Duds she stole from Border Drug.

"No thanks." I know if I take the scarf from my face I'll gag.

"Better get used to it," Cammy says. "That's the smell of sex."

When the movie is over, we wander out the front door with the rest of the crowd. The usher glares at me. "What are you doing at an R-rated movie?"

"Fuck off," Cammy says, walking past him. "Who are you, the police?"

Out on the sidewalk, under the bright lights of the marquee, we light up right away. "Let's smoke one before the bus," Cammy says. "God, I can't sit through a movie without a cig. But I didn't want that usher breathing down my neck. What'd you think of the movie?"

"Too sad." I picture Lady sticking the needle into her veins, the bruised smudges under her eyes. Bone-thin like Lenore, her hands quaking. Suddenly everything looks lost, the trash cans outside the theater, the black front window of Downtown Shoe Doctor, the crumbling brick of the old buildings, the snow heaped up along the sidewalk. "I'll never touch drugs."

"Everyone says that when they're a kid." Cammy tosses her hair back, rests her arm across my shoulder. "It's just a movie. There's nothing better than a good high. In fact, that movie made me thirsty. Let's go down to Lord Leo's. I know where we could score some grass. You'll love it; just give it a try."

"It's the middle of the night. Don't you think Lenore will wake up and worry?" I wonder if Lenore woke up already, sweating from some frightening dream, screaming for Cammy. It's Cammy's name she calls now.

"Who cares?" Cammy says. "She's lucky I'm living there at all. I'd be long gone if it wasn't for you."

"Really? What about all the days you spend together? And your private conversations when I have to leave the room? It seems like you do fine without me."

"I'm here to raise you," she says, kissing my forehead. "That's all. You got to grow up, you can't stay little forever."

"Can one of the teachers be a sponsor?" I ask Mrs. Lajoy. I'm staying in to help her over lunch recess, correcting spelling tests while the rest of her class plays outdoors. I lick the back of the GOOD JOB sticker, press it on the corner of the perfect paper.

"No. It's a relative usually, or a friend of the family." Mrs. Lajoy records the scores in her book.

"My relatives live far away."

"In San Diego?" Mrs. Lajoy asks, barely glancing up at me. She's the only teacher who stays busy while we talk, the only one who doesn't insist on staring into my eyes. Even Sister Linette suspects me of something ugly. She hasn't spoken to me since I missed her Midnight Mass.

"Yes."

"They might come for it," she shrugs. "We have plenty of sponsors come in from out of town. If not, somebody else will fill in. Family friends. Anyone would be honored. But this really isn't your problem. Naturally it's up to your parents to ask."

"I was just wondering about that page in my booklet. How soon do I need to have it done?"

"April is still a long way away." Mrs. Lajoy closes her record book, sets her pencil down on her desk. She doesn't know yet how much of my book is actually missing. My baptism. Photos and certificate. My first communion. Same thing. A picture of my sponsor. I've only shown her my stories of saints, the illustrations, the books I've read for research. "You're a good student, Faina. I'm sure your book will be fine."

When their recess is over, I help her students hang their coats on their hooks, dry their mittens on the radiators, line up their wet boots along the wall outside the classroom. The children gather in a circle at Mrs. Lajoy's feet to sing "Where Have All the Flowers Gone?" Mrs. Lajoy leads them through the song, her fingers gently strumming the guitar strings, her voice soaring above theirs like an angel's. I love their happy faces flushed with cold, their pudgy hands folded in their laps, their eyelashes still wet from snow.

"Faina, you'd better run along now," Mrs. Lajoy says, snapping her guitar case closed. "Your class is in from recess. Sister Cyril doesn't want you to be late."

Upstairs the kids are still stuffing their coats into their lockers; the boys slap each other's butts with long winter scarves. I try to sneak past them, my arms barred across my chest. If I step too close, the boys knock me into the lockers, elbow my chest. Sometimes they bat me between them like a pinball. "Oh, sorry," they laugh, as if it's all by accident.

When the bell rings, Sister Cyril appears in the hallway. "Children, take your seats. We haven't got all day."

"So how's third grade?" Emmy Atwood asks. We're the only ones left at our lockers. "Learn to count yet? Isn't it embarrassing to sit downstairs with the little kids? I'd die."

"It's not so bad. I like the break."

"Well, we're having a blast out at recess. You're missing out on all the fun." She covers her lips with Vaseline. The only make-up Sister will allow.

"Yeah, a blast. Watching the boys throw a football in the snow." This winter, the seventh-grade girls spend their time lined up along the wire fence that divides the boy's piece of blacktop from the girl's. Cheering. Getting ready for next fall.

"I'm going with Dave Fadden now. He asked me last weekend." Emmy takes a copper ring out of her jumper pocket, slips it over her finger. "See? He gave this to me. Kind of like that sailor you were so busy with when you first came. What happened to him anyway? Or that sister of yours? Is she still off modeling?"

"No. She's home."

"We know," Emmy says. "I was just giving you a test. We know everything."

"So, I guess you received the gift of prophecy," I say, slamming my locker shut.

"What's that supposed to mean?"

"The Lord is my shepherd," I say. "Somebody's already watching me."

"Did someone from my school call here?" I ask Cammy. We're in the kitchen getting dinner ready. A canned ham warmed in the oven, frozen corn, scalloped potatoes made from a box. While Cammy stirs the corn, she lets her cigarette hang loose from her lips, the long ash snaking then fluttering down to the floor.

"Yeah. They called. One day. They asked for my mother."

I take the cigarette from her mouth and set it on the ashtray. "You'll burn down the house." At night when I leave Cammy smoking alone in the living room, surrounded by candles and incense, I imagine the flames swallowing us in our sleep. "What did you say? Why didn't you tell me?"

"I didn't say anything, Guinevere." She abandons the cooking spoon at the edge of the pan, takes a break at the kitchen table. "I'm cool about schools. I know the scene. I wouldn't give the phone to a drunk."

"Did they ask who you were?"

"Yeah. I said I was your sister. So what? Am I a secret?"

"Was it Sister Cyril? Did she say what she wanted?" I slip the quilted cooking mitt over my hand, pull the sizzling ham out of the oven. "When did you put this in, Cammy? It's burnt."

"No, it was a guy who called. The archbishop, I guess."

"The archbishop?" I pry the charred bottom off the cookie sheet. "Why would the archbishop call me?"

"Shit," Cammy says. "Too bad, man. We'll eat the top."

"Did you go somewhere today?" I ask. "You seem strange." It's like she's in a trance, or about to drift off to sleep.

"Give me a break," she says. She folds her arms into a nest, rests her cheek against them, closes her eyes. "I'm just wired. It's boring as hell sitting here all day. Why can't you stay home and keep me company? Keep me out of trouble."

"What did he say?"

"Who? Jimmy?" When she says his name, she bites on her arm to muffle her laughter.

"Jimmy? Was it Jimmy who called here? I thought you said it was the archbishop."

"It was." She keeps giggling, but I don't join her. I can't find a funny word in this whole confusing conversation.

"Cammy," I say, poking her in the back with a fork. "Cut it out and answer me."

"I was kidding about Jimmy. But why won't you tell him about me? I'm ready to meet him. I could use a diversion. Even if he is, what? Thirteen? I like them young." She loops her hair around her ears, rubs her hand over her face to keep from laughing. Then she walks over to the stove, eats a spoonful of corn straight out of the pan. "Do you think he'd like me?"

I hate the way she talks about Jimmy, her constant questions when I come in from the fire escape at night. "How far did he go? Have you frenched yet?" The stories I'm forced to make up so she'll leave me alone. "Cammy, the phone call? Come on. Who was it?"

"That pastor guy. The one with the strange name."

"Monsignor?"

"That's it," she grins. "Do you think I might be his type?"

Cammy Closing the Circle

I knew the truth about Jimmy, though I made up my mind to let Faina have her little secret. I'd watched them on the fire escape sharing those sweet night smokes. Right away I took him for a New Directions kid. They all had the same shaggy look; I'd hung with enough of them through the years to know it. How could I avoid hooking up with them, their house across the alley, the steady stream of stragglers doing time at Kenny's? Most were good-looking in a ragged way, and Jimmy was no exception. Of course he was too old for her. Not just in years. In life. But she loved him; she wore it on her face. I would have known it without the diary.

"So what's happening?" That's what I said to Jimmy when we met that afternoon in the surprising sun of late January. A break in the worst winter, something we didn't expect. I was hanging out at the bus stop, killing time, waiting for him to cross Dakota Avenue for his shift at Kenny's.

"Who's asking?" Sometimes I can still hear him, his voice lifting a little at the end of each sentence, every question marked by a half-squinted eye.

"Me. Got an extra smoke?" Close up he was cute enough—too young for me, too small. But I knew what she saw in him. He had a way with his eyes. Drilling them straight into me so that I had to squirm a bit, while he slouched in his leather jacket, smoking. He reached into his pocket and tossed one to me. He was playing a poor game of hard to get, keeping his eyes steady, refusing to blink. I'd mastered this dance, the little dares, the long stares that raised the stakes. Jimmy Cordova was small time compared to me.

114   What gave away his edge was the slight tremor in his hands, the way

the match shook when he lit my cigarette. That day I took it for nerves, though it never left him.

"I'm Faina's older sister," I said. He blinked then, several times, his eyes wide and startled. I was ahead.

"Who?"

"Cammy McCoy. Faina's older sister." Now he squirmed, looked over my shoulder at the cars splashing down Dakota.

"I didn't know she had a sister."

"Well, we all have secrets." I flashed him my sweetest smile. He was nervous, no question. Grounding out one butt, and lighting another. I tried to read his face to see what he felt for her. He was too old to have any real interest. "Do you have some kind of a thing for her?"

"No," he said, choking on a deep drag. "She's a kid." He wiped his palms on the front of his jeans. "What's this about anyway? Is she okay?"

"Sure she is. She's off at her little school, like always. Just thought I'd introduce myself. You know, be neighborly." I let my fur jacket fall behind me on the bus bench. I'd dressed for the weather, and for Jimmy. A short T-shirt that showed some skin, my favorite jeans. I yawned, stretched my arms up over my head so Jimmy could get a good look at me. Check out the family. "Isn't she a little young to be smoking out back with a guy from New Directions? Seems to me that could lead to trouble."

Jimmy laughed, smoothed his hair back off his forehead. Water rushed down the gutter and into the sewer like a river. "What are you asking?" Again the squint. "Is she safe with me?"

"It's a big-sister thing."

"Well, big sister, catch your bus," he said. The 6B was rumbling toward us down Dakota Avenue. "I'll let you know when you need to worry."

It screeched to a stop, splattered mud down the front of me. The driver flipped open the door, "Coming?"

"Why not?" I shrugged. I climbed the steps, threw two dimes into the meter and grabbed the first seat. It was a day ripe with promise; I could go anywhere, be anybody. I slid open the smudged window, threw my head out into the warm wind and screamed, "Don't tell her about us, Jimmy."

He nodded his head at me, lifted his hand in a salute. I knew I'd won. He was easy.

We met in the afternoons. Jimmy managed to add an imaginary hour to his shift, some story about stocking produce. New Directions was the end of his line, and he said the counselors were loose there, at least with him because he was playing it straight and just a few months shy of freedom.

We made it in the storage room, surrounded by the musty plywood lockers stuffed full of Papa Roy's stuff. Green light filtered in through the glass-block window, the one Hank had replaced since my summer visit. There were spiderwebs everywhere. When we were finished, Jimmy liked to fool with the padlocks; he could crack a combination in seconds.

He wasn't bad in bed, but he wasn't Tony. It was a fling, a cure for cabin fever. She'd taken my dad. But even Jimmy wasn't a fair trade.

"You ever think about what you're going to do when you get out?" We were spread out on my old quilt, the cement cold against my back, my head on his stomach. I tried not to look at him. He was so thin, girl-like, with a smooth, sunken chest.

He was staring up at the ceiling, silent. Conversation wasn't his gift. "Join the service, I guess. If they'll take me."

"Couple of years and you can come home and marry Faina. We can be a threesome, star in our own porn flick."

"Why do you say that kind of shit?" He stood up, grabbed his jeans, and stepped into them. "What's wrong with you anyway?"

"Jimmy, I'm just kidding." But he couldn't take a joke about anything, especially Faina. "Come back down here with me. I'm cold alone. And we've still got fifteen minutes before your little schoolgirl comes home. She won't find us. Take it easy."

He zipped up his pants, threw his shirt on and buttoned it. "She's just a kid. Leave her out of this."

"Stay," I begged, rubbing my cheek on his leg. "I bought you something." I pulled the joint from my cigarette packet. It was crumpled a little in the middle, but I smoothed it out between my lips. Jimmy stopped stuffing his shirt into his jeans.

"I can't," he said, but he was wavering.

"Jimmy, it's a gift. From me." I ran my hand along the back of his skinny calf. He'd told me he'd been clean two years, since the beginning of his stint at Red Rock. I'd made a special trip down to Lord Leo's to break his losing streak.

"No," he said, shaking his head. He was lacing up his boots, determined to leave. But he kept glancing at it, that thin joint suspended between my teeth.

"Jimmy," I said. "Smoke. No one will know." I tugged on the waist of his jeans until he surrendered and toppled down next to me. "That's better," I said. "You take the first hit."

"Don't," he said, batting my hand.

I lit the joint, wrapped the quilt around my naked body, closed my eyes and let the warm tingle of grass soak through me. "More for me. I'm just going to sit down here and get stoned. Maybe your little girlfriend will join me."

"You get her stoned," he said, "I'll kill you. She's a kid. Why can't you leave her alone?"

That was our last blast; he never came back. I was bored, but it didn't break my heart. I could have blown his cover. Told her what a loser he was. Lousy kisser. Too quick. But we were just coming together then, just being sisters. They had their cigarettes. Their fantasies. So what?

I was glad when the Starlight gave me an escape. I was tired of watching through the window, tired of standing outside their little circle. I hated the way he leaned toward her to light her cigarette, the way he laughed at her stories, the way he tugged her braid. They looked like brother and sister, family. Both small and dark, his arm resting on her narrow shoulder, her head tilted toward his chest. Brother and sister. It was something I could never explain.

Lenore Survivors

It was Cammy who forged the field-trip permission slip. But when the Cathedral secretary called to say my signature looked suspicious, I lied and said it was mine. I didn't want to sound the alarm.

Certainly I saw through the conspiracy. Cammy plotting behind my back, Cammy turning Faina against me. Divide and conquer, that was Cammy's disease, and she'd done it since she was a child. Jealous, she'd tried to come between Papa Roy and me. She couldn't help it.

"So where is Faina?" I asked Cammy, the second I hung up the phone.

"At a protest march." Cammy had a bizarre sense of humor; she loved to jangle my nerves. "She knew you'd say no, so she asked me. Big deal. You're too paranoid to let her do anything."

I hated when Cammy accused me of holding Faina prisoner; she didn't know about the accident, didn't know the worries that weighed on my heart. "Where is she really?"

"I already told you. Some protest march."

"A protest march? At her age? What is she protesting?"

"Abortion, I guess. I told you that school was a cult."

Abortion?

Every time I tried to close my eyes I had visions so vivid and violent I couldn't sleep. I saw my little Faina dead in the snow at the State Capitol, some hysterical hippie screaming over her, a famous photograph that would become history. I kept waiting for the phone to ring, the knock on the door to announce she was dead. I imagined her handcuffed by riot police, locked in the back of a squad car, our troubles beginning again, the authorities snatching my children.

"Faina, I could have lost you," I said, when she finally came home at

3:30. She had a strange pink plastic baby pinned to her coat. "You could have been killed today. Haven't your teachers ever heard of Kent State?"

"It was important," she said. "They took the upper grades on a bus. All of us. Before we left Cathedral, Dr. Atwood led a prayer rally in the gym. He showed slides of unborn babies sucking their thumbs. He said he'd abandon medicine before he'd take a child's life."

"God above." I stifled the urge to strike her. "What are you babbling about? You're a twelve-year-old. What does this have to do with you?"

"Everything. What if you had killed me?"

"Killed you? I didn't. You're here."

"But you could have. If it was legal, like it is now. What if I'd never had a chance to live?"

"Faina, enough. I haven't slept all day. You're alive. What more do I need to say?"

Brainwashing. I saw what was happening. But what breed of people would suggest such a thing to a child?

Faina Stew

At night, Cammy disappears to her job waiting tables at the Starlight Lanes. "We need the money," she tells me. "We can't depend on Lenore."

While she gets ready, I lounge on the floor, watch as she scrunches the pantyhose together at the toe, inches them slowly up over each leg, bends at the knees to yank them up over her hips. The elastic top cuts into her flat white stomach. Then she sits half-naked in front of the make-up mirror, the round white bulbs turning her bare skin blue. She spits on the end of her eyeliner brush, rubs it over a little black cake, draws thick lines around her eyes. "Highlights," she says, opening them wide to dry. "Now they're almost as dark as yours."

I stay by her side, flip the record albums, light her cigarettes, help her unwind hot rollers from her hair. Now that she's gone for long hours, I miss her.

"Are you sure you have to work?" I ask her.

"The cash will come in handy," she says. "You wait and see. My mother's loaded, but it won't trickle down to us. Besides, I'm buying you a confirmation dress with my tips; we'll go shopping at Sears on Lake Street." She nods toward the giant plastic beer bottle already heavy with silver. "Anyway, you've got your Jimmy. That virginal boy from Cathedral. Can't he keep you company at night?"

"But Lenore and I are lonely when you leave."

"You're starting to sound like my mother."

Before she leaves, she sprays musk perfume over her body, under the pink waitress dress, between the top of her uniform and her bra, behind the back of her neck. I hold my breath when she bends down to kiss me. "Good-bye, little sister," she says, her lips sweet with Close-up tooth-

paste and watermelon gloss. "Don't wait up for me."

But I do. Ever since her first night, I've set my alarm so I'm awake when Cammy comes home. I watch for her out our bedroom window, the parking lot dreary and deserted, the garage lights shining on the snow. I watch while the strange cars bring her home, idle outside in the cold, exhaust clouding out of their tailpipes, windshields fogged over with breath and ice. Sometimes the driver roars the engine, and a loud muffler explodes into the silence. Other than that, nothing happens, so I close my eyes and wait for the sound of her footsteps stumbling up the back stairs.

When she comes into our room, I pretend to be asleep. I open my eyes just a little so she doesn't know I'm watching her kick off her spongy white waitress shoes, pull her uniform over her head. Then she peels off her pantyhose and stands in the city light that streams through our window, and lets the shadows fall over her beautiful body. Cammy.

Cammy smoking to get to sleep. Cammy playing "Stairway to Heaven," over and over, her husky night voice singing along with the song. Cammy climbing into our bed finally, her skin cold against me, her full breasts pressed into my back, her leg looped, as always, over my hip.

In the morning when I leave for school, Cammy's still asleep face down in her pillow, her long blonde hair spilling over her bare shoulders, pooling in the small curve of her back. Now it's me, again, who brings Lenore coffee, it's me who helps her hobble to the bathroom, it's me who delivers dry toast and a juice glass of vodka.

"Don't mention this to Cammy," Lenore tells me. "I just need a little sip to get going."

"You shouldn't drink in the morning," I say to her.

"I know," she says. "But someday you'll understand. It's this damn cough. A drink is the only thing that helps." Ever since Cammy's come back, Lenore seems weaker, hacking all the time, her voice faint and scratchy like she has laryngitis.

"I wish Cammy wouldn't work," she says. "I worry so when she goes away."

I look at Lenore's spindly arms poking out of her covers, her thin fingers nothing more than knobby bones. "Cammy is home with you all day."

"But she won't stay. Mark my words. She'll be gone when she gets some money."

"Monsignor wants to see you." Sister Cyril is waiting for me outside our classroom. "He's down in the nurse's room."

The nurse's room is a small dark closet at the end of the hall, next to the girls' lavatory. Inside there's only one small cot covered with a crisp white sheet, and an old metal desk. Sometimes the girls in my class pretend they have cramps, so they can skip class and sleep on the cot. Not me. I don't want to get my first period at Cathedral, I don't want to stand in that dark closet while Sister Cyril pulls a Modess pad out of the metal desk.

"Monsignor wants to see me?"

"Are you hard of hearing?" Sister Cyril clucks her tongue, tucks her hands up into her huge sleeves. "He's waiting."

Inside the dim room, Monsignor is perched on the edge of the cot, his hands pressed together, the tips of his fingers tapping on his chin. "Come in, come in."

I stand in front of him, glance down at the brown spots dotted over the top of his bald head. He lifts the tiny paper-covered pillow and places it on his lap. "Have a seat, young lady," he says, patting the white sheet.

I don't want to sit down next to Monsignor with his woody brown teeth, the gray whiskers sprouting out of his nostrils and ears. I've stood close to him before, in November, when he handed out our report cards, one by one, in front of the class—the agonizing wait while he examined my grades, the quick pat he gave me on the back when he was done.

"I don't mind standing."

"No, sit, please."

I take my seat on the cot, out of his reach, and stretch my uniform skirt down over my knees.

"There has been some concern about your confirmation training." Monsignor slides his glasses up the bridge of his nose, clears his throat. "Sister Cyril says you haven't brought in your baptismal certificate."

"How would she know? She's not the one doing my confirmation training."

Monsignor frowns. "I don't know. Perhaps she heard it from Mrs. Lajoy." I look past him at the poster of the four food groups. The cow, the bread, the red apple, the glass of pure white milk. *Eat well. Build a healthy body.* "At any rate. Do you have your baptismal certificate?"

"My mother's looking for it. We might have lost it in the move."

"Yes. I phoned your mother, twice, but she never responded to my message. She can write and request your certificate from the parish where you were baptized. You were baptized?"

"Yes. My mother has been busy. She started a new job."

"Wonderful." Monsignor cups his hands in his lap. "Maybe she can clear up some of that back tuition. We like people to stay current. We can't run a school on good intentions. Just bring that certificate in so you can be confirmed. Will you do that for me, missy? I'm a busy man, let's put this matter to rest."

"Yes."

The cot heaves beneath us as Monsignor rises. He stands over me, his wrinkled hands resting on the top of my head. "May Almighty God bless you. In the name of the Father, the Son, the Holy Spirit." he says. "There has been altogether too much stew stirring around you. I can't remember another child who came to Cathedral with so much trouble."

"Was I baptized?" I ask Lenore. We're lounging in her bed again, like the old days, the two of us sipping our bowls of chicken-noodle soup, the TV tuned to *Truth or Consequences.*

"Baptized? I don't know. You might have been. When you're my age you'll see you can't remember much."

"Was Cammy?"

"She was christened. That's what we called it then. Mother arranged it. She bought a beautiful white gown from Young Quinlan. It seems to me there was a luncheon afterward at the Minikahda Club, but I could be confused."

"Then I was christened too?"

"I suppose you must have been. Though everything's so different with the second. You wait and see when you're a mother. The novelty wears off."

"I need a certificate. In order to make my confirmation."

"A certificate? Faina, this is getting crazier by the minute. Sponsors. Papers. What do these people want from me?"

"Well, do we have it?"

"If we do, it would be in Papa Roy's papers."

I wait until Cammy's at work and Lenore's asleep to go searching. I need to find this certificate, the slip of paper Monsignor requires for my confirmation. I open the deep file drawer of Papa Roy's desk. It's full of green folders, each one with a labeled tab. Household. Dry Cleaners. Employee Taxes. Social Security. Insurance. Medical Records. Legal.

The folders are stuffed with old papers, none of which mean anything to me. I pull out the file marked Legal, hoping it might contain family documents, the certificate I desperately need.

I don't understand any of it. Will. Purchase Agreement. Order to Terminate Parental Rights. My dad's name, Robert Martin McCoy, and my name, Faina Margaret McCoy, written in bold ink. *The party requests parental rights be terminated. The party requests to be absolved from further financial, legal, and physical responsibility.* It's signed by Lenore and my dad. January 23, 1965.

"Faina," Lenore calls from her sleep, and I slip the file back in the drawer, quietly sliding it closed.

When I've settled her in again, I go back to take a second look. This time I hide the paper under my shirt, tip-toe past Lenore's door and into my bedroom. It's a technical document; most of the language I can't understand, but the general meaning is clear to me. Request to terminate parental rights. What I want to know is whose idea was this? Lenore's or my dad's? Who ordered her out of my life? Does it mean she isn't my mother now?

I know if I go into her room, shake her awake and insist on an answer, she'll blame me for snooping through Papa Roy's things. She'll say it's ancient history. She'll tell me she doesn't remember. So I write to my father. My father will tell me the truth.

"Do you have secrets in your family?" I ask Jimmy. We're sitting on the fire escape stairs, my back pressed up against his knees, my quilt wrapped around me like a cape to keep the cold from seeping into my bones. This Minneapolis winter has lasted forever, this wind that burns like fire, this chill I can never escape.

"I suppose. You know, the usual. Don't tell your mother. Don't tell your father. Don't tell your sister. But everyone knows, because as soon as they've said that, they're the ones that go blabbing the news."

"I don't think my dad kept secrets from me. But now I can't remember anymore. It felt like we told each other everything; there wasn't that much to tell. You want to get under this blanket with me?" I lift up my arm to make room for Jimmy.

"No thanks. I was born here on the tundra," he says, his teeth chattering.

"Do you think secrets are a bad thing?" I'm happy I have my back to Jimmy, happy I can concentrate on the two cars stalled down in the alley, their hoods propped open, the occasional whine of an engine that won't quite start. A familiar sound in this city. "Bad?" Jimmy says. "That depends. Not if the truth would hurt somebody."

"What if telling the truth would hurt you?"

"That's self-protection. It's necessary. You do what you got to do. What is this, a question on your religion quiz? I remember this shit from my Catholic school days."

"Do you think there's a difference between secrets and things you just don't say?"

"Jesus Christ. I'm failing. Where the hell is this going?"

"I have a sister," I blurt out. The words puff out of my mouth like smoke. "I didn't want to tell you. Because she was gone for awhile, and now she just came back, and I didn't want to mention her when I didn't know for sure where she was."

"So?" Jimmy says. "What's that to me? I don't need to know all the details of your family."

"Just that I should have mentioned it sooner. Probably. Because she's home now, she lives with us, my mom and me while my dad's away. And you'll meet her someday."

"Why would I? I'm not bringing you home to meet my folks. They need to give up," Jimmy says. "That battery's dead." I glance over at the two men still struggling to start the car. "I'm going to give them a hand," Jimmy says, standing up and stepping over me. "My brother was great with engines. Go on inside now."

"So you don't care that I never mentioned my sister?"

"No," Jimmy says. "Your sister means nothing to me."

Back in the apartment, I boil water for cocoa, toast a slice of Wonder Bread, melt the peanut butter over the top while it's hot. I plug in the Christmas lights still tacked up along the living room window, and watch the colors blink across the frosty glass. Now that Jimmy knows the truth, the secret is behind me; I won't have to worry he'll discover Cammy sometime through the window of Kenny's and hate me for hiding my beautiful sister. I won't have to worry, as long as they never meet.

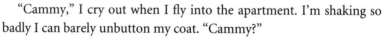

"We seen her." I don't need to turn around to look; I recognize Hank's growl immediately. I try to pry open the door to the building, but he's got his ape hand clenched around the iron handle. "Not so fast, little lady. We seen it all. The comings and goings. Frances and me. Not much you can sneak past us."

I'm glad I've given up walking home through the alley, I'm glad I'm out on Dakota Avenue where people can rescue me. If he tries to grab me again and throw me into the basement, I'll scream.

"You ladies got some company upstairs. Thought the police took that girl away for awhile. They let her out already?"

"I don't know what you mean."

"She can't stay here. The papers say two tenants only. Been like that since the old man died. Lenore signed."

"I'm just visiting."

"Yeah, you said that six months ago. We're trying to keep this building clean. She's back, and we got the same losers showing up here at all hours of the night. People smoking dope. Your old lady's lease is up in June. Tell her to start looking." He squeezes the back of my neck. "You got me?"

"Cammy," I cry out when I fly into the apartment. I'm shaking so badly I can barely unbutton my coat. "Cammy?"

"What?" Cammy screams. "I'm in a hurry."

"Come here a second. Please." I don't want to talk to her in our bedroom, or in our hallway, or anyplace else Lenore might hear us.

"What the hell?" Cammy stands there in her nylons and bra, a hot-roller pick clenched between her teeth. "I got to catch my bus in fifteen minutes. Al will have my ass if I'm late for my shift."

I wave her toward me into the narrow entrance. "It's Hank," I whisper. "He says Lenore has to leave. He says her lease will be up in June."

"He's been saying that since I can remember. He's crazy."

"He means it, Cammy. He says she should start looking. Three of us can't live here, it's not on the lease."

"He hates us. Always has. Because Lenore's loaded. They all do. Blow him off."

"Did something happen with the police?"

"Which time? I got to get ready." I follow her through the apartment, down the hallway, back to our messy room. Cammy's jeans and shirt in a heap on the floor, the covers bunched up on our bed. "Cool it," she says, lighting a cigarette and handing it to me. "Hold this for me. Take a drag, it'll calm your nerves."

"Faina, is that you?" Lenore's wobbly voice floats from her room.

"I'll be right in," I scream. "I'm just hanging up my uniform. Hank means it, Cammy. He hates us."

"Not us. Hank hates *me.* Here's the short story. A while ago, I was running with some guys who broke into the bakery. Kicked in the back door. It was a joke; we were stoned and hungry. Frances lost maybe a hundred bucks and a few jelly rolls. So what?"

"They knew it was you?"

"Couldn't prove it. Never confess. They can't pin anything on you without a witness."

"You stole from Frances?" Frances with the accent, Frances with the crown of braids across her head. No wonder she asked me so many questions.

"I've got a gift." Cammy pulls her uniform over her head, straightens her hair in the make-up mirror, takes the cigarette from my fingers for one last drag. "You know that. I've lifted from everybody. Border Drug. Kenny's. You've helped me, St. McCoy. Those that got it don't miss it. Get my drift? Hank can keep his plumbing supplies; I'm not into pipes. Not that kind anyway. And still, baby sister, I got to work for cash. How do you explain that?"

She leans over and kisses my forehead, rubs her thumb over my skin to wipe off the gloss. "I told you, I'm buying you your confirmation dress. Now keep all this crap from Lenore. It'll just make her nervous."

"I know."

"You worry too much," Cammy says. "I'll see you when I get home."

But she doesn't see me when she comes home, and she doesn't see what I see. The car windows steaming over during her long hours in our parking lot, the different men who deliver her to our alley. Doesn't know I've seen her totter out the car door, lead different men by the hand across the snowy lot, their shoes making prints in the snow, her rabbit jacket hanging wide open. Doesn't know I've crept out into the hallway, spied on their secret sounds down in the stairwell. All those men who are buying my confirmation dress, all those men who leave her good tips, the money I get to count in the morning, the grand total I tally on a slip of Dahl Cleaners paper. The same tablet I used this summer to keep score of our card games. Cammy doesn't see all the fear I carry in me, the truth about Lenore's termination, Jimmy, the missing baptismal certificate. I can't tell my story to anybody. Not Lenore. Not Jimmy. Not my dad. Not Mrs. Lajoy. I can't even tell Monsignor, in the dark closet of his confessional, my face hidden behind a curtain and a screen. Because he might recognize me. My voice. The sound of the girl swimming in stew.

Cammy Sweethearts

We worked Faina's assembly line. My mother clipped out the brown construction-paper dogs with her manicure scissors; I attached the tails with little gold fasteners she'd dug out of Papa Roy's desk. Faina printed the message on the dog's stomach: BE MY DOG-GONE VALENTINE. It was a design she'd mastered the year before in San Diego; she was wild about the way the tail wagged.

My mother rose from the dead for this type of activity. The two of them had already wasted hours gluing paper hearts and Christmas ribbon on a sunken shoe box. I couldn't believe we were at the valentine project again.

"Faina, you're so clever," my mother said, wagging one of the tails. "I can remember how much I loved Valentine's Day as a girl. In our gang we wrote little poems, sayings mostly. *Yours till Niagara Falls.* You know. If a boy liked you, he left a sweet in your pocket. Of course, I always had a handful: saltwater taffy, licorice sticks, lemon drops. For most, chocolate was hard to come by, but then, we lived in Kenwood. We didn't often go without. Mother said she didn't think the boys would love me with rotten teeth, but I ate it anyway."

I passed Faina my stack of finished mutts. She'd been allowed to set up shop on my mother's sacred vanity, the mirrored perfume tray pushed to the side. "Maybe Jimmy will get you one of those cheap cardboard hearts filled with bad candy," I said, just to stir her up. "You know, the kind you gouge your fingernail into before you eat it."

"Jimmy?" my mother asked. She was hooked that fast. She dropped the manicure scissors, forgot the clever wagging dogs. "Now who's this Jimmy? You girls and your secrets, you never tell me anything. Cammy and I used to love to talk about her beaus. Didn't we Cammy?"

"Yeah, really," I said. When I was a kid, she lived for "beau talk." *Tell me about the boys at school. Who has a crush on you? Who chases you at*

recess? With your face, you can't tell me all the little boys aren't begging for
a kiss.

130

Sheila
O'Connor

Faina shot me that pissed-off scowl she'd perfected. "Jimmy's just a kid at my school," she said. She was a master liar, never blew her cover, never got her stories crossed.

"A boy at Cathedral, huh?" my mother sang. "Well tell me. Does he like you, too? I didn't think you were interested in boys, yet. I thought you were a late bloomer."

"I'm not," Faina snapped. "He doesn't like me. Cammy was just making a joke."

"Everyone wants a sweetheart," my mother said. "That's nothing to be ashamed of." She wasn't one to let a subject die. "But if you're really interested, you should fix your face. And you could make him a very special little doggie. I think I've got a stick of Juicy Fruit in my purse you could tape to the tail. Cammy, hand it to me."

I grabbed her pathetic white patent-leather purse from the closet doorknob. I'm sure it'd been there since the sixties. She liked to keep it within easy reach, to pay the Dakota Liquors delivery boy, or write checks for the monthly bills.

"I don't want the gum," Faina insisted, with that black stubborn voice my mother always ignored. "He's a boy at school. That's all." She inspected the next dog, wagged its tail. "Cammy, don't bend the fasteners back so far."

"You don't pay enough to complain," I said. "Bend the fasteners back yourself."

"Girls, don't bicker," my mother said. "This is a special occasion. Faina has a new sweetheart. Here it is." She held up the stick of Juicy Fruit like a great treasure. "Tape this to the tail. Let him know how you feel."

"Cammy, did you check the mail?" Faina asked. School was done for the day; the big valentine bash was behind her. She stood in our bedroom doorway, clutching that ridiculous box to her chest.

"Nothing came for you. How was your big party? Did Jimmy give you anything at school?"

I was rushing to get to the Starlight early. Al was expecting a flood of lovers, regulars pouring in for the Sweetheart Special: Two for One Burgers and Beer. Wives eat free.

"There was nothing in the mail for me?" Faina slumped down on the edge of the bed.

"Don't worry about Jimmy," I said. "He's no great catch."

"It isn't Jimmy. I was the only one who had homemade valentines." She pulled the lid off the top of her box. I glanced at the collection of little cards and candies. They were store-bought, cartoon characters, the same junk I'd passed out in grade school.

"So what?"

"I want to go back to San Diego." She threw her box of valentines down on our bed, ran to the bathroom, slammed the door.

"So go." I shouted. I'd wasted my night off making those stupid little tails. It was impossible to make her happy. "I didn't get a valentine either. Do you see me bawling like a baby?"

"I'm sorry," she sobbed. "It's just that my dad always remembered."

"Remembered you, maybe. But he never remembered me."

I couldn't bear her little-girl disappointment; maybe it reminded me of some earlier time in my life. Whatever, I'm sure it was her tears that made me stop outside the Starlight, and lift that wretched kitten from the cardboard box marked FREE.

It was an ugly thing, clumps of mangy orange fur and a white splash over one of its red-rimmed eyes. An albino look almost, a pink nose, tiny pink paw pads. Patches of pink skin showing through the fur. I took it in with me.

"Hey, where you going with that?" Al asked, when I strolled past the front desk with the kitten poking its ugly face out of my apron pocket.

"It's a Valentine's present for my baby sister." I lifted the kitten and nuzzled it to my nose.

The Starlight was decorated big-time for the holiday, red foil hearts at the end of each lane, red crepe-paper streamers strung from the ceiling.

"Not in here," Al said. "The health department will shut us down."

"Have a heart," I laughed.

"Ha ha," Al said. My charms were wasted on him. He would've unloaded me the first week, but he saw the way I sucked in the customers. He was a fat old pig, on his fifth wife already, owned a house with a pool somewhere out in the suburbs. He was pure bottom line, money. He called the Starlight *Slum City,* but it certainly kept him in cash.

"Get rid of it, Cammy." He was cashing out the register from the lunch crowd. "We're looking at a big night. The Sweetheart Special."

"Are we taking the sweethearts at their word, or do you want me to ask for a marriage license before I give them two beers?"

"You're a royal pain in the ass," he said, trying to slap my butt.

"Keep your mitts off me," I said, hitting his arm.

"Don't screw with me, Cammy. Get rid of that cat. Or it's your last shift."

In my locker I made a nest for her with my rabbit jacket. Gave her a little cereal saucer of milk. If I was lucky, Al wouldn't hear her meowing. If I wasn't, he could toss me. Serve the sweethearts himself.

It was a tough night; tips were always low when guys came in with their wives. It made me sick to see the old bags, their hair still showing curler lines, their painted eyebrows, their polyester pantsuits. "Sweetheart Special," I said, slamming their orders down on their tables. I didn't bother with friendly when there wasn't money involved.

We closed up earlier than usual; the guys didn't hang around with their wives on their arms. I threw my tips into my macrame purse. I could tell a bad night when I wiped a table.

"Meow, meow," I said, walking out past Al, and lifting the kitten's paw in a little wave.

"Your days are numbered," Al said. He was settling back in his manager's chair, a big leather swivel thing where he sat to smoke his shift-end cigar. "Your luck is running out."

I flipped him the finger and stepped out into the February night. The wind was so bitter my skin felt tight, my fingers stiffened to stone within seconds. I'd never taken the bus home; there was always a warm car out front waiting for me. Sometimes two or three, and then I got to take my pick. I tucked the kitten inside my jacket to keep her cozy. It was too late for cat food; I'd have to send Faina to Kenny's in the morning.

The bus was dead at midnight, one of the last ones running. The driver was a grandfatherly type, reminded me a little of Papa Roy. I'm sure he was bored skidding down the same icy streets, sipping his thermos of coffee. "Don't bother," he said, when I tried to drop my dimes through the slot. He even let me hold the kitten on my lap.

"A girl your age shouldn't be out alone at night," he said. "It isn't safe in this city."

"I usually drive. But our car wouldn't start."

"I tell you what, this has got to be the worst winter. There's black ice at every intersection. And the snow. Lord above. Will it ever quit?" The streets were banked with mountains of snow, so thick and deep they'd outlawed parking along Franklin Avenue. The snowplows had been running for days straight, and still there were drifts you could hardly climb. "It's days like this make me hate my job."

"Me, too," I said. I ran my nails under the kitten's chin.

"Girl pretty as you shouldn't need to work. You got to find a man to take care of you."

"My mom's sick," I said. "I'm supporting my family."

"Don't see that much anymore," he said. "Your mama raised you right."

When the bus slid to a stop in front of Kenny's, the driver reached under his seat. "Happy Valentine's Day," he said, handing me a box of candy.

"Thanks," I said. I didn't want to tell him I'd never eat that cheap cream-filled crap.

"I'm diabetic. Can't eat it anyway. One of the regulars on my route gave it to me this morning."

"It's really nice." He reminded me so much of Papa Roy, I almost cried. I'm sure it was the night, the bad tips, the couples.

"I hope I see you again," he said. "I'll give you a free ride any time you need it. You're sure a pretty little thing. Maybe I'll even come in bowling when I get a night off. How would that be?"

"That'd be great." I could tell he'd be a big tipper.

Inside the apartment, everyone was asleep, as usual. My mother could wait until morning. I knew it'd take some talking to get her to go for the kitten. But it was Faina I wanted to surprise.

"Get up," I whispered in her ear. "Valentine's Day is still here."

She was wiped out, like always. She rubbed her fist over her eyes, sat up in our bed. She was wearing that striped flannel nightgown with the ruffles across the chest, the one my mother had ordered for me years ago from the Sears catalog. Faina had found it in the back of my closet, still wrapped in cellophane.

"Be my sweetheart," I meowed in a squeaky little voice, before I set the kitten on our bed.

"For me? Where'd you get it? Cammy, can we keep it?" It was the happiest I'd seen her.

"It's your valentine, baby sister. From me." I pulled my greasy uniform over my head, tossed it into the corner. "Move over, I'm freezing," I said, crawling down under the covers. I snuggled in next to the two of them, Faina's soft flannel warm against my bare skin.

"Now are you happy?" I kissed the back of her head, rubbed my frozen feet along her bony leg.

"Yes," she said. "Thank you, Cammy."

"See, Minneapolis isn't so bad." I wrapped my arm around her waist. "You think she's too ugly to love?"

"Not to me." Faina rolled over and settled the kitten between us. "But how do you know it's a she?"

"Remind me to teach you the difference someday."

"She purrs like a little machine. Listen." Faina held the kitten up to her ear like a seashell. "Purr. Persephone."

"What the hell is that?"

"Persephone. You know, the goddess who ate the pomegranate seeds. Get it?"

"You're a major head case. I don't give a shit what you call her, she's yours. But I'm not learning to pronounce it."

She stroked her cheek along the kitten's fur. The name meant something to her. What did I care? I called the cat Per. That was name enough for me.

"Oh, I almost forgot," I said. "There's a box of fancy candy by my purse. It was sitting outside our door when I came home from work. There's no card. Must be a mystery sweetheart. But I bet it's for you. From Jimmy."

Hi there Catholic girl,

Twelve years without religion and now this? Confirmation? If you're looking for a name, try mine. Saint Roberta? How's that sound? I'm sorry I can't be there for the show. Have Lenore take some pictures of you all dressed up, send them to me. I'd give anything to see your face. I can pass them around here, show the office folks the gorgeous broad who writes me all those letters. Sometimes I read them in my bunk at night, the old ones. I go back over them, just to hear your voice. Don't worry about that sponsor business, have some friend of Lenore's stand up for you. What difference does it make? Wiley says he'd be happy to do the honor. Well, I'm throwing this in the mail before we hit the town. It's no picnic keeping up with the young guys, they go all night, end up seeing morning at some stranger's house. The whole group loaded to the gills, playing guitar and singing. Not me, I'm always half asleep. Wish I had your voice. Wish I could be with you. Dad

Faina The Message

Per makes us happy. All of us, even Lenore, who lets Per nap beside her on a satin pillow. Cammy teases Per with a string, a rolled-up ball of newspaper. "Come see this," we call out to each other; then we gather at the bathroom door to watch Per catch drops of water from the faucet, or lick her pink tongue over her tiny saucer of milk.

"I don't know what I'd do without her," Lenore says, stroking her hand over Per's arched back.

"She's a mangy little stray," Cammy says, lifting up Per to kiss her nose.

"She'll be beautiful someday," Lenore scolds. It's the same thing she says about me, which makes Per and me family. Per with her tufts of duck-feather orange fur, me with my dark skin and scrawny body.

"She's mine. Give her to me."

"She's yours, all right," Cammy says, tossing her into my hands. "You can clean her litter box, Dr. Doolittle."

For confirmation I've decided to take the name of the patron saint of cats. I know from my studies there is a saint for everything: St. Jude, the patron saint of desperate causes; St. Anthony, the saint of lost things; St. Cecelia, the saint of music. Mrs. Lajoy keeps a shoe box full of plastic-covered saint cards. Each card has a painting of the saint and a prayer to recite. We're allowed to sift through it for ideas.

"You'll each get your own for confirmation," Mrs. Lajoy tells me. I'm staying in again for recess to continue my saint research. "Have you made a decision, Faina?"

"About my sponsor?"

"No, about your name?"

"Actually, I was wondering. Do you know the name of the patron saint of cats?"

"What about St. Francis of Assisi? He's the one in the box with the birds on his shoulders. It's my understanding he's the patron saint of animals in general. I'm not aware of one who covers cats in particular, but we could probably ask Monsignor."

"That's okay. I'll look in the library."

"I'm a fan of cats, too," Mrs. Lajoy says. "I treat my own two like children. They're my only family while my husband's in the Army. But Francis is a fine name." She rummages through the box looking for the saint card to show me.

I can't take Francis, not after Cammy's burglary or the way Frances forced Lenore to send me to school.

"What about Persephone?"

"Persephone?" Mrs. Lajoy rests on my desk, her delicate fingers curved around the edge for balance. "Where did you hear about Persephone?"

"I had an elective in Greek mythology in San Diego. I like the name. A lot."

"There is a big difference between myth and religion," Mrs. Lajoy says. "Monsignor would be appalled if he knew you suggested such a thing." She lifts my booklet off my desk, flips the pages with her thumb. "If I were you, I'd settle on a name and get going with the rest of your booklet. Monsignor is still waiting for your baptismal certificate. Sometimes I wonder if you look for trouble."

"My mother sent for it. She said she expected it to come any day."

"I hope so." Mrs. Lajoy pauses at the blank page labeled "First Communion." "Don't you have any pictures of this day?"

"We left so much in storage."

"Faina, it isn't my business," she says. "You're Sister Cyril's responsibility. But if I were you, I'd tread carefully."

A hard pounding jolts me out of a deep sleep. When I open my eyes, our room is so dark I think it's still night. "Cammy," I whisper, jabbing my elbow into her stomach. "Get off me. Somebody's knocking."

"Girls?" Lenore screams from the other room. "Girls, what's happening?"

I slide my hand under Per's belly, set her in the closet behind Cammy's boots and close the door. "Be a good girl," I beg. "You don't want them to take you away." I jerk the pillow out from under Cammy's head. "Come on."

"Girls?" Lenore screams again.

"Just a minute, Lenore." I shout. "We're coming."

"What the hell is this?" Cammy says. "I didn't get in until three in the morning."

"Put on some clothes and go see."

"Stop with the bongo routine," Cammy moans, nestling deeper into the blankets. "My head is throbbing."

"It could be a fire." I tug at her arm, try to get her to stand.

"I hope this whole damn place burns to the ground."

"Cammy!" Lenore calls. "It's six o'clock in the morning. What is it? What's happening?"

I stop in Lenore's doorway, flip on her light. "Don't worry, Lenore. I'll go see."

"Faina, don't let anybody in. Not anybody. Do you hear me?"

The door is locked, dead-bolted twice and chained. I stand on my toes to look through the peephole. It's Hank's face, distorted, his lips purple and swollen, his red nose twice its size. "Yes?" I say. "What is it? We were asleep."

"It's Lenore I want to talk to, little girl. You get her out here."

"She's sick. What do you need?"

"I want to talk to her."

"I'll give her a message." I know things will be worse if I bring Lenore to the door.

"I want the money. To pay for the damage. Every last cent of it. In cash this time."

"Damage?"

"Vandalism. It's a crime. I'm calling the police."

"We didn't vandalize anything."

"Maybe not you. But it's your fault we got trouble in this building. I want the money for the dumpster. I'm coming back for it."

"Okay, I'll tell her," I say.

"I mean it."

I wait until I hear the last clunk of Hank on the steps, then the door to Dakota Avenue opening and closing.

"What is it?" Lenore asks. She's leaning against the kitchen counter, holding her worn bathrobe closed, an empty glass trembling in her hand. "Is it Persephone? Are they taking her away?"

"No, it was Hank. He said he smelled smoke somewhere in the building. Wondered if we smelled anything."

"Hank," she sighs, rolling her eyes to the ceiling. "That man ought to be committed."

"Go back to sleep. I'll wake you before I leave for school."

"Faina," Lenore says, laying her head on my shoulder. "I don't want any trouble."

When I get back to our room, I open the closet door, and Per scampers out to greet me. I nuzzle her against my chest. "Don't worry," I whisper. It's cold in our room, our windows covered with a layer of ice, and Cammy's wrapped in our blankets like a mummy. "Get up," I say, shaking her shoulder. I yank a corner of the blanket away from her.

"Give me a break," she mumbles.

"That was Hank. It's something about vandalism or damage. Cammy, what happened last night?" I've given up waiting for her to come home. I don't like seeing her stagger out of strange cars, I don't like smelling the sweet smoke that clings to her clothes.

She opens one eye. "I saw it when I came home. It's no biggie, but I knew it'd piss Hank off."

"Saw what?"

"Out in the parking lot. Take a look. It hasn't disappeared by morning."

I scrape at the frost on our window. In the winter, the early mornings look like evening; everything's nickel-blue and shadowy, the snow the green of the ocean. But even in the darkness, I see it immediately, the fluorescent pink spray paint scrawled across the dumpster. SLUT. "Oh, no," I say, sucking in my breath.

"So what?" Cammy laughs. "It's not us. No one even knows I live here."

"People know," I say. "What about all those rides home? Those different men that park with you out back for hours. One of them probably wrote it."

"How would you know?" Cammy snaps at me. "Maybe it was Jimmy. Ever think about that?"

"Not Jimmy. Jimmy wouldn't do such a thing."

"There's more to Jimmy than you think. Anyway, who the hell cares?" Cammy says, covering her face with her pillow. "I've been called worse."

I know Cammy is wrong. This has nothing to do with Jimmy. Still, I don't want him to see that word written on our dumpster. Not about me. Or my sister.

SLUT. The word follows me to school, through the deep snow, down Dakota Avenue, past the clusters of public-school kids waiting for their bus. It follows me under the thorny bare branches of trees, past the evergreens, up the icy steep steps of Cathedral, and into Sister Cyril's room. I feel like I wear it on my face, the hot-pink paint, SLUT, a word they all see when they look at me.

When I open the top of my desk there's a present waiting, Papa Roy's hunting cap and "Deer hunting?" scribbled on a scrap of paper. I know Tom Payne and Dave Fadden left the message for me. I lower the top of my desk quickly, before the other kids discover my secret. SLUT.

"Class, please." Sister Cyril orders. "Let us rise now for prayer."

The students shuffle up to the front of the room, hold out their hands for the circle. "And you?" Sister says, looking over the top of her glasses at me.

I leave my desk reluctantly, keep my eyes on the speckled tile so I don't have to look at anybody. When Sister drops her chin to her chest, I shake off my classmates' sweaty hands and step outside their circle. "Our Father, who art in heaven," Sister chants. The words spill out of their mouths like nonsense. Like nursery rhymes. Hickory dickory dock. Baa baa black sheep. I'm done praying with them. I'm done being one of their sheep.

"Let's go get your dress," Cammy says to me. She's sitting cross-legged on our bedroom floor, counting out quarters into perfect stacks of four. "I've got twenty-eight dollars. That ought to cover it."

"You don't need to spend your money on me." When Cammy suggests *shopping* now, I try to find an excuse to stay home with Lenore. I hate her macrame bag filling up with make-up and jewelry, skimpy lace bras, and gifts for me.

"Come on," she says, slapping the back of my head. "I told you that's why I got a job. Get that cat off your lap; let's live a little." She opens her hands like claws. "Shoo," she hisses, startling Per from sleep. "Get lost."

"Leave her alone." I try to grab Per, but she slips away from me.

"Oh, Christ," Cammy says. "What a baby. Forget the dress." She whacks a box of Marlboros against her knee. "I'll spend the money on me. Lenore can hem up another costume for you. Like your uniform. That looks real cute."

"I'm sorry," I say quickly. I've learned to give in to Cammy's sudden fury, the eyes of fire she had that day at the Elm Tree Room. "I just don't feel well today." I lift her hand to my forehead. "A fever maybe."

"You feel fine to me. But suit yourself. You don't want the dress, then we'll skip it. It's no skin off my nose what you wear to that ridiculous church." She scoops the money up off the floor and holds it over the jar, letting it fall between her fingers like rain.

"No, we'll go. Don't put the money away."

"No." The quarters clang against each other.

"Cammy, please," I beg. Lately Cammy is either dazed or angry, foggy or furious. Nothing in-between. I want her to go back to the Cammy who first came home. The Christmas Cammy. "Please. I want to go to Sears. Don't put away your money."

"Okay," she says, standing up suddenly. "I'll tell my mother we're going. But don't give me any more of your shit."

At Sears, we take the escalator up to Teens. It's a big department store, but nothing like Daley's downtown. It smells like a circus, hot dogs and popcorn, peanuts and ice cream. Instead of mirrors and chandeliers, there are lawn mowers and refrigerators.

"I used to work here," Cammy says. "When I was living with Tony." I pretend I'm hearing this for the first time, although it's a story she's told me before. "They taught me how to cut keys, mix paint. It was okay. But the money's better at the Starlight. If I were you, I'd go for waitressing right away. If you can drum up some charm, you'll make plenty in tips."

"I don't want to be a waitress."

"Why not? You can't beat the cash."

"I want to be a writer."

"Yeah," Cammy say. "And I want to be Linda Lovelace."

"Who's that?"

"Forget it," Cammy says. "You're not as smart as you think."

In Teens, all of the dresses Cammy chooses are wrong for me. Polyester prints with deep scooped necks, psychedelic minis. When I try them on in the fitting room, they're huge, even the size threes. "Don't tell me you still shop in the kids' department," Cammy says.

"Nothing fits." I hunch in front of the mirror, the low neck dipping down over my bare chest, the waist drooping over my hips. The purple ribbon around my neck looks ridiculous.

"Come on, Buster Brown," Cammy says, tugging the dress over my head. "Let's go find you a baby-doll outfit."

Down in Girls 7–14, she grabs a handful of size tens off the racks. "Why not?" she says. "Something's got to fit."

"I don't know." I shake my head at the dresses she's chosen for me.

"You have no taste. Leave the fashion decisions to me."

While I model her assortment, she scrunches up in the corner of my dressing room, lights a cigarette, ashes on the carpet. "That one," she says, pointing her cigarette at me. "It doesn't make you look so flat."

I like the dress, the sheer lime-green fabric, the wide bell sleeves, the bow fastened to a thick sash. "I'll put a couple of thin braids down the side of your face. It'll look cool. Really hot."

"Okay," I say. "But it looks a little wild for confirmation."

"You're not a nun," Cammy says. "We'll get you some platforms to go with it."

"Not today," I beg. "That fever is coming back."

Cammy counts out her quarters for the cashier. "These baby clothes are cheap. I guess the Starlight Lanes is good for something." She hooks her arm around my neck, kisses me on the lips. "You can write about me."

On the first floor we stop by the food counter. "I got to get some chocolate-covered almonds for my mother. They're her favorite. Papa Roy always bought them for her whenever he came here shopping. You get whatever you want." I choose a flat, rainbow-swirled sucker because it looks like candy from a fairy tale.

"What about you?" I ask. "What are you getting?"

"I'm not hungry," Cammy says, rubbing her stomach. "I think your fever is wearing off on me. Come on, I want to show you my old department." Cammy takes a pot of frosty gloss out of her purse. "How do I look?" she asks, painting it on her lips with her pinkie finger, then smacking.

"You look great." I try to picture Cammy working in this dreary department store, stamping price stickers on the cans of paint, stocking the shelves. I remember all those long months I waited for her, how I imagined her in some exotic place, a model in Spain. Not cutting keys at Sears.

"Cammy." I turn to look at the slow-motion voice calling her name. The man looks as slow as he sounds, bug eyes bulging behind thick black-rimmed glasses, a red Sears smock, pliers in one hand. "Cammy."

"Hey, Clayton," she says, smiling.

He plods toward her awkwardly, holding out his arms shyly, as if he's hoping to hug her. "Oops," he grins, and drops the pliers into his pocket. "Can I have a hug?"

"Sure," Cammy says. But when he puts his arms around her, she's stiff as a tree.

"I've missed you," he shrugs, as she steps away. "I'm sorry my mom made you leave."

"It's okay, Clayton. I'm home with my old lady. It's not a bad way to pass the winter."

"But she was so mean to you." Clayton stares at me while he speaks. "I wish my mom had let me keep you in my room. I've sure been lonely."

"Yeah, I've missed you, too. This is my baby sister." She shoves me toward Clayton. Giggles. "Isn't she cute?"

Clayton blushes. "Sure. But not like you, Cammy."

"Give her some time; she's a late bloomer."

"Cammy, can you come down and have lunch with me soon? My treat."

"Yeah. Hey, Clayton, Tony ever come around here asking for me?"

"Nah. They got security guards now at Sears. They don't want him coming around. He steals."

"Shit," Cammy sighs. "I was hoping he'd lend me some money."

"You shouldn't take money from him, Cammy."

"I know. It's just that we're a little desperate. We need to take a cab home, and I spent all my money on my baby sister's church clothes." She takes the lime dress out of the bag and holds it up for Clayton. "She's making her confirmation. The dress cost a lot. But I want her to look pretty."

"It's nice," Clayton says. He reaches into his back pocket, pulls out a worn leather wallet. "I can pay for your cab. Look," he says, carefully holding up a long strip of black-and-white snapshots of Cammy. "Remember when you took these in the photo booth for me?" In the pictures, Cammy's making clown faces, her tongue stuck out in one, her lips puckered in another. In one she's giving the camera the finger. "I wish my mom would've let you stay."

"Don't sweat it," Cammy says, handing him back the snapshots. "Do you have the money?" Clayton lifts a crisp ten-dollar bill from his wallet. "Is that it?" Cammy puffs out her bottom lip. "I don't think that'll get us home. We live way out in the suburbs now. But we can go find Tony."

"No," Clayton says, handing her another ten-dollar bill. "You know my mom keeps most of my money." He drops his head, stuffs the wallet back into his pocket. "When will you come down and have lunch, Cammy? Can I call you?"

"I'll come real soon," Cammy says, taking me by the hand. "My mom doesn't like the phone to ring. But thanks, Clayton, you saved my life." She blinks her crusty black lashes at him. "Again."

Out in the Sears parking lot, Cammy starts running. "Hurry," she screams. "It's the 21A. It's too damn cold to miss our bus."

I stop, look over my shoulder toward the entrance to Sears. He's there, watching us run past the cab stand.

"Cammy," I pant. "Clayton knows."

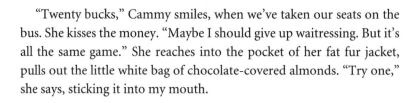

"Twenty bucks," Cammy smiles, when we've taken our seats on the bus. She kisses the money. "Maybe I should give up waitressing. But it's all the same game." She reaches into the pocket of her fat fur jacket, pulls out the little white bag of chocolate-covered almonds. "Try one," she says, sticking it into my mouth.

"No thanks." I pull it out. "I don't eat almonds. Cammy, he saw us get on the bus." She props her wet moccasin feet on the seat in front of us. Gritty snow melts down the red vinyl cover. "He knows we didn't take a cab."

"So what?" she says, tossing her hair back. "That's love. That creep is crazy about me. How much money have you gotten from Jimmy?"

Cammy Luck

I had to sober her up and bring her in. She had a hundred excuses. All of them connected with money. No health insurance, bankruptcy. "They'll take every cent Papa Roy left me. Then what? Lose the apartment? Live on the streets?" I was too young to believe her. I took it all for booze talk. Paranoia.

"It's a county hospital. They have to treat everybody."

Besides, I knew she could afford a private doctor, but she'd inherited Papa Roy's crazy cheapness. And his fear of records. She refused to see the same doctor twice. "If you go too much they keep track of you." Mostly, she was afraid of what was inside of her. The knife she swore was just below her right rib cage. She'd blown through an old bottle of Papa Roy's Valium, and still the pain wouldn't disappear.

That morning, I had my own fears. Social workers. Clipboards. A thousand questions. It was the same scene with every agency. Christ, you couldn't get treated for the clap without telling them your whole sordid history.

And it hadn't even been a year since the last time I'd dragged her into emergency, hadn't been a year since they'd ordered her into treatment, then called the county to dump me in protective custody. Find a nice foster family for the truant and thief. Hadn't been a year since they'd forced me to run, to scrounge on the streets.

"I can't go in with you." I'd waited until we were outside the hospital to tell her the truth. "They can't know you've got kids at home. Don't mention Faina or me. You live alone. And don't let them admit you. Just tell them about the knife. Ask for the Valium."

In the last few months, she'd shrunk down to nothing. Barely the size of Faina. All skin and bones except for the puff of pouch that hung from her stomach. "You need to go in now. Don't let them see the bedsores."

She nodded slowly, blinked. Even healthy, she'd never been a match for me. Holding my hand on the sidewalk, dressed in that long wool coat with the velvet collar, she looked more like my daughter. A little kid wearing her mother's clothes. But her face was old, her skin the color of beer, her lips cracked and smeared with too much lipstick. She looked worse than I'd ever seen her, worse then the last time they'd thrown her in detox. I didn't know how she'd gotten so bad.

"I'm too scared to go in without you, Cammy. I can't remember everything you told me to say."

"Pay attention. This isn't a game. If you screw this up today, they'll take Faina and me. Do you want to lose me again?" I pushed her silk scarf up off her forehead. "Remember, use your mother's name. Your mother's birthday. Your mother's social security number. You live alone. You have no money. The pain's on your right side, just below your ribs. Don't sign anything."

"Come in with me." Her hands were shaking wildly.

"You know I can't. Remember what happened last time? It'll be worse if they know you have a daughter."

"I need a drink." She looped her arm through mine. "One drink. Let's stop in at that place across the street?" She pointed to the Whirlpool, a dumpy bum bar with a boarded front window, the sign hanging loose on one hinge.

"You know what they'll do, they'll put you in detox again if they smell the booze. You need medicine. Ask for Papa Roy's Valium. Tell them about the knife in your stomach, the nights you can't sleep."

In the cloudy winter light, she looked half-dead, her teeth chattering, her yellow eyelids swollen and heavy. "Go now," I ordered, shoving her through the sliding glass door. "Check in at the front desk. I'll meet you out on Sixth Street in two hours."

She twisted the gold watch on her wrist, another gift from Papa Roy. Her initials engraved on the back. "But it's not even ten o'clock yet."

"I'll be back here at noon. It's a county hospital. This is a slow operation. You're competing with bullet holes. Just sit down, read a magazine. Let them help you. There's no other way."

Walking away from her, I had a hole in my gut the size of a grapefruit. The wind tore between the tall buildings, but even as it hit my face, I felt hot and woozy. I needed sleep, a warm bed. I hated downtown on weekdays, businessmen with their briefcases rushing past me, women in dull pumps drumming down the sidewalk. I needed coffee. A place to pass the hours. I was tired of taking care of her. Tired of watching her die.

"Where you been hiding?" Tony's voice seemed to rise out of thin air. But there he was, slumped in the orange booth in the basement of Wentworth's, sipping coffee and finishing a plate of runny eggs. When he looked up at me and smiled, his gray eyes foggy, his wild hair tangled in frizzy curls, my old rage faded.

"Must be my lucky day," I said. I crawled in next to him, let him nibble a little on the base of my neck. An old habit. His skin still smelled like sandalwood incense, cigarettes.

"I came down to finagle food stamps. Lines get too long late in the day. Hungry?" He pushed his plate of leftover eggs and toast crust toward me. "You look like you need something."

I felt my luck turning. Something good had led me to Tony. I knew he'd rescue me, Faina too, like he did last summer. I thought about that first night I'd met him, stoned at a backyard barbecue. I'd followed the music, wandered into it looking for food. I'd already spent a few nights sleeping under a Lake Street bridge with some other kids. Hard living. I'd been Papa Roy's angel, and there I was begging for food.

"Aren't you a barefoot beauty?" Tony said when he saw me. He fed me a burnt burger, then took me in without question. It wasn't his way to dig too deep. "The past is past," he told me, like it was some great philosophy. "The now is all we've got."

Now, in Wentworth's restaurant, when he stuck his rough tongue between my teeth, I covered my mouth and gagged.

"What's with you?" he asked, sliding away toward the corner of the booth.

"I don't know. I think it's the flu."

"Well, you look like shit. You still running?" He grabbed my stomach, squeezed a handful of skin. "Let me buy you breakfast. You're too thin."

"You got money?"

"For you, I do."

I ordered Rice Krispies, dry toast, warm 7-Up, but by the time they came I couldn't eat them. We talked about the good times: getting our clothes at the Free Store, the pink-feathered boa and rhinestone sandals he picked out for me, the great money we made last summer dealing, the steak dinners we split at the Tempo bar. He held my hands between his, kissed my fingertips every few minutes.

"Cammy, come back to me," he said. "I'm sorry."

I'd been waiting forever to hear those words. "Why didn't you say that sooner?" I rested my head on his arm; his skin was so hot it burned through his shirt. "Maybe we weren't good for each other."

"Not good," he said, smiling. "You got a bad memory." He kneaded the inside of my thigh. "You didn't even call me."

"You don't have a phone."

He reached in his coat pocket, ripped a check out of his wallet, scribbled a number across the front. "I do now. For business."

I read the name on the check: Steven Lang. It figured Tony didn't have the credit for his own account. "No wonder you offered to buy me breakfast."

"You know me, Cam. I'm a man of multiple talents."

I folded the check and tucked it into my back pocket. "Me, too. I'm waiting tables at a supper club in Richfield. My old lady bought a house there. I'm turning suburban."

Glad as I was to see him, I wasn't ready to scam his next scheme.

Wentworth's was starting to buzz with the lunch rush; the line snaked back to the cosmetics counter. It'd been a good half hour since our waitress had splashed hot coffee into Tony's cup. I knew from experience she wanted to turn our table over for the next tip. "Well, that's it," I said, helping myself to Tony's last cigarette. "They're spent." According to the Pepsi clock, it was already 12:30. It was Tony's fault I'd lost track of time. I wanted to slide into bed with him, cuddle under his musty covers, forget about my mother, the last few months of hassles.

But then I thought about her, that sad little girl standing outside in the cold, waiting. "I got to go. I'm meeting my old lady at Daley's to shop for spring clothes."

"You really have gone suburban." He wrapped a strand of my hair around his finger. "Come back to me."

"Maybe." I shrugged. If my luck went sour, if they nabbed my mother, Faina and I might be there tonight.

"Call first," he winked. "Just to make sure I'm free." Then he pressed a dime into my palm. "Do me a favor," he whispered into my ear. "Keep this between your knees for me."

I found my mother curled up on a couch in the corner of the emergency-room lobby, her purse tucked under her cheek, a pool of drool next to her mouth, her coat draped over her back like a blanket. If it hadn't been for the other bums that cluttered the lobby—psychos mumbling to themselves, old ladies with black trash bags—she might have attracted some official attention. I jiggled her arm; I wasn't hanging around long.

"Where were you?" she asked, wiping her glove over her wet face.

"You were supposed to wait outside," I whispered. "Not sleep. I told you I don't want them to see me."

"I waited outside until my feet were so frozen I could hardly walk." She coughed a low, rattling cough; I heard the gurgle inside her chest.

"Come on, let's go. We need to get home."

She was easy to boost to her feet. But standing, she couldn't keep her balance. I wedged my hand under her armpit to stop the wobbling. "Mother. Pay attention." Her breath reeked of Listerine. "You've been drinking." She'd found booze somehow, though I'd searched her purse and pockets before we'd left this morning. "Did a doctor see you like this? Did you tell them anything?"

"I'm scared, Cammy."

"Who isn't? If you screwed this up, Social Services will be at our door."

I hooked her purse over her arm, but she let it drop to the floor with a thud. A nurse glanced up from the main desk. "Is there a problem?" she asked, cradling the phone between her ear and shoulder. "If you wait a minute, I'll call security. Looks like she might need a wheelchair."

"No," I said. "She's okay."

I hurried her through the glass doors into the harsh wind. "That ought to sober you up some," I said.

She pulled her velvet collar up close to her chin. "In like a lion, out like a lamb," she muttered. "I can't go outside in winter; this climate is too hard on me."

"It's April," I said, setting her down on the bench inside the bus shelter.

"It stinks in here. Papa Roy would want me to take a cab." She was coughing again, holding a handkerchief over her mouth to catch the spit. The hot air from the overhead fan mixed with the stench of garbage and piss. My stomach turned. Flu maybe, or too many cigarettes on an empty stomach.

I lifted her chin, stared into her muddled eyes. "Papa Roy's dead, Mother. What about the knife? Did you get a prescription for Valium?"

She brushed my hand away. "I told you I'm dying, Cammy. I'm dying, and nobody cares."

Lenore The Whirlpool

It was Cammy's fault for leaving me scared. Scared of the papers, the doctors touching my naked body, scared of the cotton robe, the questions, the way they trapped me the last time. I didn't care about the knife; I didn't want to lose her again.

I waited until she crossed the street and disappeared around the first corner. My beautiful baby. My first little girl.

It was dim inside the Whirlpool, dim and smokey. I sat down at the bar under the Grain Belt Beer light, paid the bartender in cash. On TV, they'd stalled out the Watergate hearings for the Patty Hearst story. "Turn it up," I said. I couldn't get enough of it, the kidnapped college student, the heiress, the hostage who'd joined her captors and changed her name. Tania. The fugitive. The girl with a machine gun robbing a bank. She looked so much like my little Faina, dark hair, dark eyes, that same sort of beret. And now it was Faina who was changing her name.

"How do you keep them safe?" I asked the bartender.

"Never had kids of my own," he said, emptying my ashtray.

"It's impossible nowadays. Look at Patty, she was home, wearing her bathrobe when they took her away. Her bathrobe. Now they've brainwashed her. Blackmailed her family. It's money they're after; an heiress is never safe. I have the same fears for my own girls. Papa Roy had it with me."

"I'm sure, " the bartender said. "Either way, it's over for her. Patty Hearst is screwed."

I lost track of time. An hour, maybe two. When I'd spent the last of my money, I went back to Hennepin County. The lobby was warm; I took my place in a line of people waiting for free chest X-rays. Why not? That was close enough.

It was easy to answer their questions, I gave them Mother's name, my old address in Kenwood. Anyone could change their identity. Let them try to trace a dead woman. I don't know what it was, some kind of lung cancer or TB screening. I just took my seat, wrapped my coat around me. It was an oven in there, but I couldn't stop shivering. Eileen Dahl. I figured I'd wake when they called my name. But it never came to that.

Hi Honey,

Who could believe a little cat. You hassled me for a pet so many years, I thought you'd given up. Persephone? What kind of name is that? She sounds like a beauty, but don't let her take all your love away from Croc. Remember, he came from far away. He needs a home.

Honey, I know when I first left I said one year, but it's going to be a little longer. What can I do, they won't give me a ticket back. Besides, you got to be out of the country a year and a half to skip the income tax, and the company only wants guys who can commit to two. I thought I'd give it a try, see if you were all right. And things are working out great for you. I'm happy. Some ups and downs but isn't that just life? I knew you would survive. I'm the one in hell. Working twelve to midnight all this week. I'm sure Lenore will keep you, but I'm going to tell her later, when I've sent some $. I bet she's pissed I haven't sent much yet. But I'm saving. I'll pay off all the sharks when I get back. Then we'll be free. As far as that legal bullshit goes, there's no dark secret. Forget it. I think it had to do with her old man's money. He didn't want us to touch it. We lived fine without it, so I signed. Anyway that's court stuff. It's got nothing to do with us. Lenore's your mother either way. No paper in the world can change that fact. We live the way we want. Got me? Remember that I love you. Dad

Faina Protect Us

My book is nearly finished. I've replaced the missing photographs with stories of my baptism and first communion. All of my writing is done in ink, skipping a line in-between like Mrs. Lajoy ordered. I loop thick green yarn through the three holes punched out along the side.

"Just in time. Now all we need is that baptismal certificate," Mrs. Lajoy says, taking my book from me. "It's your last day with me; confirmation practice starts on Monday." She pages through my book. "Your cover is especially well-done."

"Thank you." I like it, too—the gifts of the Holy Spirit colored in marker; my title, HOLY SACRAMENT, printed in bold, three-dimensional letters I learned how to draw at my old school.

Mrs. Lajoy stares at me. "Has this school year gone by fast for you?" She crosses her legs and rests her hands on her knees. "I mean, it's April already. Maybe it's just me, but I'm already counting down the days until June 7." Mrs. Lajoy looks like April in her long, cloudy Easter-colored skirt and her muslin shirt. "And you, you made it through your first Minnesota winter. That couldn't have been easy."

I nod, busy myself snapping the caps back on my markers.

"I think it's been a stretch for all of us. I'm glad I teach third grade; there's something simple about it. You're at a hard age—seventh grade, it's tough. Someday you'll look back and see that. And what you'll see is, you survived it."

"You think?" I glance at Mrs. Lajoy through the curtain of hair I've let fall across my face.

"Definitely. Life's full of strange things. And I'll tell you something else. This wasn't the place for you, Faina. You'll look back and see that. We're all good people. You, me. The other students here at Cathedral. Sister Linette, who really cared about you. But good people don't always fit together. It doesn't make anybody wrong. Do you follow me?"

"Yep." I arrange my markers carefully in their box. Dave Fadden, Tom Payne, Emmy Atwood, Sister Cyril, Monsignor. They aren't good people to me. Neither is Sister Linette, who hasn't spoken to me since I skipped Midnight Mass. I try to imagine the *someday* Mrs. Lajoy means. The *someday* when I'll feel differently.

"But I'll always remember your gifts," Mrs. Lajoy says. "We all will, even those who don't want to admit it."

I nod again. What gifts? I feel like I'm at my funeral. "I don't think they all will."

"They will," Mrs. Lajoy says, solidly. "What I'm trying to say is, next year, you'll make a fresh start. I hope, I don't know how to say this, I hope it's a wide place. A place big enough for a girl with your spirit."

"A wide place?" I'm lost now. Did Lenore tell them I was only here for the year when we registered last September? Or does Mrs. Lajoy somehow know my dad was supposed to come back for me? Next year won't be a fresh start, but I don't know how to explain that to Mrs. Lajoy.

"Whatever's ahead of you. Who knows? But keep in mind, this wasn't the right fit. Don't blame yourself."

"I won't." I slip my markers back in my pencil case, zip it closed. Recess is over, and outside Mrs. Lajoy's classroom, the hallway hums with the rush of her kids. "I should go upstairs now. Sister Cyril won't want me to be late."

"Faina, could you wait?" Mrs. Lajoy says, rising to open the classroom door. "I've got to get the children settled, then we'll finish."

When the kids dart into the classroom they run up, rope their little arms around my waist. "Hug, hug," they scream, shoving against each other to get close to me.

"Give her some space," Mrs. Lajoy laughs. Now that it's spring, the kids smell like sun when they come in from recess. I miss the old smell of snow and sweat, their faces wet with cold. "Everyone, let's gather."

I stay at my little desk in the corner. I know when the kids are settled, she's going to take me out in the hallway and ask about my sponsor. Since no one knows Lenore is my mother, I've decided to have her stand up behind me when the archbishop sets his hands on my head, and if they ask, I'll say she's my aunt from California. I know she'll agree, for one day she'll get dressed and come to church, because she won't want outsiders snooping into our business.

Mrs. Lajoy takes her guitar out of her case, strums a chord for attention. "What shall we sing today, my little angels? Raise your hands."

I want to go back to third grade again, to be one of Mrs. Lajoy's angels, to sit in her room with the giant stuffed bear, Pandy, the glass jar of jelly beans, the little clay pots of grass seed lined up along the window ledge. I want to sit at Mrs. Lajoy's feet, my legs crossed, my hand raised, waiting for her to call on me.

"Why don't we let Faina choose today?" Mrs. Lajoy says. "Since it's her last day downstairs with us."

The kids all turn to look at me, their eyes bright with spring, their bodies squirming. "Boo," they hiss, their thumbs pointing down toward the floor. "We don't want her to go."

"I know," Mrs. Lajoy says, strumming again for silence. "Class, quiet please. Is there a song you'd like us to sing for your last day?"

"Sure," I say, trying to decide quickly what my request should be. I love all their songs, the way they really do sound like angels when they sing with Mrs. Lajoy. One last time, I'd like to hear Mrs. Lajoy sing her favorite. "What about 'Tis the Gift to be Simple'?" I like the mystery of this song, the words that don't make any sense, the graceful melody.

Mrs. Lajoy smiles at me. "A girl after my own heart." She scoots her chair around to face me. "Okay, class, let's sing."

'Tis the gift to be simple, 'tis the gift to be free, 'tis the gift to come down where we ought to be. Mrs. Lajoy sings the first verse solo. She stares straight into my eyes today, as if it's a song she's written for me. "*And when we find ourselves in the place just right, we will be in the valley of love and delight.*"

Her angels join in at the chorus. "You sing, too," Mrs. Lajoy calls out to me. "We know you have a beautiful voice."

When the song is finished, Mrs. Lajoy's class claps. "Faina, you should be proud of your voice," Mrs. Lajoy says. "It's one of your God-given gifts. Use it."

"Thanks," I say. "That was great." I grab my pencil case and my notebook. As much as I loved their song, I want to get out of here before Mrs. Lajoy returns to the question of my missing sponsor.

"Wait," Mrs. Lajoy says, setting her guitar down into her case. "There's one more thing. Could you come here, Faina?" She reaches down into her guitar case and pulls out a tiny gift-wrapped box. "We wanted to get you something. To thank you for all your help. Didn't we, class?" The class claps again, bounces up and down on their butts. "Open it," they scream.

I'm so flustered from it all—their song, the gift, the classroom full of kids staring at me—I can hardly unwrap the present. Under the paper there's a small, black velvet box. When I push against it with my thumb, it pops open.

"It's a St. Christopher medal," Mrs. Lajoy says. "For protection. I know it's not your saint, but we voted on it as a class; it's the one we wanted you to have."

St. Christopher Protect Us is written on the silver. "Thank you." I want to say more, but the words are caught in my throat.

"I'll help you put it on," Mrs. Lajoy says, taking the box from me.

She stands behind me, guides the silver chain around my neck and fastens it. Then she rests one soft hand on my head. "What do you say, class?"

"Thank you for all your help," they shout out, as if it's been rehearsed.

"Run along now," Mrs. Lajoy says. "Don't worry, Sister Cyril knows that you'll be late."

Today, when I go home, I hardly notice the dumpster. Usually that word is a rock in my chest, but today, it's different. I can't wait to wake Lenore and tell her about the medal and the music. I wish Cammy were home, too, so I could tell her everything, but she's pulling longer shifts at the Starlight, waiting lunch and dinner for extra tips.

Per is asleep in her usual spot on the pillow, her head tucked next to Lenore's cheek. "Hi, girl," I say, scooping her up for her after-school kiss. I run my hand over the tiny bones poking through the top of her skull. No matter how much we feed her, she's so skinny her ribs still ridge through her fur. "We got to fatten you up, Per."

"Faina," Lenore mumbles, opening her eyes. "Why are you home so early?"

"It's my usual time. How are you feeling?"

"My mouth is so dry," she says, touching her tongue to her lip. "No matter what I drink. Nothing makes a difference." As soon as she speaks the coughing starts. She beats her fist against her chest. "This damn thing," she sighs. "Hand me a cigarette."

"You shouldn't smoke with a cold."

"I know, I know," she says, patting my hand. "Damn death sticks. They've got me hooked."

I pass her the pack of Salems. Ever since her cough started, I've quit smoking. Even with Jimmy. Sometimes I miss the peace it gave me, the cool minty taste on my tongue, but then I think of Lenore hacking and gasping, spitting yellow phlegm into a Kleenex, and the thought of cigarettes makes me gag.

"I want to show you something." I lift up my medal for her to see. "It's a St. Christopher medal. Mrs. Lajoy gave it to me for helping down in her classroom."

"Oh, Faina. I'm so proud of you," Lenore says, her eyes tearing up. "I'm so happy I sent you to that school. It's the best decision I ever made. You've done so well there. It's been a good year here, hasn't it? I mean all and all. You're happy to finally be home?" When the coughing fit hits again, she squeezes my hand.

I lift the warm glass of water to her lips. "Swallow." The thin trickle of water gurgles down her throat. "Lenore, I think you should see somebody. A doctor."

She crinkles her nose, shakes her head. "I know this year won't make up for everything. But we've been so happy. Together. Will you remember me as a good mother?"

"Sure," I say. She's never called herself my mother. I brush her matted hair away from her forehead. I think of last summer, all the hours I spent backcombing her hair, helping her fix her face, the classics we read together. I try to remember when it all changed, when the cough came to stay, but I can't.

"Faina," Lenore says, closing her eyes. "I love you more than you'll know."

When she's asleep, I lift Per from her bed and go out to the hall to call Cammy. In a fat, torn 1967 phone book, I look up Starlight Lanes.

"Starlight Lanes," a man hollers over loud music. "What'll it be?"

"Cammy McCoy." I say.

"She's working. No personal calls on my time clock."

"It's an emergency."

"Sure, sure. They all are. Cammy," he yells. "You got two minutes."

"What?" Cammy growls.

"It's me. Faina."

"What do you need? I got three tables waiting."

"It's Lenore. She seems really sick. Worse than usual."

"Right," Cammy says. "There's nothing I can do about it now."

"What about an ambulance?"

"No ambulance. Stay out of it," Cammy says. "I mean it. You don't know shit. I'll handle it in the morning."

"I'm running across the street to Kenny's," I whisper to Lenore, but she doesn't answer me. I feel guilty leaving her, but I've sat in her bed for hours waiting for her to wake up. Besides, I need to get outside, breathe the spring air, see Jimmy.

When I get to the fire escape, he's already waiting there, perched on the top step, staring up at the stars, smoking.

"I wish you'd quit," I say, taking my place beside him. "Haven't you ever read the warning on the side of the package?"

"That's bullshit," he laughs. "My old man's been smoking since he was ten and he's healthy as a horse. It just gives the government something to do. Like the war on VD. Besides, I've kicked everything else. I'm so clean I squeak."

I rest my cheek against the cold metal railing, let the warm chill of the night wind brush across my face.

"I thought April would never get here," Jimmy says. "I can't believe how fast this year's gone. When I first got to New Directions, the end seemed a lifetime away."

As happy as I am to be out here with Jimmy, to fill my lungs with the spring air, to know the dark wall of winter's behind me, I can't quit thinking about Lenore's cough and what Cammy plans to do in the morning.

"What's with you?" Jimmy says, shaking my shoulder. "We'll see each other again."

"What do you mean?"

"After New Directions, you know. Maybe I'll come to San Diego like we planned. I want to see that ocean you're so crazy about. What do you think?"

"Great," I say.

"Will your sister be going back with you?"

"I don't know." This is the first time Jimmy has mentioned Cammy since the day I told him she was home. I wonder if he's discovered the beautiful girl I've hidden from him. "Why?"

"Just wondering. I've seen her around. Coming and going from your building. In that pink waitress uniform. That's her, right?"

"Yeah."

"She's hot, but she doesn't look anything like you. Doesn't act like you either. You sure you got the same old man?"

"Jimmy, I've got to go now. I still have homework to finish." I don't feel like talking anymore; I want to crawl into my bed and hold Per against my chest. I want Cammy to come home from the Starlight.

"Hey, you stay on the straight and narrow," Jimmy says, tugging my braid. "Don't let that sister of yours screw you up."

"Screw me up?"

"See that?" Jimmy asks, nodding toward the dumpster where the fluorescent SLUT glows in the streetlight. "That's for your sister. It's written all over her. Have I ever steered you wrong?" Before I can answer, Jimmy bends down and kisses me on the lips. It happens so fast, I miss my chance to kiss him back. "I've been wanting to do that since Christmas. There's four years between us. Maybe three and a half? So what? That won't seem like much when you're older. We'll wait for each other. You saved my life this year."

"You've saved mine," I stutter. It isn't exactly what I mean, but it's all that comes to me. As soon as I say it, I wish it were true. I wish he could save me.

"That makes us even," he says, taking my hand. "Now we're connected for life."

In the morning, I wake up to the sounds of spring floating in through our window. Rain on the sidewalk, car doors slamming, delivery trucks idling outside in the alley.

"Cammy?" I call out in a hushed voice. She should be next to me sleeping. I feel around the covers for Per, but she isn't there either.

"Per," I say, jumping out of bed to go find her. "Per?"

"What're you looking for?" Cammy is standing in Lenore's doorway, already dressed in a T-shirt and jeans.

"Per." I peek my head into Lenore's room. They're both asleep; Per's rolled up next to Lenore on the satin pillow. "She never sleeps in here until after I leave for school."

"Well, today's a new day," Cammy says, combing her hair with her fingers. "Get used to it." She looks tired this morning, her eyes pale and puffy, her lids sandy with sleep.

"What are we going to do about Lenore?" I whisper.

"We?" Cammy nods her head toward the kitchen. "I've got to get coffee before I can see through the cobwebs."

The two of us sit down at the kitchen table. I brush the old toast crumbs into my hand. This afternoon, I'll clean the apartment like I did last summer, and Cammy can make Lenore that baked chicken dinner she loves.

"I'm taking her in," Cammy says, slurping her china cup of strong coffee. "She's been like this before, worse maybe. It'll pass."

"Taking her where? I want to go with you."

"No. She won't want a circus. Her doctor's downtown. Dr. Lang. He'll know what she needs." I'm worried about Cammy's odd calm, the sleepy slow way she's talking.

"Have you looked at her this morning? Last night when I went to bed she was breathing funny, gurgling."

"She's my mother. I slept with her all night. I know the score, Faina. You're a visitor here. Go to school. When you come home this afternoon, she'll be on her way to getting well."

"Can I talk to her?"

"She's sleeping. I'll give her a message. Look at the time. You'll be late. Go get dressed. I'm taking her in this morning."

I throw on my uniform, my tennis shoes, the gray hooded sweatshirt jacket I brought from San Diego. I splash cold water over my face, squirt a dab of toothpaste in my mouth, skip the teeth. No matter what Cammy says, I'm going to see Lenore before I leave for school. I'm going to say good-bye to her and Per.

"You ready?" Cammy asks, without looking at me. She's sitting on Lenore's little vanity stool, smoking a cigarette and staring into the mirror. "It's starting to storm. Grab Papa Roy's umbrella."

"Okay."

"And Faina, keep your mouth shut about this. I'll take care of it myself."

I walk quietly over to Lenore's bed, sit down gently on the edge and sandwich her hand between mine. When I touch her, she doesn't even twitch. "Lenore," I say, hoping she'll open her eyes. "I want you to have this."

"What the hell are you doing?" Cammy says. "Everything isn't a god-damn drama."

I thread the silver chain behind her head, fasten the clasp, string the medal down until it rests flat on her chest. "It's St. Christopher," I whisper. "He'll protect you."

"I bet," Cammy says. "I wouldn't be in such a hurry to give away your voodoo. Maybe you should keep that for yourself."

"You're late," Sister Cyril announces as soon as I walk into the room. "Monsignor needs to meet with you at lunch."

Even with Papa Roy's umbrella, I'm drenched from the storm, my tennis shoes soggy, my hair plastered to my head. When I take my seat, the wet wool of my uniform prickles like itchweed. The rain rushes down our classroom window in watery sheets.

"Open your books to page 218," Sister Cyril orders. We're almost to the end of our *Practical Mathematics* book; three chapters to go and we'll be finished. Next year, another seventh-grader at Cathedral will open this book, and see my name, Faina McCoy, written in the index. I want to scratch in a little note, somewhere in the middle. *Stormed today. I'm afraid Lenore is dying. F. M. April 18, 1974.* I want to write it in ink, so Sister will never be able to erase it.

When she turns her back to the class to demonstrate the first problem on the blackboard, I tuck my book into my lap, flip back a few pages, and scribble it.

"You can't do that," Emmy Atwood says, leaning over my shoulder. "They'll make you pay for the book."

I hide my hand behind my head and give her the finger.

"Ooohhh," she says. "You're so cool."

I don't care anymore what they do to me. I don't care about my lunch meeting with Monsignor, or the baptismal certificate, or the sponsor, or the confirmation. I just want to be home, out of these sopping clothes, warm in Lenore's bed with Per between us on the pillow. I want to bring Lenore her medicine, run her bath water, help her to get well.

"It's quite simple, girls and boys, ladies and gentlemen," Sister Cyril says, turning to face the class, and tapping one gnarled finger against her temple. "If you use your head, there's a solution to every problem."

By the time lunch rolls around, the shocks of lightning have stopped, and the rain has died down to a drizzle. I wonder if Lenore is home from the doctor, safe in her bed, swallowing her first dose of medicine. I want to believe what Cammy told me— "She bounced back before"— but then I remember how cold Lenore's skin was, and the way she didn't even open her eyes, and my stomach sinks to the floor.

"We're meeting in Sister Barbara's office," Sister Cyril tells me when I pull my mushy brown lunch bag from my locker. "You'll have to eat later."

"Sister Barbara?" I've never been down to the principal's office; Sister Barbara has barely spoken to me, except once or twice out on the playground, when she asked if I was able to keep up with my homework.

"I'm walking the students down to the lunch room. I'll meet you there in a moment."

When Sister Cyril waddles down the hallway, I make up my mind to escape. I'll race down the front staircase, past the principal's office, and home to Lenore and Cammy. But when I reach the bottom step, Monsignor grabs me by the collar. "Slow down, young lady. We don't run in the halls."

There's a group of people gathered in Sister Barbara's office for the meeting. When I walk in with Monsignor they all gawk at me. Sister Linette. Sister Barbara. Mrs. Lajoy. Even Mrs. Atwood. The only one missing from this nightmare is Sister Cyril. Monsignor and I take two chairs at the end of the long tan table. Sister Barbara folds her hands. "Shall we begin with a prayer?"

Together they rattle off the Our Father.

"Have a seat, Sister." Sister Barbara says to Sister Cyril, who's just arrived. "Faina," she continues, bowing her head toward me. "First, this isn't a lynching. We requested your mother's presence, but I'm sorry to say she declined."

She declined because she can't breathe, she can't stop coughing, she can't get out of bed. "She has a new job," I say.

"So you told me," Monsignor adds. "Although she's still months behind on tuition." His bald head glistens.

"It's my preference to be direct," Sister Barbara says, glancing down at the yellow notepad on the table in front of her. "I'm an administrator, not a social worker. It's obvious to all of us you have family problems, but there are things we can take care of at Cathedral, and things we can't. We're a private school. We don't have the funds to serve troubled children. The archdiocese does offer social services through Catholic Charities and I'd be happy to make the referral at your, or your mother's, request. But right now, my job is to see that this school runs efficiently."

When I glance up at Mrs. Lajoy, she's half-sad and half-smiling, the same way she looked yesterday, when she sang that song into my eyes.

"Faina," Sister Barbara continues, "it's no secret we've received complaints about you since the day you arrived. I don't know how much of it is rumor and how much of it is truth. I'm well aware stories have a way of taking on a life of their own. Nevertheless, we've received calls about you smoking, going to R-rated movies, roaming the streets with an older girl, who apparently appears quite questionable. Your sister? Several parishioners in your neighborhood have seen you with a teenage boy from some sort of detention center. Your classmates' parents have heard endless tales from their children, most of them so shocking they're better left unsaid. Still, despite this, the children have reached out to you. Sister Linette went above and beyond the call of duty. She even gave you a solo in the Christmas program, a part that should have been awarded to one of our better students. Everyone's made an effort to welcome you into our community. Beyond the outstanding tuition, this is obviously not a good fit. Do you care to respond?"

"No." I glare at Sister Barbara, clench my teeth. I hope she can read the hatred in my hard eyes.

"Then we're done. It's for the best." Sister flattens her palms against the tabletop. "Our doors are open to any Catholic child who resides within our parish boundaries, but we also have the right to dismiss those who don't toe the line. You'll be released at the end of this year. We can't sacrifice our values to keep you. I have no doubt you'll fare better at the public junior high. By all accounts, you're a good student. I pray you put your brains to better use."

"Great," I shrug, to show how little I care. I hide my hands in my jumper pockets, so the judges can't see them trembling. "Can I go eat lunch?"

"Faina," Mrs. Lajoy says, sweetly. "We still want you to make your confirmation with us. I know how much it's meant to you."

"But first," Monsignor stammers, "let's put this business of the baptismal certificate behind us, once and for all. There seems to be some question as to whether or not you're actually a Catholic. We've seen no evidence of church attendance. No offerings given in your family's name, though the envelopes were mailed in September. No record of your baptism. One of the children told me, in confidence, you asked what to say at communion. Without the baptismal certificate, we're back at square one. Unless of course you secure your own, I've asked Dr. and Mrs. Atwood to stand in as your godparents. Dr. Atwood is president of our parish council, and Mrs. Atwood heads up our P.T.A. They have a soft spot in their hearts for children; they've generously agreed, with ample misgivings. Many of which, I admit, I share. But Mrs. Lajoy has interceded on your behalf. We'll gather at the church this Saturday. Two o'clock sharp. Your mother's presence is welcome, and requested, of course. Following your baptism, you'll make your sacraments of first eucharist and penance. Neither of which you should have been participating in this year."

"Faina," Mrs. Lajoy says weakly, raising her eyebrows at me. "I'd like to be your confirmation sponsor. If you'd let me. I think we share a special bond."

"I don't care." I focus on the dull wooden cross behind their heads, the dry palm leaves tucked behind it, the sterile beige walls. "Can I go now? I'm hungry."

"Your response confirms my decision," Sister Barbara says, shaking her head. "I feel confident we're on common ground."

Cammy Running

The cough was killing her. She blamed me for it; she claimed she'd caught it the day she waited outside Hennepin County while I made my sweet peace with Tony. "I told you not to take me in the first place. I knew the doctors wouldn't help."

"You're sick," I said, as I held her head over the pan. Her hair was greasy with sweat, her skin cold, her vomit pink and foamy. "You could be bleeding internally."

That's what the emergency nurse had told me over the phone when I called Hennepin County hospital. *She needs to be seen as soon as possible.*

She couldn't catch her breath between coughs.

"Sit back." I propped the pillow between her and the wall. "Close your eyes and try to rest."

Her room smelled like death, the way I imagined it: open sores, puke, the body getting ready to quit. I hated to touch her; she was so skinny now her clammy skin hung off her bones. Each breath gurgled like she was under water, like she was drowning.

I closed her bedroom door, went into the living room. I needed to scream until my throat hurt. I got down on my knees, buried my face in the couch cushion and howled. I wanted to cry, but my eyes were dry and gritty. I guess I'd forgotten how.

It's true, I saw it coming. Even on that Christmas morning, when I stood at the side of her bed, I knew our little house on the prairie was temporary. I knew we were going to crash. But this time I was ready; I had money, tips and wages from Starlight Lanes, the few extra twenties I'd lifted last night from the register to help us escape. I had enough to get us out of this city, halfway to San Diego at least, and I figured we'd hitchhike from there.

And if everything failed, I had Tony's phone number. Steven Lang. I knew he would take us in.

When I went back to her room, she was still coughing. I sat at the edge of the bed, held my breath to keep myself from retching. My stomach had been whirling for weeks.

"I need to call an ambulance for you. You're not strong enough to get there by cab." I dabbed the spit from her lips with a Kleenex. "Let me get you another cold cloth."

She wrapped her weak fingers around my wrist. "Don't send me away, Cammy. If I go, I'll never come home."

"Don't be stupid. You'll be well in no time. You're not going to die, Mother. You'll be home before you know it."

"Will you come with me?" She kept her eyes closed when she talked to me, as if she were off in a faraway land.

"I can't. You know that. I'll wait at home for Faina. When she gets home from school, we'll take the bus down to visit."

"I don't want to go alone." A tear trickled down her temple, dropped to her pillow.

"You'll be all right. You can come home in a few days. I'm going to call now, and then I'm going to wait downstairs until the ambulance comes. I'll leave the door unlocked for them. But I can't be here. Don't mention my name."

I had to take off before the cops showed up to ask the tenants questions, check out our place. Once they ran our address through their system, they'd know our story.

"Watch over her," I said to Per, setting her down on the pillow. I don't know what I thought a cat could contribute, but it gave me some relief to know she wouldn't be alone.

"Sleep," I said, pulling the sheet up to her chin and kissing her cheek.

"Cammy, I've always loved you most of all."

"I know," I said. "The same goes for me."

And then I made the call.

"Out like a lamb." That's what came to me the minute I stepped out into the alley. It'd been raining all morning, but the clouds had suddenly cleared, and that minute, April felt more like June. Almost overnight, the snow was gone from the sidewalks, brown grass covered the neighbors' yards, cars drove by with their windows open, music blasting.

I didn't wait for the sirens; I just threw Faina's duffel bag over my shoulder and started running. I had to get her from school, make tracks, before the cops came looking for us.

In my mind, I saw the whole circus. Hank stomping up from the plumbing shop. He was bastard enough to want to be there when my mother went down. Frances rushing out of the bakery, blabbering about the robbery, the marmalade twists, how that's all that woman would eat. I knew they'd fill the cops full of stories. About me, always in trouble. And the good little girl from California. Some sort of shirttail relation. But what kind of parents would let their daughter live with people like that?

I heard it all, their voices slamming together in my mind as I ran the eight blocks to Cathedral. Dogs snarled and barked from their back yards, a few old folks glanced out from their kitchen windows. If luck was with us, it would take at least an hour for the details to stack up. I felt the same hot terror I'd felt the last time I ran, the last time the hospital called in the county, the last time I tried to save her, the last time I nearly lost her.

I had an excuse to free Faina from school, Papa Roy's funeral, it had worked for me through the years. But a block from Cathedral I saw her, crossing Twenty-second Street, already headed toward home. Faina, the good girl, the genius who never cut class.

"What are you doing? Skipping? I thought you were such a stickler for school?"

"Cammy," she whimpered, like she already guessed my mother was lost to the county. "What did the doctor say?" Her face was streaked with tears. She was always too quick to cry. When she noticed the duffel bag, the fear I'd predicted flashed in her eyes. "Cammy, what's happening?"

I grabbed her arm, snapping it so fast I heard it crack. "We got to get moving. I'll tell you on the way."

"But Lenore," she said. "I want to know if she's okay."

As soon as we'd made it to an alley off Dakota, she planted her feet on the ground, refused to keep moving. She was panting. "Where are we going? I want to see Lenore."

"Lenore's gone," I said. "The ambulance came for her. Took her downtown. It had to be done. I don't even know if she'll make it."

"But I want to be with her." She looked so pathetic standing there in that uniform, that stupid thick hem, that rumpled gray sweatshirt, that pink plastic baby still pinned to her chest.

"Faina. Listen to me. I know the system. They'll take us, lock us up in JD. Do you want to end up like Jimmy?" If she didn't start moving, I'd slap her across the face.

"Jimmy?"

I knew I'd tripped up on my story, but I was too wired to care. "Forget about Jimmy, for once. I've got money to buy us bus tickets back to San Diego. We'll go down to the Greyhound depot now, stash our bag in a locker, get something to eat. I'm starving." I hadn't eaten since last night, a salami sandwich on dry rye bread, and little specks of light floated past my eyes. "We'll hang out in San Diego until my dad comes back. It's just a couple more months. We can stay with the coffee-shop guy. The one you like so much. I'll work for our rent."

"No," she said. I hated her stubborn streak. "I'm not leaving Lenore. I want to go to the hospital and see her."

"Okay," I lied. "I'll take you there now. We'll go downtown, make sure she's okay." I needed to make her move. I couldn't show up in San Diego without Faina, my father's one daughter. He wouldn't want me without her.

"We can't go to San Diego," she said, wiping her tears with her sleeve. "He won't be home for another year."

"Liar." I saw through her trick. She was stalling, scamming a way to stay, to nursemaid my mother. "He's supposed to be back in June. My mother told me."

"No. It's a two-year contract. He was going to tell Lenore pretty soon, when he sent some money. I've got his letter at home. I'll show it to you. Cammy, it's the truth." Her chin quivered.

I wanted to wrap my hands around her scrawny neck and choke her until she changed her story. She was unraveling my plan, ruining everything. "It doesn't matter," I said. "We can't stay here. We'll find someplace to live while we wait. Guys will take us in. That part will be easy. We don't have a chance in this city. They've got files on me. Shoplifting, truancy. And you're here illegally. You know as well as I do my mother doesn't have rights to you. I found the papers in your drawer. Even if she pulls through, they won't let her keep you."

I knew I had broken her. I could see her desperate search for a trap-door, her beady black eyes darting frantically. "Who knows that?" she asked.

"It'll be right in our file. Hennepin County has everything on record. They'll take you, Faina. Lock you up in some kiddie prison where I can't protect you. You want some creep with zits humping you while you sleep? I'll be eighteen in a year or so. Free. But you're going to be the one serving the long sentence."

"Per," she said. "Where is she? I won't go without her. I won't."

"Forget Per. Someone will take her in. Feed her. Some sucker like me."

"No," she said, dropping down on a crumbling concrete wall. We were losing too much time; if we didn't catch the 6B for downtown soon, the cops would be on us. "I'm going to go get Per. And then you'll take me to see Lenore?"

"Don't be stupid. The cops will be at the apartment."

"I'll wait until they leave. I'm not going without Per. I'm her mother. I'd never leave her alone."

"Okay. Go get her. Let them haul you away." I hated that cat. I should have left her to die that night in the cold. "I'll wait for you in the bathroom at Dakota Park. I'll give you an hour. If you don't show up, I'm leaving. I'm not letting you take me down."

"Can't you come with me?" she begged, her eyes filling up again with tears. "I'm scared, Cammy."

"I got to save my own ass," I said. "You want that cat, you go get it." I didn't think she'd do it alone.

Faina Empty

First, I check Dakota Avenue for cop cars like Cammy told me. There's no sign of anything, not police, not an ambulance, not the crowds I imagined. Not even Frances or Hank. Maybe Cammy made up the whole story to get me to go to San Diego, maybe Lenore is still up there, struggling to breathe, just waiting for us to come home. Through the big glass window of Kenny's, I see Jimmy loading groceries. If I really am boarding a bus for San Diego today, I need to say good-bye to him, to let him know I didn't disappear. Jimmy, the only true friend I have here; Jimmy, who said I saved his life.

In the back alley it's quiet, too. Everything is just the way I left it this morning. The dumpster still screaming SLUT, the wet blacktop, the soggy cigarette butts left over from all the nights Jimmy and I talked out here, perched up on the fire escape, staring out over the rooftops and into the sky. Sometimes cloudy, sometimes full of stars, the moon always changing its shape. The things I'll miss. Jimmy's last kiss, the way he tugged at my braid to tease me, the little gold cross earring shining in the streetlight.

When I open the heavy back door, Hank's there, blocking the sea-green staircase, the one bare lightbulb swaying from a frayed cord above his head.

"Fina," he stammers. "You're home early. Looks like your ma's real sick."

Then it's true. My heart drums against my chest. "She's not my mom."

"Well, whatever she is. She's real sick."

I try to squeeze past him, but he blocks me with his thick body, his filthy hands.

"What's your hurry?" He squints at me.

"I want to go upstairs to see her."

"Not there. Ambulance took her to Hennepin County drunk tank, I bet. Same place they take them all. You can't live up there alone now. You know it's against the law." He clicks his tongue against his teeth. "The older girl's gone. Took off with a duffel bag. Didn't even stay to see if her own mother lived or died. Anyway, those two won't help you. Bad blood the both of them. Crazy. That Lenore ain't fit to raise a dog."

"I'll stay with a friend. Don't call anybody, please."

"Ain't up to me. I just own the plumbing shop, caretake the building. I was up there when they came. The girl left her alone, close to dead. They needed your names."

"Our names?"

"I answered what I could. I'm not here to mind your business. You kept the place up real nice. I don't blame you. I seen you go off every day in your uniform. Cathedral. That's my church. We've got that in common. It's that older girl who ruined it. I saw it coming the minute she showed up."

"I have to go," I say. "I'm sure Lenore needs me." I know Cammy's starting to worry. I don't want her to give up and leave without me. I don't want to have to find my way to the Greyhound depot alone.

"That cat. The lease said no pets. I'll keep the damage deposit to pay for the cleaning."

"Per. Is she okay?"

"The ambulance folks left her alone. I got pets of my own. Nobody messed with her. You should be so lucky."

I have never been alone in the apartment. Never been here without Lenore. I'm terrified by the silence. I dead-bolt both locks, draw the chain.

When I look in her room, her empty bed seems like a dream. I want to believe that she'll hobble out of the bathroom, ask me to turn on the TV. I stretch out in her spot, next to Per, who meows at me. I press my face into her pillow, so I can breathe her memory. The sad, sour stench of sickness. Smoke, vodka, Final Net hairspray, White Shoulders perfume. On her TV tray, the little white bag of chocolate-covered almonds she never ate, this week's *TV Guide,* her ashtray, finally empty.

I wonder what it's like in the emergency room, if she's scared or lonely, if she's worried I might not come. I wonder if they've fixed her breathing, if she's swallowing food, if the gurgling has stopped. Hank said the drunk tank, but that's not what Cammy told me. I know Lenore will feel better once I get there, when I can hold her hand between mine, tickle her arm until she falls asleep. Maybe then, Cammy will change her mind. She'll see Lenore needs us, she'll let us stay home until we're sure Lenore is finally well.

I open Lenore's closet slowly, half-afraid a stranger will pop out and grab me. Hank again. Or Tom Payne. Her purse is there, just like Cammy told me it would be. I empty it on the bed: the Juicy Fruit she wanted me to glue to Jimmy's valentine, the fake leopard-skin cigarette case she never used, Papa Roy's lighter with his initials engraved on the front. Old Kleenex, lipstick, loose tobacco. I open her red vinyl wallet. The checks Cammy told me to bring are there. In the small plastic rectangles, there are school pictures of Cammy. Cammy as a little girl in pin curls, Cammy in bangs, Cammy with pink barrettes, Cammy in pigtails, Cammy with her hair pulled back from her forehead, Cammy with straight hair draping her face, Cammy with blue eye shadow, Cammy refusing to smile. All the years they lived without me. I open the dark slot, pull out the money, her social security card, a little square photo of me in kindergarten. My first school picture. My hair cut short as a boy's, my front teeth missing, that silly crooked grin. *Faina, age 6,* my dad printed on the back in pencil. Maybe this is the same picture Lenore told me about, the one Papa Roy carried in his wallet until the day he died.

I take her wallet with me, throw it into a brown Kenny's bag. In our room, Cammy's clothes are scattered everywhere, on the bed, the floor, spilling out of her dresser drawers. I add my uniform and blouse to the mess, pull on my dirty jeans, one of Cammy's ripped T-shirts. I fill the paper bag with the things I can't leave. My diary, Per's food, her little china dish. My dad's letters. The napkin with Keith's address. My Shepherd Psalm bookmark. Lenore's family Bible. Croc. The wooden boomerang. My winter boots. I leave the confirmation dress hanging in my closet. I wish we could take it back to Sears, get our money. I wish I could cut it into a million pieces, throw them on the steps of Cathedral, let Sister Barbara figure it out.

I double Jimmy's choker, tie it around Per's neck for a collar, pull the string from my sweatshirt jacket and attach it for a leash. If Per had a little nametag with our address, I could never lose her. Even a stranger would know where to send her home. But there is no home now, not for Per or me. She scratches her back paws against the choker frantically, rears backward to wriggle out of the leash. "It has to be done, Per," I tell her. "Please." I dump out Eileen's wicker sewing basket, the one we used last summer to hem my uniform. The day Lenore told me I'd need to be a sheep.

All of this I do quickly, afraid I'll hear the front door open or footsteps on the stairway. I know Cammy's in the bathroom at Dakota Park, angry. I know I have to get there before she leaves.

When I step out of our apartment, I have Per tucked up against my chest, the sewing basket looped over one arm, the bag of keepsakes cradled in the other arm. I don't bother locking the door. Why should I? We're all gone now. Forever. Sometime soon, someone will come here and find us missing, will load our things into boxes marked MCCOY just the way my dad and I did in San Diego. Hank probably. Or Frances. They'll pack Papa Roy's *Great Poems of the English Language*, Cammy's record albums, Eileen's rosebud china, Lenore's mirrored perfume tray. Boxes and boxes of belongings. And a year from now, no one will remember we lived here.

As soon as we step into the sunlight, Per digs her claws into my skin, then leaps down to the sidewalk. She's never seen spring, never smelled the rain, or put her paw in a puddle, never been startled by cars, or pounced on litter fluttering past her feet. I'll never make it all the way to San Diego with Per scrambling at the end of her string. I tuck her into the sewing basket, fasten the lid closed. "Per," I whisper between the cracks. "I'm sorry. But we have to hurry."

Across the street, Jimmy's loading groceries into the trunk of a gold Cadillac, helping a white-haired woman into the driver's seat. "Take it easy," he says, slapping the hood of her car.

"Jimmy," I call out, hoping he'll take a chance and talk to me.

"What're you doing home from school already?"

Just as he says this, a hand lands on my shoulder. I see Hank standing in the doorway of his plumbing shop, pointing toward me, Frances spying through the bakery window. I don't turn to look at the person who's holding on to me; I just keep staring at Jimmy, the fear and confusion splattered across his beautiful face.

"Faina?" When Jimmy steps out into the traffic, cars screech to a stop.

"It's okay," I scream, waving him away. He just stands there, frozen. "Go back to Kenny's. I'll tell you about it tonight." I know there's nothing he can do. In a few days, he'll leave New Directions, go home to his family. "Go on. I'll tell you the whole story tonight."

"Fina McCoy? I'm Officer Williams. Can I ask you a few questions?"

Maybe I could run from him, the way I did today from Cathedral, make it the few blocks to Dakota Park. But he'd trail me, on foot or by car, and Cammy would never forgive me. So I follow him to the squad car parked at the end of the alley, behind Hank's Plumbing.

"I haven't done anything," I say.

"What you got there?" he asks, pulling his pad from his belt holder. "In that little sewing basket?"

"My cat."

"Your cat?" He unfastens the latch, lifts the lid a crack. Per pokes her little orange face out to sniff the sun. "You taking her for a walk?"

"Yep."

"Like that? And the bag? Mind if I take a look?"

I set it down on the ground, careful to find a patch of cement that's dried since the morning storm. He reaches in, takes a look through my things. "Locked, huh? Got a key for this?" he asks, holding up my diary. "Just in case we need to take a look."

I reach down under my T-shirt and pull out the purple ribbon. It hasn't been off me since I left San Diego. Not even in the shower. I pull it over my head, clutch it in my fist.

"I suppose you wouldn't want me to read it. Private. That kind of thing," he says. "But I need the key. Don't worry. I'm just going to hold on to it. Keep them together. You have a seat." He opens the back door of the squad car for me.

I balance Per's basket on my lap, prop the rumpled paper bag between my feet. The steel-mesh grille between the front and back seats reminds me of Monsignor's confessional. Only there's no velvet curtain to hide my identity.

He twists around in his seat to look at me. Lifts the handset to radio in my story. "You're not under arrest or anything," he smiles. "I'm really just here to help."

Help. Like Mrs. Lajoy. Like Monsignor. Like Sister Linette and the Atwoods. Like Frances. Like Hank. Today I've had more help than I need. "I haven't done anything wrong," I repeat. He can't arrest me for carrying a cat and some keepsakes. I'm sure it's Cammy they're after, Cammy with her record for shoplifting and truancy. I know if they put me in prison, my dad will come for me. He won't let it go that far.

"We're also looking for the older girl. Cammy McCoy. Is she your sister? There's some confusion. Your caretaker isn't sure; your school says she is."

My school? He's already been to Cathedral? I don't know what to answer.

"Yes, she's my sister. I don't know where she is. At work maybe?"

"Where would that be?" All the time we're talking he's writing notes in his heavy black book.

"I'm not sure of the name. Some kind of bowling alley."

"And this is your mother, then? The one in the hospital?"

I stare out the window of the squad car. From here I can see New Directions, the upstairs room I always imagined was Jimmy's. I've told so many stories this year, some I can't even remember. Is this my mother?

"Yes," I admit. "It is."

"And your father?"

It's too late for me to tell more stories, too late to remember my lies. "He's on an oil rig in Australia. I'm just visiting here while he's working."

"Australia? You're visiting? From where?" I can tell he doesn't believe me.

"San Diego."

"Okay," he grins again. "Well, you're certainly far from home. Then your mother doesn't have custody?"

"No," I sigh. "I don't think so."

By now, I'm sure Cammy has quit waiting. She's left the bathroom at Dakota Park for the Greyhound bus depot. At five o'clock, she'll be on the bus headed for San Diego; she'll work at Keith's Coffee Shop and wait for my dad. Without me.

He closes his pad and sets it down on the seat beside him. "Fina," he begins.

"Faina," I say. "It's Faina."

"Faina, then. Your mother's quite sick. They've taken her down to

Hennepin County Medical Center and admitted her to ICU. It's too early to tell what will happen, but there are good doctors watching over her. Some of the best."

"I want to go see her."

"Not today, I'm afraid. They don't allow patients in her condition to have visitors. Let's give her a few days to get on her feet, and then we'll see what can be arranged."

"A few days?"

"We're going to need to place you in protective custody. There's no one home to take care of you. Child Protection will handle your case until your father can be found. Do you have an address or anything?"

"Yes." I reach in the bag and pull out one of my blue airmail envelopes.

"We'll try to contact him. Let him know the situation. Hopefully, he'll respond."

"He'll respond." When I look down the alley, there's Cammy, poking her head out from behind Mead's Mortuary. "What's protective custody?"

"We'll put you in a temporary shelter. Good Shepherd Children's Home if there's room. You'll have a social worker on your case, someone to watch out for you. Someone to recommend what should be done."

"Done?"

"You know, in terms of a guardian. Don't worry about that now. Let's just get you settled into a place with food and a nice warm bed. Everything will look better tomorrow."

"Is this a prison?"

"No," he laughs. "It's to keep you from ending up in one. But the cat," he says. "It can't come with you."

"She has to. I'm her mother. I can't leave her." No matter how hard I try to stop them, tears stream down my face. I hug Per's wicker basket to my chest. He already took my diary key; I'm not going to let him have Per.

"It's regulation. Isn't there a neighbor who can care for her?"

"A neighbor?" Frances or Hank?

"Just someone to keep her until you can pick her up in a few days. When your dad comes for you. A day or two, that's all."

I tug at my eyelashes to stop the tears. The only one I can think of is Mrs. Lajoy. "One of my teachers might take her."

"That brown-haired lady? With the curly hair? She seemed pretty concerned when I spoke with her. She offered to help if she could."

"She might take her. She has cats of her own."

He looks at his watch. "Okay," he says. "Let's go ask her."

"I don't want to go back there."

"I'll handle it," he says, turning the key in the ignition. "You can wait in the car."

When we pull out of the alley, Cammy's gone. Jimmy's standing on the sidewalk in front of Kenny's, watching us drive away. I lift my hand in a little wave.

In front of Cathedral, I slump down in the car seat. "Do you have to park here?" I ask. I'm sure in minutes Emmy, Carolyn, Tom Payne and Dave Fadden will circle the squad car to jeer at me. "I'll hurry," he says, locking the doors.

I take a last look at Cathedral. This school I hate. I think about Mrs. Lajoy saying I wouldn't always feel this way, how one day I'd look back from a distance and see it differently. But I won't. It's burned in my mind forever, and someday, I'm going to tell the whole story. To anyone who will listen.

When Officer Williams comes out of the building, Mrs. Lajoy is with him. He unlocks the squad car, lets her slide into the back seat. "Faina," she says, "I'm so sorry about your mother. We all are. You should have told us she was sick. If only you'd told us, things would have been different for you. It's all been a terrible mistake."

"I need someone to take my cat. Just for a few days. I know you like them. I couldn't think of anyone else." I don't want Mrs. Lajoy to see me here, in this squad car, my face wet, my eyes puffy and pink.

"Yes, of course," she says. "I'd be happy to. And I'll take good care of her, I promise. What else can I do?"

"Fina can get the cat if her dad comes for her."

"He's coming," I insist.

"Sure," he nods. "But you know how it is," he says to Mrs. Lajoy.

"I'll watch her indefinitely. I'll even let her sleep with me. Okay?"

Mrs. Lajoy opens up the basket to take a peek. "Faina, she's beautiful," she says, petting the top of Per's head. "What's her name?"

"Per," I say. "Persephone."

Sheila
O'Connor

Cammy What Was Ahead

Faina? Of course I went back for her, but when I saw her trapped in the squad car, I knew our days together were done. There was no San Diego without her, no ocean, no beach, no chance to escape this sad city. I waited until she saw me, until she knew for sure I'd never desert her. Faina. My baby sister. The dark girl I'd grown to love. I lifted my fingers to my lips to blow her a kiss. I wanted to hold her, to crawl into the squad car next to her, to press her small face to my chest. But I left.

Tony's basement place was dark and musty, just the way I remembered it. I needed a break from the heat, the steam that was rising off the wet sidewalks. My head was throbbing, my stomach a boiling pit. I grabbed a Budweiser from his little refrigerator, the box of Cheese Nips off the card table, and crawled into his bed. Our bed, the sheets dank and sticky. It still smelled like Tony. Sweat. Cigarettes. Sex. I knew he'd keep me. Knew it that morning at Wentworth's. At least while I was worth something, at least while I could work a good scam.

When I closed my eyes, the bed was spinning. I was spent from running, spent from the drain of the day. I laid my hand against the cool cement wall, but I couldn't stop twirling. Stale crackers and beer turned in my stomach. But there was something else in there, something eating me alive from the inside. Not Tony's. Not anybody's. Just a dark-eyed dream like Faina or Jimmy. A pink plastic baby pinned to Faina's chest. And who would help me? Cammy McCoy? No mother. No father. No sister. Who would save me from what was ahead?

Lenore Intensive Care

There were tubes everywhere, nurses waking me to check my temperature, my blood pressure, measure the fluids in the clear plastic bags. The constant beep of machines, a needle through my back to drain out the lung. Pneumonia, they said. Maybe liver. Cirrhosis. Like Mother. But I was too young to die. When I asked about Faina and Cammy, no one would answer me. "You need to run that past the doctor," they said, scribbling secrets about me in their chart.

"I'm going home as soon as I feel better," I told them. "I have daughters. I can't stay away too long." I wanted to leave, to sneak a cab home, but I couldn't. I knew they were stealing my money while I was under their spell of sleep. "I want to see my girls," I insisted, but they never let me.

"Okay, Mrs. McCoy," the doctor said, straddling the chair like a cowboy. "I'll give it to you straight. Your lungs are shot, your liver is shot. It's going to take a long-term solution to turn that around." It was the first I'd seen of him, some kind of bearded young hippie with a ponytail. Earth shoes. A turquoise eagle medallion. A Mexican smock. A false sense of familiarity. A typical county doctor. Too low to have his own practice. "You need to get out from under this problem. You'll be dead in a year if you don't. I'm sending a counselor from detox intake. The first open bed will be yours."

"I can't stay," I said. In a day or two I'd regain my strength, go home to Faina and Cammy, home to our little apartment, and Per sleeping on the pillow beside me. My girls would watch over me; the two of them would help me get well. "I have children."

"Not for long," he frowned. "The county can't let you keep them in this condition. They're going to look at your stability. Your history.

This is it. Your drinking days are done." He clicked the top of his pen, slipped it behind his ear. "You clean up. Heal. Kick the booze. It might take a few months, even a year to get you back on your feet. The real work is up to you." He winked at me, patted my leg through the blankets. "First things first. Kick the booze. Then you can go back home."

Faina Shelter

My social worker, Therese, has good news for me. The doctors at Hennepin County have given me permission to see my mother. *My mother.* That's what I call her now.

"As it stands, we'll go after dinner," Therese says. We're sitting on the lawn in the Good Shepherd courtyard for a special counseling session Therese has requested. "But remember, it's a first visit. Don't expect too much."

"After dinner? Why so late?" I want to skip this day I know will drag on forever. Morning studies, where we work in small groups according to our ability. Midday Mass, where the pregnant girls waddle in and slouch in the back pews. Lunch. Always meat, mashed potatoes and gravy the wrinkled nuns scoop onto our trays. Social responsibility. Sponging down the tables in the dining room, emptying wastebaskets, mopping the tile floors. Afternoon rec. Softball out in the hot spring sun. Canteen. Mail call and candy. Study hall. Counseling. Dinner. More meat and mashed potatoes. Food I'm too sad to swallow. Evening free time. Ping-pong or old movies flickering out of focus.

"I've already gotten you out of morning studies," Therese says, leaning back on the grass, tilting her face toward the sun. "What more do you want from me?"

"My dad?"

"Your dad," she laughs. "Haven't I already told you I'm doing my best?" I like Therese, her white cotton-candy hair, her hoarse voice, her short denim skirts. She's promised to bring my dad home.

"So my mother must be better," I say. "If she can have visitors. She'll be out in a few days." I can't wait to get out of Good Shepherd, go home to the apartment and nurse Lenore back to health. I don't want to end up like Jimmy, living in a halfway house without Per, or Lenore, or Cammy.

"Better?" Therese repeats. She has a habit of always repeating my words before she answers me. As if she didn't quite get it straight the first time. "I only know what they've told us. She has a rough road ahead of her, Faina. These things take time. But there's good people willing to help her, she won't have to do it alone."

"Like me. I can help her as soon as they let her come home."

"Like you?" Therese says gently. "You know that really isn't your job. As much as you might want it to be. You're a twelve-year-old. Someone should take care of you."

"Almost thirteen."

"All right," she laughs, closing her eyes. "Almost thirteen."

"What about Per? Can I visit her, too?"

Mrs. Lajoy sent a letter from Per. She made believe it was Per writing to me, telling stories about Mrs. Lajoy's cats, Shadow and Kitty, how they lick her ears in the morning, how they've made room for her at the foot of Mrs. Lajoy's bed. Per said Mrs. Lajoy feeds her little fish treats to fatten her up. "I miss you Faina. Meow," she wrote. At the end of the letter, Mrs. Lajoy drew a picture of Per with her orange crayon fur tufting out of her little duck head.

"You and that cat," Therese says. "You have so many requests. Let's tackle one thing at a time. Today, you have a full plate."

"Tomorrow?" I say. "Tomorrow could I go see Per?"

"Tomorrow?" Therese sits up, folds her legs beneath her little skirt, concentrates on the plaster statue of Jesus holding a lamb. "Faina, Mrs. Lajoy called this morning. I didn't realize your confirmation ceremony was tomorrow. She said you worked hard to prepare for the day; she said she'd be happy to be your sponsor. Trouble is, I'm not sure if I can make that happen."

"No," I say. "Please. It doesn't mean anything to me."

"You're sure?"

"Yes. Just don't mention it to the sisters." If the sisters find out there's a sacrament, they'll force me back to Cathedral.

"Okay," Therese sighs, clapping her hands together. "No confirmation. Anyway, we have bigger fish to fry."

"Is our session finished?"

"Anxious to get back to morning studies?" Therese asks suspiciously.

"No. I just thought, maybe, if we were done talking, I could pick some lilacs to bring to Lenore. My mother."

"Your mother," Therese repeats. "You do that." She gives the toe of my tennis shoe a little pinch. "I'll just grab some sun while I supervise." She stretches back out on the grass. "Don't run away now," she calls to me. "I'm just inches from getting you out."

Jesus stands in front of the lilac shrubs, one delicate hand hooked under the lamb's wooly belly. I tear off a few stalks, imagine how happy the lilacs will make Lenore. I have so much to tell her. I need to say how sorry I am I wasn't there when the ambulance took her, how sorry I am she's been alone in the hospital so many days. I want to tell her I have the family Bible, and not to worry about Per, who seems happy at Mrs. Lajoy's. I want to know if there's been any word from Cammy, a phone call maybe.

"Don't wander off, Faina," Therese shouts. "Remember, you're going to be one of the lucky ones."

When afternoon rec is finished, we haul the sacks of softball equipment back to the storeroom. "Excellent exercise, girls," Sister Marie says. Then she announces, "Canteen," and everyone rushes off for candy. Today I don't care about mail call, or banana taffy, or syrupy bottles of strawberry soda we yank out of an old machine. Instead, I sneak off to the dormitory—a field of bunkbeds twenty girls share. Today I need privacy, a chance to be alone before dinner, to think out the things I need to say to Lenore.

I pull my diary out from under my mattress. Press in a few lilac petals to save for a memory.

I wish I had something nice to wear tonight so Lenore could see me *dressed decent for once.* My first day here, Therese took me "shopping" at the Agape Store, a room in the basement where kids can pick any clothes they want for free. Most of it was junk, stained and worn out by the kids before us. I chose an old pair of Levis with shabby knees, a couple of baseball jerseys, a pilly pair of stretchy red shorts. Nothing Lenore would like.

"What about it, Faina? You think you're ready?" It's Therese grinning in the doorway, her tan arms folded across her chest.

"Now? I thought you were taking me after dinner."

"Me too," she says. "But there's been a change in plans."

"I just want to do my hair before we leave."

"Now?" Therese says. "Forget about your hair, you look great."

"It'll only take a minute." Quickly, I weave it into the single braid Lenore begged me to wear to school every day, the tidy look she liked best on me.

"You've got beautiful hair," Therese says, putting her arm around me.

I hide my diary back between the mattress and the sharp metal springs. "You're the first person who ever said that to me."

"Well, I won't be the last," Therese laughs. "Now let's hurry. There's someone waiting to see you who's already waited too long."

I reach for the clump of wilted lilacs. "I should have put them in water."

"Faina," Therese says. "None of this matters." She takes my hand and pulls me out into the hallway. "Come on."

"Sweetheart," he roars. "What the hell's happening?"

When I hear his voice I can hardly believe it. It's him. My dad. Right here in the Good Shepherd lobby. My dad, his skin brown and leathery, his hair shaved down to his scalp, his body bigger than I remember. Solid and sturdy.

"Were you two going to make me wait forever? What kind of operation you got going here anyway?"

"Dad," I shout, running to grab him. "I can't believe it. You came."

"Who else?" he says, throwing his arms open and swallowing me up in a bear hug. "Jesus Christ, Faina. This is the last place I thought you'd end up." I bury my face in his stomach, stay still while he kisses the top of my head again and again. A hundred kisses. He's really here. My dad is home.

"Honey, honey," he mumbles into my hair. "What the hell happened?"

I wish I could tell him the whole story, but I'm not sure I know it myself.

"I told you I'd bring him home," Therese says. "I just wasn't quite sure how long it would take, and I wanted to save the surprise."

"So is she free?" he asks Therese. "Do I need to post bail or something?" He keeps his arms around me, squeezes my neck while he talks.

"No," Therese laughs. "You've signed everything. I'll process the paperwork. The county will be happy to be done with one, believe me. We're always glad when we can make a relative placement, let alone a custodial parent. Unfortunately, there are plenty of girls waiting for her bed. Faina's one of the lucky ones; I just told her that this morning."

"Lucky?" my dad says, ruffling my head. "That's one way to put it. Let's pack up and get moving. I'm sure you've had enough."

"What now, stranger?" he asks, pulling a cigar from his shirt pocket. We're in the Good Shepherd parking lot, the rental car map spread open on my lap, my paper bag of belongings in the back seat. "I think I can make it without pictures," he says. "Don't forget I just traveled across the goddamn world. Besides, I did my own short stint here; Minneapolis isn't exactly the big city."

"What about the oil rig? Do you have to go back? What about the two-year contract? The money?"

"Money," he grunts, spitting the tip of his cigar out the window. "I've done enough for money. And look where it got us. Broke and broken." He pulls me across the hot vinyl seat until I'm nestled in the cave just under his damp arm. "Sweetheart, how long is it going to take for us to set this all straight? To turn it around? A lifetime?"

"I don't know," I say. How long will it take?

He blows the sweet smoke out into the spring breeze. "Pretty nice wheels," he says. "You think they'd miss it if we drove it home to San Diego?"

"San Diego? We're going back to San Diego?"

"What else, honey?"

"When?"

"Today. We sure as hell can't stay here."

"But we have to stay. For a while at least. Just until Lenore gets well."

"Sweetheart," he says. "We can't. We need to go back. I've made a dent in my debts. Not what I hoped for, but I did my best. I can line up work; the marina will probably take me. At least we'll find a place to crash. We're out on the red-eye at midnight. The tickets are bought. I blew my wad on them. It cost a bundle to bust out of Australia."

"But Lenore," I beg. "I'm supposed to see her today. She's waiting; Therese was taking me after dinner. Dad, I can't go without saying good-bye. And Per, we have to pick her up at my teacher's place."

"You got a lot of demands for an ex-con. It's up to the airline if we can fly that cat. And Lenore," he huffs, with a heavy short breath. "You can send her a line."

"No, no. I have to see her. I can't just leave her like this."

"Suit yourself," my dad says, driving past the tall iron gates of Good Shepherd. "But leave me out of it. I couldn't stand to see her on a good day."

"I'll hang right here," my dad says, holding open the hospital door. He pats me once on the butt. "Have at it, honey. Go write your last chapter. And then we'll hit the road."

At the front desk, the secretary jots down Lenore's room number on a small scrap of paper. "Fourth floor." She points to the elevators. "I hope you're twelve," she says. "I know they don't allow children."

The hospital stinks like the janitor's closet at Cathedral, disinfectant mixed with sweat and sickness, the same smell that followed Lenore. I've never been in a hospital before, and the bare walls, the waxy floors, the people in white uniforms, the cart with the sheet-covered body, all of it terrifies me. No wonder Lenore was afraid to come.

When I step off the elevator on the fourth floor, I'm stopped by a stern nurse in a white cap. "May I help you, young lady?"

"I have permission to see Lenore McCoy today. I'm her daughter."

"Yes," she says, studying me. "And you're twelve?"

"I am."

"Well, you certainly don't look it. Didn't somebody bring you? Someone from the county?" She cranes her neck to look behind me. "I understood you'd be supervised."

"My social worker is downstairs," I say. "She needed to stop at the bathroom. She'll be up any minute. Can I just go in alone?"

The lilac stems droop in my hand.

"Your mother shouldn't really have flowers. Why don't you give those to me? If they last beyond tomorrow, your mother can come out and see them when she feels stronger."

"Okay," I agree, handing them over. Therese was right: None of it matters. I just want to see Lenore.

"It's the third door on the left. Remember, you can't stay long."

Lenore is propped up, her hospital bed at a slant, a starchy pillow under her head. Her eyes are closed; she's sleeping. One tube snakes out of her arm, another ropes out from under her sheet. Her skin is a tawny clay color I don't remember. I listen to her breathe: There's still a faint trace of gurgle, but nothing like the last morning I saw her.

"Lenore," I say, lightly tapping her bony shoulder. "It's me, Faina."

"Faina." As soon as she speaks the cough starts, a dry, rough hack, not the rattling one she couldn't shake. I don't understand why she looks so shriveled and sick here. I thought she came to get well.

She reaches out her trembling hand. "Let me kiss you." I bend over the bed so she can touch my cheek. It's the first time she's ever kissed me, the first time it wasn't my lips brushing obediently against her powdery skin. "Faina," she whispers into my ear as if it's a secret. "There's just a curtain between us." She points to the long blue sheet dividing the room into sections. "Someone's always listening on the other side. Be careful."

"Okay," I say.

"Now tell me," she whispers, forgetting the kiss. "What's happening? They've mixed up everything. I don't understand a word of it."

I wish I could explain it to her, but none of it makes sense to me either. I can't understand what happened, all the things that went wrong in our lives.

"Where's Cammy? Where's my beautiful baby girl? No one will tell me."

"I don't know," I say, which for once is the truth. "Hiding probably. Waiting until you come home." I don't want to tell Lenore that Cammy might be in San Diego already, or that Cammy left her alone to die. Cammy my sister, Cammy who held me in sleep, Cammy who ran when she saw I was caught.

"I worry about her," Lenore says to me. "She's so beautiful and wealthy. Look at what happened to poor Patty Hearst."

"I'm sure she's safe," I say, taking Lenore's hand in mine. "Cammy can take care of herself."

"Cammy," Lenore says, "my beautiful, beautiful baby. And you, are you all alone at the apartment with Per?"

"No," I say. "Not really. I've been at Good Shepherd."

"Good Shepherd? Is that something those people at Cathedral arranged?"

"Yes," I lie. "In a way."

"All in all, those Catholics have been good to you, haven't they? That school was worth every red cent. I keep thinking of how Cammy's life might have been different if we'd had some religion. But what did I know then? Catholics are like another country to me."

Lenore pats my hand nervously, coughs again, struggles to catch her breath. "Faina," she whispers. "Come closer." Her breath reeks like a fly-speckled fish washed up on the beach. "They're plotting to lock me up here. For months. Even years. I don't know what these people have up their sleeve, but I have to play along for a while at least. I'm sure they're after Papa Roy's money."

"You just need to get well," I say.

"But how can I do that under these conditions? Faina, when you come tomorrow, sneak me in a little sip of something. I'm sure you understand."

"Per's staying with my teacher," I say to change the subject. I move my head away from her so I don't have to listen to her hiss and rattle.

"That's wonderful," she says, smiling weakly at me. "I'll bet little Per is lonesome for me. That kitten was such good company. Just like you. Do you remember all the fun we had together last summer?"

My eyes are starting to burn, my throat hurts. "Yes."

"Do you know, is Hank taking care of the apartment?"

"I think so." I can't tell her about the eviction, the boxes of keepsakes some stranger will take.

"I need to arrange to get him May's rent. As soon as you fall behind those sharks swim in for the kill."

"I have your wallet," I say, pulling it out of my back pocket.

"Good girl," Lenore says. "You're so clever, Faina. So cunning. Hide it in the back of the drawer, will you? And don't tell anyone you gave it to me. The help. I'm sure they steal."

I hide it in the drawer of the bedside table, behind a blue plastic half-moon tray. The tray is filled with Lenore's personal belongings: her gold watch from Papa Roy, toothpaste, toothbrush, a sample-sized tube of hand lotion. Underneath it all, the silver St. Christopher medal from Mrs. Lajoy.

"Do you want me to fix your hair?" It looks terrible, glued to her head with grease.

"No," she says. "Let them earn their keep. Besides, I don't want to lose a minute with you. Scoot closer."

My chair is already so close to the bed the metal rail jabs into my knee. "Lenore." It's time to tell the truth, to set things right before I leave. Tomorrow she'll wait for me to sneak in the little sip, and I won't be able to come. "My dad is here."

"Bobby," she shrieks, clutching the baggy hospital gown to her chest. She jerks the blanket up to her chin. "Don't let him see me like this, please."

"No," I say. "Don't worry. He's outside smoking."

"Thank god," she sighs, smoothing the side of her hair. "He can come for a visit when I'm better. When I've had a chance to put on my face."

"He wants me to leave. For San Diego."

As soon as I say this, her groggy eyes blur with tears. "What do you mean leave? But what about me? Who will help me get well?"

"I'll come back," I promise, gently rubbing her shriveled arm. "Maybe in a few weeks."

"You won't. I know what's happening. Bobby wants to steal you from me. But we belong together. The three of us. You, me, Cammy. We've been so happy, haven't we? You're a girl. What does Bobby know about raising a daughter? You can't leave when I'm in this mess with my liver. Or lungs. Or whatever it is. Thank god you didn't inherit my health."

She's coughing now, so hard and fast she's choking. I lift the plastic glass of water, tuck the straw between her lips. "Drink." I listen for the gurgle while the water goes down, but it's gone.

She takes a few swallows, shoves it away. "Maybe it'll take some time like they say, a few months to really get me back on track. I'll play their game. Then we can be together. You're my daughter. And you'll want to continue at Cathedral, get a private education. Grow up to be valedictorian. This place." She pinches her nose. "It's a public facility. You can see for yourself what that means. Papa Roy would die if he saw the conditions. And still, they're robbing me blind."

"Excuse me," the nurse says, poking her head into the room. "Your mother is a pretty sick lady. She needs her rest. Why don't you say your good-byes?"

"They always think they know everything," Lenore says, batting her hand at the air. "That's why I hate having strangers in our business."

"I brought you lilacs," I say. "They're out on the desk. It's finally spring."

"I'm glad winter's done," Lenore says. "I don't think I could survive another one. *When lilacs last in the dooryard bloomed,*" she recites. "The rest escapes me. It's Wordsworth. Or Whitman. All those W names. But it's just as well about the lilacs, they've always given me violent headaches."

"Please get well," I say, bending over to kiss her cheek.

"I'll see you tomorrow then," she says, clutching my wrist. "You'll work it out with Bobby. I'm not brave enough to do this alone."

"I know." I can't tell her I'm leaving. I can't even tell her I love her. I wish I could crawl back into bed with her one more time, read a chapter from *Little Women* until she drifts off to sleep. I wish we could start all over, not just this year, but at the beginning. Change the story. Make sure it turns out happy.

"I can't be alone," she says, turning her back to me. "I need my little Faina McCoy."

"So," my dad says when I step out into the sun. "How'd it go?"

I shrug my shoulders, try to swallow. "I promised we'd stay. Just for a few days. A week or two. Just until she's back on her feet. She needs me."

"It's done, Faina. It's finished."

"We can change the plane tickets."

"We can't. I've already seen enough of Minneapolis to last me a lifetime." He smooths his hand down my hair.

"Please." I'm ready to drop to my knees, rope my arms around his leg and plead. Right here, right on this busy street.

"She had her day. You don't owe her anything. Lenore is a grown-up, for Christ's sake. She'll have to fend for herself."

"But she can't get well without me."

"Or with you. She can't get well either way. We're burning daylight; let's get this show on the road."

"This is it," I say, as soon as we pass the mishmash of smashed cars at the Auto Trade lot. "Right there at the end of the block." My dad swerves toward the curb, slams on the brakes. Across the street, the bakery window shade is pulled down for the evening. Frances won't be there to squish her nose to the window and watch.

"This is it?" my dad says, raising his eyebrows at me. "This?"

"Yep," I say. "Above the bakery."

"Lenore really went down. She was a rich chick when I knew her." He drums his palms against the steering wheel. "It's a little rougher than I imagined."

"This is where she moved with Papa Roy after they sold their big house in Kenwood. It's pretty nice inside, lots of old furniture, china, antiques that belonged to Papa Roy and Eileen. That's Lenore's room on the corner. I slept with Cammy in the back bedroom by the alley." I can't take him back there; I don't want him to see the dumpster, the SLUT that was meant for me.

"Papa Roy. Jesus, that name drove me crazy. Even in the grave," he laughs. "She's still calling him that. So we going up to get your stuff or what?"

"No," I say. I don't want to see the empty apartment again, Lenore's bed, the week-old breakfast dishes still in the sink. I don't want to know if Hank packed our things already. "Everything I want is with me. Except Per. We still have to get her."

"Then what are we doing here, sweetie? Sightseeing?" He knocks his knuckles on the dash impatiently. "Faina, I'm done in. I've been traveling for over two days."

"Can you wait just a second? I need to run into Kenny's."

He digs down into his pocket, passes me over two quarters. "I remember about your boyfriend," he says, giving my leg a quick squeeze. "Pick me up a beef jerky, I'm starving. And make it fast. I'm jealous already."

Inside Kenny's, there's no sign of Jimmy. He's not at the cash register bagging groceries; he's not back in produce arranging apples or in the soup aisle stocking the shelves.

"Will this do it?" the cashier asks, when I set the beef jerky down on the counter. She's a regular, the one who sold me Lenore's Salems without a note. She knows me, the girl with the funny accent, the girl who lives across the street. By now, the whole neighborhood probably knows our story. The ambulance. The police. Cammy disappearing.

"Is Jimmy working today?"

"Nope. He served his sentence; they set him free."

"When?"

"Couple of days ago. Wednesday, I guess."

I put the quarter down on the counter. "You mean he's gone? He left New Directions?"

"Sorry," she says, snapping her gum between her crooked front teeth. "But I think he was happy. Who wouldn't be?"

Outside Kenny's, my dad leans against the painted white brick, a fresh cigar clenched in his lips. "Just thought I'd stretch my legs. We got a lot of sitting still ahead of us." My dad winks. "So, is this Jimmy of yours coming out to meet your old man?"

"No. He's not working."

"Night off, huh?" my dad says, wrapping both of his big arms around me. "That's too bad, honey. You can send him a postcard from home."

I rest my back against his stomach, settle my head on his chest. There are so many things he doesn't know or understand. Like Jimmy's gone for good. And I can't send a postcard, because I don't have an address. And Lenore can't take care of herself, can't make it without me. And Cammy showed me the ropes, but not in the way he imagined. I can't ever tell him this story, the life I lived on this street. Dakota Avenue. Home. Our old brick building. The neon palm tree of the Paradise Club. Dakota Liquors, their weekly deliveries. Border Drug, where I bought my stamps and Cammy stole Milk Duds before the movie. Rusty's Tavern, the leftover smell of beer and hamburgers on my way to Cathedral each morning. The bus stop. 6B. The marmalade twists from the bakery. Hank's Plumbing. The constant hum of traffic outside my window. The alley. The fire escape. The place where I first saw snow, where I first kissed Jimmy.

"That's it, then," my dad says. He draws his rugged thumb along the scar on my eyebrow. "It's history now, Faina. It has to be."

Faina McCoy

I go back to San Diego for my beginning.